An Alternative His

Michael Goodwin

2022 White Bird Publications, LLC

Cover by E. Kusch

Published in the United States
by White Bird Publications, LLC, Texas
www.whitebirdpublications.com

ISBN 978-1-63363-565-4
eBook ISBN 978-1-63363-566-1
Library of Congress Control Number: 2021952765

PRINTED IN THE UNITED STATES OF AMERICA

To White Bird Publications for having guts
and an open mind in a publishing world
that has become close-minded, insular,
and asleep in its woke orthodoxy.

VICE VERSA

An Alternative History of the 2020 Presidential Election

White Bird
Publications

You may not be able to alter reality, but you can alter
your attitude towards it,
and this, paradoxically, alters reality.

—Margaret Atwood

"I hope
that if alternate universes exist,
it will still be with you
and me
in the end. I hope that
there will always be an us.
In every world,
In every story."

—Tina Tran,
Let us always find each other.

Chapter One

LOOSE LIPS

May 2020

FBI Director Bernard "Barney" Cummings leaned his six foot-four-inch frame over the golf ball and gimlet eyed the hole six feet away. He shifted his feet like a cat on soft fabric and slightly adjusted the angle of the putter face. Just as he was about to pull back the club, the intercom on his office desk phone trilled.

"Director Cummings," his secretary, Sheila said, "Deputy Director Fisherwood is here to see you."

"Okay, send him in," Cummings answered. He then quickly put away his putter and the targeted coffee cup turned sideways just as Karl Fisherwood tapped on the closed door while simultaneously opening it.

"What's up Peckerwood?" Cummings asked,

referring to his deputy by the affectionate nickname he had given him when they attended University of Alabama law school over twenty-five years before. A photo of him and Fisherwood outside the clubhouse at the Trump National Golf Club in Charlotte, North Carolina occupied a space on Cummings' wall behind his desk and presented an odd couple, Fisherwood several inches shorter, balding and slightly pudgy next to the lean as a rail Cummings who had a helmet of salt 'n pepper hair.

Cummings plopped into his high-back, black leather, ergonometric, swivel chair behind his cherry wood desk, while Fisherwood took a seat in one of three government-issue chrome and leather chairs that were arrayed in front of the expansive desk. The sunlight pouring through the large office window highlighted the grim expression on Fisherwood's face. Scowls regularly weighed on his rotund face, even though his blue eyes would easily lend themselves to cheerfulness.

"Field office in Seattle got a tip from one of its Chinese assets."

"Yeah?" Cummings muttered as he pressed his fingers into a tent.

"Xi and the Chinese government are getting ankle deep into the 2020 election. Bots, trolls, cyber espionage, the whole shebang."

Cummings' finger tent collapsed, and his hands interlocked with each other.

"Looks like they're going all in for Biden. Here's an example of some of the stuff they're spraying out there." Fisherwood fiddled with his smartphone and then handed it across the desk to Cummings.

"This one is called 'The Great Orange Turd.' On

some Instagram account, DumpChumpTrumpsRump! It's gone viral."

Cummings stared at the smartphone screen, on which a cartoon figure of Trump gradually morphed into a giant orange fecal pile as various Trump tweets were read out loud by a voice mimicking the president's. "Crazy Joe Biden is acting like a tough guy. Actually, he is weak, both mentally and physically, and yet he threatens me, for the second time, with physical assault. BRING IT ON, SLEEPY JOE! YOU'LL GO DOWN FAST AND HARD, CRYING ALL THE WAY!" And "How amazing, the State Health Director who verified copies of Obama's 'birth certificate' dies in a plane crash today. All others lived. Hmmm..." And "Sorry losers and haters, but my IQ is one of the highest—and you all know it! Please don't feel so stupid or insecure, it's not your fault." The tweets weren't limited to politics: "Everyone knows I am right that Jamie Fox should dump Katie Holmes. In a couple of years, he will thank me. Be smart, Jamie!" And so on for another two and a half minutes as the shit pile got bigger and more orange.

"Disgusting, isn't it?" Fisherwood said.

Cummings handed Fisherwood's phone back to him. "Kinda funny I have to admit."

"What's not funny is that Seattle says they're trying to hack local election commission computers. Get all kinds of voter info. Social Security numbers, addresses, party affiliation. They got that Apartment 3 hacker gang in Guangdong working overtime on this."

"That's some serious stuff, Karl. Who's sourcing this?"

"A Brit named Daniel Copper. Used to be a top agent with MI5. Worked out of Hong Kong. CIA used him for some clandestine operation in Macau a couple years back. Said he also did some really good work on what the Chinese would do about the Hong Kong protests. They fully vouched for him."

"We need to verify this before we do anything with it. Vet it up and down, in and out. And no friggin' leaks to the media. And don't let POTUS know. He'll go ballistic and push me to eat it before it's even half-baked."

"Got it, Boss," Fisherwood said.

His deputy director always called him "Boss" because of their long friendship. Addressing him as Barney would be too casual on the eighth floor of the J. Edgar Hoover Building. So, he settled on "Boss," just ass kissing enough but not too officious.

"Just giving you a heads up," Fisherwood said as he rose to leave. "As far as leaks, you know I run a tight ship with tight lips."

After Fisherwood had left, the Director shook his head and muttered "Damn. This is not good."

Next day…

Gary Wang picked up the ringing phone at Biden Headquarters, New York. Since Coronavirus had come to town, he had been working out of his apartment in Astoria, Queens, acting as a volunteer receptionist for headquarters, the 888 number and direct line automatically rolling to the phone in his apartment.

"Hey Gary, you busy?" Amancia "Manny" Carleton asked.

"Hey there, not really. Wazup?"

"I'm hearing some crazy shit. Wanted to run it by

you. Are you free to talk? You're not on a recorded line or anything like that, are you?"

"Uh, no. Nothing like that."

"Okay..." Manny said, pausing for a few seconds. "Got wind of some scuttlebutt here at Fox News."

"Yeah, and what's that?" Gary asked as he anxiously stood from his desk. Manny was an assistant guest coordinator for the Fox weekend broadcast. She often called to give him tidbits.

"I was in a stall in the restroom, and I heard who I think was Dana Perino and some other woman talking about the campaign and something about the Chinese supporting Biden."

"When you say support, what exactly do you think they meant?" Gary asked.

"I'm not sure, but they sounded alarmed."

"What I can't believe is that they didn't check under the stall walls to make sure there weren't any feet there. But they didn't mention any details?"

"No, not really. Can you see that happening? You got a better feel than anyone I know about what the Chinese are thinking," Manny said.

"Well, they certainly don't like Trump, we all know that. You think Fox has enough to run with anything?"

"I don't know. I'm not in a position to know. I know everyone here is a Biden supporter, so I think they would be really careful before running a story that might hurt him."

"Yeah, Fox is the lone voice in the wilderness. All the other media hates Biden. It's so ridiculously flagrant. Probably nothing to this, just some scuttlebutt, like you said."

"I hope so. Hey lover boy, you coming over

tonight for some fun?" Manny asked.

Anticipation flushed through Gary. He and Manny had been together for less than a month. She was faster at getting more than acquainted, but he was ready to catch up.

"Sure. What time you get off?"

"Hopefully by 8:00. I'm helping out on a segment we're doing about Trump. Dig this, we got some guy who says Trump likes hookers to pee on him."

Gary burst out laughing.

"Source doesn't want to go public but that smells about right."

"It smells awful," Gary said.

"We're figuring out how we can present it with at least a modicum of credibility, even if from an anonymous source."

"Just do the usual and start out with, 'If true…'" Gary snickered.

"Yeah, the Edward R. Murrow in me frowns at that," Manny said. "Like isn't it the reporter's job to find out if it's true before reporting it? But whatever for the cause."

She didn't have to state the cause for Gary to know that it was stopping Trump from getting re-elected. "Anyway, I'll buzz you around eight," Gary said.

"Cool. I'll get a six-pack of Red Stripe and reheat the Jamaican jerk chicken I had last night. Mama's recipe."

"Yummy."

"Yummy? What, me or the chicken?"

Not expecting that retort, he paused a second. "Both!"

"You're so bad! See you then babe."

He couldn't remember the last time a woman had called him babe, if ever, but he sure liked it.

The day after the day after…

Slade McClintock sat at the red leather banquette in an alcove corner of the restaurant L'Ambassadeur on 10th and Q. The owner/maître'd, Antoine, was excited to have the Republican Chairman of the Senate Intelligence Committee as one of the first patrons at his restaurant since DC had recently allowed the return of indoor restaurant dining at fifty percent capacity. But if truth be told, he secretly let one of his most prominent patrons inside to dine a couple times before despite the lockdown because, well, he was the Chairman of the Senate Intelligence Committee.

"Senator, would you like another Manhattan?" Antoine asked.

"Sure, why not. Thanks A."

Slade McClintock was the senior US senator from the state of Arkansas. He was seventy-four years old with an ostentatious bourbon belly. Most striking about the senator's physical appearance was his hairline, which started as a V at the upper middle of his forehead and uniformly swept back from there, like The Werewolf's. Like most senators and congressmen over the age of fifty he dyed his hair, in this case a ridiculously unblemished brunette color. His tenure as a representative of the people of Arkansas was inaugurated forty years ago.

Senator McClintock looked up and said, "Well, here arrives Boy Wonder," referring to his aid, Avi

Silverman, approaching the alcove. Senator McClintock's running joke with Avi, a graduate of Cornell, was to ask, "Are you sure your alma mater's an Ivy League School?" Avi's answer was always something like, "I believe so, at least that's what they told me."

One might wonder if the senator would have hired Avi if he had known for certain that Cornell was an Ivy League School. He once said to Avi, "You know, back in the day Ivy Leaguers ran the government, Wall Street, the media. But all those wet-behind-the-ear kids figured out that just about every American institution is irredeemably corrupt and systematically racist, so they only work at non-profit advocacy groups or in academia now. And guess what, Avi? No one in government, on Wall Street, in media seems to miss them much."

"Sorry I'm late, Senator," Avi said as he sat down, "but the bus service really sucks since Covid hit."

"Holy smokes, is that mask big enough you're wearing? What is that, an N-95? Take that ridiculous thing off, will you."

"Oh, sorry Senator, I forgot I was wearing it," Avi said as he removed his mask. "You can't enter a restaurant without wearing one."

"Oh, hogwash, those masks don't do shit. I even heard Fauci say they didn't before he said they did. A bunch of virtue signaling by pussy progressives."

"Maybe so, Senator. Anyway, I wanted to give you some info on what I heard from my contact at CNN."

"Alright. You did sound a bit breathless when you called me to meet."

Avi fidgeted in his seat and said, "You're not going to believe this, but I'm being told—"

At that moment, Antoine came over and asked Avi if he wanted anything to imbibe.

"Uh, make it a diet cola, please."

"Avi, I told you before that tee-totaling is not good for your health, especially mental health," the Senator said.

After Antoine departed, Avi continued, "So I'm hearing from CNN that China is putting tons of money toward getting Biden elected."

McClintock took a long sip of his drink as he eyed Avi with a dead aim stare over the crystal glass rim.

"Who at CNN told you this?" the senator asked, his cocktail buzz suddenly dissipating.

"Gale Sturmstrom."

"Ole Gale, huh. She's really moved up in the world from the rag hag she was when I first met her twenty years ago, working at the *New York Post*. Where's she getting this from?"

"She said she couldn't say, at least not right now."

"Why she's telling you about this?"

Avi shifted in his seat. "We're friends."

McClintock's pale slab of jowls shuddered as he chuckled. "Friends? You mean you're fucking her?"

Avi blushed and looked at his diet soda a waiter had just placed on the table. "Uh, well, not really, or you know, we're friends."

"That's okay, Avi. I don't need to know more. You won't be the first lamb that cougar devoured. Anyway, back to the Chinese. We should probably feel out the FBI on this. I might have to give ole Barney a call."

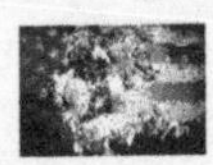

"What the fuck, Peckerwood!" Director Cummings

exclaimed. As a deacon at the First Baptist Church in Fairfax, Virginia, he avoided cussing as much as he could, but sometimes he just couldn't help it.

"That old ogre McClintock called me buzzing with stuff about Chinese paying and playing for Joe Biden. Not even two whole days since you told me." Cummings stood in front of the window with the Washington Monument in the distance while Fisherwood roosted in his chrome and leather nest.

"Damn, I dunno who could have leaked," Fisherwood said.

"Yeah, tight ship with tight lips my ass."

"The only person in the agency who knew about it besides me was Samantha Wilson in the Seattle office who got it from Copper. And of course, Copper knew, but he'd blow his cover talking to CNN."

Cummings rubbed his chin as he stared out the window. *Doesn't it always happen this way, things about to blow up just as I'm less than a year away from retiring? Twenty-five years working for the government at half of what I'm worth, and now some sweet job at a DC law firm, or lobbying outfit, or hedge fund is in jeopardy over some leak.*

Cummings turned toward his subordinate. "Find out who's pissing this information out, Peckerwood. Bird dog this like our careers depend on it. And hurry up before the Orange Turd calls, pushing me to the wall to go public with it.

Chapter Two

GLOBAL FISSION

June 2020

Peter Aliasione walked down Pine Street in Seattle on a bright June day. Summer was the only time he would visit Seattle because gloomy rain and clouds sapped his energy. He needed his energy as a politically well-connected lawyer with a contact list on his iPhone that spanned the globe.

The acrid aroma of burning plastic and plywood filled the air in downtown Seattle, a lingering reminder of the recent Darrell LeMay riots and looting, er, protests. LeMay, who had recently been laid off due to Covid-19 as a short order cook at the Rebel Diner in Dalton, Georgia, had been shot and killed by local police. Responding to a domestic disturbance call at

LeMay's apartment, the officers thought the cell phone that LeMay pulled out was a gun. This being the twelfth killing of an unarmed white person by police in the US so far that year, protests across the country erupted.

Aliasione walked past empty storefronts afflicting block after block like missing teeth in the city's mouth. The good denizens of the "Pioneer Square'' business district had not gotten around to bleaching away all the graffiti that stained the ground level facades of skyscrapers that were once shiny with optimism. Like tattoos etched by a drunken tat artist, the loopy spray-painted letters variously read: "Kill Killer Cops! Seeg Hell Fuher (sic) Trump." Across Old Navy's plywood window was scrawled, "White Privlege (sic) Forever!" An armless mannequin man *sans* clothes was propped against a No Parking sign, a stunned dumb expression on his face.

Normally, Aliasione attended business meetings attired in one of the Armani suits that lined his closet like soldiers arrayed for combat. But today he was attired in beige cargo shorts and a Rice University t-shirt. He wore sandals instead of the usual loafers adorned with the golden Gucci horse bit. He dressed down to keep the one or two panhandlers that seemed to occupy every corner of downtown Seattle from hitting him up for some dough. Meanwhile, the Patek Philippe wristwatch stayed snug and secure in one of his cargo shorts giant pockets, so as not to tempt one of the corner bums, as he uncharitably called them.

Notwithstanding his everyman attire, Aliasione's brisk stride, arms swinging, and head held high, betrayed a man who had places to go and people to see. Finally, he espied the appointed meeting place, a Starbucks, and there, sitting outside at one of the clusters of metal chairs and small tables, was the man he was to see, Daniel Copper. He happily noted that the only other person in the seating area was a guy slumped over one of the tables, apparently out cold with a syringe dangling from his forearm.

"Ah, here he is, my favorite secret agent man," Aliasione said. As Copper began to rise from his seat, Aliasione waved him down, "No, no Danny, don't get up."

Copper was dressed in a cream-colored linen suit, no tie, shirt unbuttoned two buttons down, revealing some dark chest hair. He wore a necklace bearing small white objects, an accessory that people would have called a puka-bead necklace three decades before. The Ray Ban aviator sunglasses that he wore brought Joe Biden to Aliasione's mind, in both cases the aviators signifying Top Gun "dudeness." His long, raggedy hair hung down to his shoulders and his thick goatee showed a few gray streaks. This was the third time he had met Copper, and for the third time he wondered if Copper's appearance resulted from his idiosyncratic fashion sensibility or from a desire to disguise his occupation as an ex-spy now doing work as a "researcher."

After innocuous chit chat that ranged from the Seattle Mariners to Aliasione's flight from Washington DC— "With Covid scaring everybody, I had the whole damn plane to myself, so why use the Gulfstream!"— Aliasione crossed his arms and got down to business.

"So, Danny, that was some good work you did for us on the Chinese sticking their fingers in the election pie."

"Thanks, Pete. A lot of effort and years went into developing a network on the mainland and in Hong

Kong. It finally paid off."

Copper's Liverpudlian accent reminded Aliasione of the Beatles.

"And I'm always happy to keep you in the flow of what's to know since you've been a paying customer in the past," Copper said.

Aliasione harrumphed, as if Copper should know enough to know that he knew just about everything worth knowing, at least when it came to the American political scene. He circulated information like the heart does blood. He was founder and managing partner of Global Fission, a Washington DC strategic intelligence firm, which was basically a fundraising and dirty works operation for the Republican Party. This fresh Biden poop, whether true or not, would help the cause, the cause being the re-election of Donald J. Trump.

It helped that he was currently having a torrid affair with a young man who worked at the FBI as an analyst and had just recently been given the task of connecting the dots relating to Chinese money spent on Facebook, per Deputy Director Fisherwood. "My little J. Edgar," Aliasione affectionately called his paramour. (However, unlike FBI Director Hoover, his boy toy didn't parade around his apartment in women's dresses.) After some cocktails and a bottle of wine and during some pillow talk, the young analyst revealed what he was working on to his sugar daddy.

"Thanks for sending it my way, Danny boy." Aliasione didn't inform Copper that he relayed Copper's intel to CNN star reporter, Gale Sturmstrom, his old friend and partner in crime, as he put it.

"Well, thank you, Peter. I do what I can."

Copper did some opposition research for Global Fission in 2018 regarding the Democratic candidate in one of California's congressional districts. Let's just say that Copper's discovery of an illicit affair that the married candidate had with the priestess of the Unitarian Church of Wiccan Socialism had made the election a lot closer than it should have been in a heavily Democratic district. Aliasione knew talent when he saw it and so kept Copper in mind for future work.

Aliasione did not know, however, that Copper had also delivered the same info to the FBI. He would soon learn that Copper's ultimate aim in all his espionage endeavors was to get paid by somebody…anybody.

A masked waitress came to the table to take the two gentlemen's orders. Aliasione ordered a tall regular coffee black while Copper went for a Peppermint White Chocolate Mocha Frappuccino.

"I hope you don't mind my splurging on a five-dollar cup of coffee," Cooper said mawkishly.

Funny how he assumes I'm picking up the tab. "No, not at all, Danny. I called for this meeting after all." The call had come the week before when Aliasione told Copper he had a job for him as a follow-up to his Chinese election interference score.

Aliasione planted his arms on the table and looked hard into the lenses of Copper's sunglasses. Aliasione's vanity did allow himself a few seconds to admire his bulging biceps as reflected in the sunglass lenses, bulges obtained from hours of working out with his personal trainer. *Chris Cuomo doesn't have anything over me when it comes to muscles.*

"Have you put together a file on this stuff yet?" he asked.

"No, not as of yet," Copper said. "I'm still doing some back checking and formatting it."

"So, no one has seen it?"

"No." Aliasione couldn't accuse Copper of lying since he had not directly given the completed file to the FBI...at least not yet.

"Good, I want an exclusive on it, Danny." Aliasione's amiable tone turned steely.

"Exclusive?"

"Yep. No one but me sees it."

"Well…" Copper slightly raised his hands from the table and looked about as if he were somewhat bemused by the proposition and seeking someone to affirm his bemusement. "I'm not sure I can do that, Peter."

"I got fifty grand that says you can."

"You'll pay me $50,000 for this file?"

"Yep. I'll wire it tomorrow. And I think that's a hellava price since someone's already leaked this all over the place like an old man full of Flomax."

Copper shook his head, obviously annoyed by the leaks, not knowing that the leaker was Aliasione's buddy, Sturmstrom. Aliasione's modus operandi was to relay intel to Sturmstrom in the hopes that with all of CNN's resources she could get a clearer, fuller picture of the situation before going on air with it. "Hey, Gale, I'm hearing some juicy gossip about Marcon…" Strumstrom would then hit up her contacts, like Avi Silverman, to verify whatever Aliasione peddled. Once enough people parrot speculation to each other, it becomes information. This perverse circular flow enabled Aliasione to spin this newly mined, accepted public knowledge for his own profitable and sometimes nefarious purposes.

"And on top of that, I've got something else you can do for me, Danny."

"Yes," Danny said, his frown vanishing.

"I got more than a hunch that the Biden campaign knows about this Chinese effort. And my batting average when it comes to hunches is 999."

"Hmm," Copper said as he sipped his Frappuccino.

"I want you to use your network to confirm that hunch for me."

"I don't know, Peter. That's a tall order. I've got nothing to go on other than your hunch, however impeccable it might be."

"I'll deposit $50,000 for what you've already put together. You need to set up a bank account in Cayman I can wire into."

"I already have one, of course," Copper said.

"Good then. You get me what I need, and another hundred grand comes your way." The $150,000 would barely make a dent in the two million dollars that the American Grass Roots Crossroads Political Action Committee to Re-elect Donald J. Trump, which went by the acronym AGRCRTRDJT, had contributed to Global Fission's 2020 opposition research enterprise.

"Hmm..." Copper leaned his head back for a few seconds, appearing to consider the matter. But Aliasione had done a thorough background check on Copper and knew enough about his financial situation to know his heart was probably palpitating at the $150,000 opportunity. Aliasione almost smiled thinking how Copper's $2500 rent on his townhouse, the $600 payment on his 2014 BMW 530xi, the alimony payment to his dear ex-wife, these and all the other monthly drains on his diminished income were gathering like the orphans in *Oliver Twist* before the enormous kettle of gruel, their cups held up.

"And when will the retainer be deposited?" Copper

slid his chair forward.

"Give me instructions, and it goes out tomorrow," Aliasione said. "I'll itemize it as an expense for the…um…for the Copper File we'll call it."

"Okay, I'll start the deep dive the day after."

Not long after his meeting with Aliasione, Copper made a call to Hong Kong. "Good morning, Meng," he said cheerfully to the female who answered the phone. "You up and about?" Since it was eight-thirty in the morning, Hong Kong time, he certainly hoped that his most important Chinese contact was out of bed.

"Professor Copper? Please, you can't call me on this number," Meng said in Cantonese. "Things have changed here. They're always listening. I will call you back."

Copper felt chastened after Meng discontinued the call. Of course, things had changed. Hong Kong was slowly being squeezed to death by the python-like Chinese Communist Party and would sooner or later be swallowed whole by the mainland government.

Copper had gotten to know Meng a few years before when she was a twenty-three-year-old associate, and he was a senior fellow at the Hong Kong based Confucius Academy of International Understanding. The Academy was renowned as a think tank where scholars, journalists, foreign service bureaucrats, could study and discuss current events in China and its place on the global stage within the relative openness that then prevailed on the island state. Copper fit in the foreign service category and Meng in the journalist. Meng addressed Copper as Professor Copper for reasons not completely clear to him, although he did give lectures at the Academy. In any case, he never bothered to correct the flattering title.

Meng had since joined the Hong Kong based Internet hosting service facetiously called Chinklink. Chinklink had access to various nooks and crannies in the dark web, and it wasn't long before Meng and Copper knew that they were both in a position to scratch each other's backs. A marriage if not made in heaven, then at least in purgatory. Copper found her to be somewhat ditzy in a nerdy sort of way, a bob hairstyle, and big, black-framed eyeglasses. But she had been able to provide Copper intel on the Hong Kong democracy movement, which Copper had relayed to the CIA. Whether Copper did this as a supporter of the movement or to get future paid gigs from the CIA didn't really matter to the agency. It found his work useful and professional.

Meng returned Copper's call a few minutes later via an encryption app.

"Professor Copper, please that number is off limits. Vulnerable to big ears," Meng said in English to Copper after he received her call.

"I know, I know..."

"So, I'm euphoric you called me this morning. Anything super special?"

Her proficiency in English did not extend to knowing how to properly modulate her adjectives.

"I got another job for us. A follow up to the work we did about Xi getting involved in US elections."

"Okay. Super-duper!"

"The client wants us to notch it up a bit."

"Notch it up?" Meng asked. "Like on a belt?"

"Uh, no…like take it to another level."

"I see."

"The client wants us to find any actual connections there might be between Xi and the Biden campaign, besides China dumping money into it."

"Oh, okay. Like collusion?"

"Ha, yeah, well, let's not get ahead of ourselves, darling. Start out with the wonton dumplings before we get to the Bird's Nest special. Do you think you can work your contacts and come up with some quality dirt along those lines? Give it the old college try."

"Yes, but I'm sorry to say I didn't go to college."

"Ha, that's just an expression, dear."

"But I must tell you something, Professor. Some bad news."

"Oh, and what's that?"

"I got suspended from my job last week."

"Meng! Did you go to work drunk again?" Meng had been suspended before for showing up at work if not exactly inebriated then at least terribly hungover with sour plum wine breath.

"No, I did not, Professor. I swear to your god I didn't. I went to Dragon Boat Festival last night. My team win, and we celebrated by drinking a little. Sorry."

"So does that mean you're out of action?"

"No mister. I still have plenty of action. I still have friends who know tons of knowledge. Like Zheng Wei. He works at MSS. He's at the party last night. He's here now."

"Meng! A guy with the Ministry of State Security's in your apartment right now?"

"He in bedroom, snoring like hog. No worry. He good guy. On our side. He gives me lots of dope."

"Dope? You mean he's a drug dealer?"

Meng laughs. "Of course not, Professor. Dope like

info. You need to better know American slang."

"What I need from you is some plausible evidence that Biden's people know about what the Chinese are doing."

"Hmm…that might be difficult. Like Chinese proverb say, 'Hard to catch big fish with tiny shrimp.'"

"I understand, Meng. But focus on one word that I said. I said plausible evidence. You know what that means?' He then said the equivalent word in Cantonese.

"Oh yes, Professor, I see it. You mean like rumor?"

"Bingo!"

"Huh?"

"I mean yes, that's exactly what I meant. It doesn't have to be one hundred percent verified, just something that makes sense."

"Fantastic. Will begin soon to find rumors. But I need one thing first, Professor."

"And what's that?"

"Money. I have no job. I need pay."

"I understand. How much?"

"For me 5,000 Dollars not Yuan."

"Okay, that's done. And if you get me some rumors, and I emphasize plausible rumors, then I will pay you another five thousand US dollars. Deal?"

"Deal. Believe in me, Professor. I am the wind beneath your wings."

After the call with Meng ended, Professor Copper couldn't help but feel less than confident. Meng had come through before, but maybe this was a mountain too high for her to climb. She put on a game face or voice, but still... What other angle could he get on whether the Biden campaign had the slightest inkling about what the Chinese were up to? Who else did he know who might know just enough, who might have a clue that could be finessed, massaged, misinterpreted into a $150,000 incrimination?

Copper suddenly jumped from his couch, almost knocking over a lamp on the side table. "Of course, you idiot!" He hurriedly opened his laptop to book a flight to New York City.

Chapter Three

LOVE AND HATE DURING THE PLAGUE

The leafy canopy of interlocking ancient American elm trees slowed the shafts of sunlight shooting through, so that by the time they landed upon Manny and Gary fifty feet below, they had dissipated into a diaphanous cloud of golden flecks.

The couple strolled along Literary Walk in Central Park, so called because of the prominent statues of Shakespeare and three other writers. On this late June day, throngs sought sanctuary in the vast green arboreal expanse from the dreary plague that kept them cooped up in tiny apartments. Most sighed with relief as they entered the park. If all those sighs had been sounded together, they would have been as audible as the cicadas in the trees.

Manny stopped and did a pirouette in the middle

of the promenade for no other reason than wanting to do a pirouette. Her light, robin egg blue summer dress fluttered above her knees as she spun with a technique polished at Manhattan's Fiorello H. LaGuardia High School of Performing Arts, an hour and half subway ride from her family's row house in Queens.

Gary smiled. "Something particular make you do that?"

"Nah, just seemed natural."

"Hey, check this dude out." Gary stood before the statue of the Scottish poet Robert Burns in the midst of literary afflatus.

"Look at his expression," Manny said. "Looks like he's having an orgasm."

Gary laughed. "Or taking a dump on that tree stump he's sitting on."

Manny bent over with giggles.

As they continued to stroll down the walk, Manny noticed other couples holding hands. She and Gary had already gotten intimate in each other's beds, but they had never publicly displayed affection. Yes, Gary was a bit of an egghead and reserved, but fuck it, Manny was going to hold his hand. When her hand reached out and casually took hold of his, she glanced sideways and saw his lips crease into a quick smile.

Manny liked his smile because he didn't overuse it. When he smiled, he meant it. He wasn't the most handsome guy around, she would admit. A bit better than okay. What she first noticed about him was his well-kept hair, its part so straight. That and something in general about his face reassured her.

When Manny took his hand, Gary's nervous system sparkled for a moment with a paradoxical frisson of awkwardness and tingling pleasure. He had been on dates before, but he had never had a girlfriend, he was embarrassed to admit. He told himself that he had more important things to do than focus on a relationship. But really, he had always felt a bit shy around girls, too worried about saying or doing the wrong thing. Manny vanquished those feelings. Like she hit a switch that turned off the bright light of his self-consciousness.

He was proud to accompany someone with her looks. Not a beauty in the Hollywood fashion sense, with all its "Kartrashian" expensive exaggeration, but in a natural way. Her slender dancer's figure met his height of five foot ten. Her hippie, blue-tinted round sunglasses occluded her green eyes. Those she had inherited from her Scot Irish grandfather who left troubled Northern Ireland for peace of mind and a little bit of Jamaican land to grow bananas.

When Gary first met Manny at a Biden campaign event, he was struck dumb for a second or two by those eyes looking at him above her mask, highlighting her brown skin and short cropped, dark curls. "Hey, I'm Amancia Carleton. People call me Manny," she had said to him then. After a couple of seconds of no response from Gary, she asked, "So what's your name?" like she was talking to a bashful little boy.

They continued to amble down the walk until they came to the mall where stood the twenty-six-foot-tall Bethesda Fountain, topped by an angel hovering over four cherubs. Manny and Gary sat on the low circular stone wall surrounding the gurgling fountain.

Manny put her hands on her knees, sat straight up, and inhaled. "What a beautiful day!"

A dozen or so people milled about, most keeping a safe six feet from others. Gary was reminded of a Chirico surrealistic painting of a plaza where solitary figures stood sentinel against some coming catastrophe on the horizon.

"So…you hear anything more about that Chinese thing?" Gary asked. His sunglasses disguised the intense interest in his eyes. They had hung out for over an hour now, and he itched to bring up the topic even though he would have rather avoided work talk during this idyllic stroll with the girl with whom he was falling in love.

"Nah." Manny shrugged her shoulders. "Probably a bunch of bullshit."

"I hope so. You know I told you I was sort of an unofficial advisor to the Biden campaign on things to do with China."

"You did," Manny said. "That's great."

"So, I can see them having me spearhead any investigation of this sewer gossip."

"So, maybe this turns out to be a good thing for you."

"But there is one fly in the ointment. I've been kinda freaked out by the stupid rumor going around because—Manny you have to promise you won't tell this to anyone," he said after pausing in mid-sentence.

"C'mon dude, if you know anything about me, you know you can trust me."

"I've been working on setting up a meeting between Biden and Xi."

"No, really?"

"You know I had a fellowship at that institute in Hong Kong after I graduated. Confucius Academy of International Understanding."

Manny smiled. "Yeah, I always dug that name."

"I've made some calls to some people I knew there, friends working their way up in the government.

They contacted some higher ups. Starting to have some real discussions about a mini-summit or something like that."

One of his drinking buddies from the Academy whom Gary had called a few days prior was Zhao Li, a mid-level bureaucrat at the Ministry of Foreign Affairs.

"Listen, my friend," Zhao had said to Gary in Mandarin, "I think that's a great idea. Something that could propel both our careers. I'm going to set up a conference call with one of my superiors, you, and me next week to work this out. And you remember Wei Kezhi from the Academy? He's working in the Ministry of Public Security. We need to get him involved too."

"Ole Kamikaze Kezhi, who liked to down like five Kamikaze shots in a row?" Gary laughed. "I'd love to catch up with him. Set up this conference call, buddy."

"Wow, that is exciting." Manny put her hand on his.

"Yeah, it's funny because, you know, I'm not usually the guy who makes things happen. I let stuff happen to me. You know what I mean?" He was tired of living the cliché of the passive, ivory tower intellectual, a go-with-the-flow guy. He wasn't a type A personality, not even a type B, but damn, he knew he could do better than type Z.

"Sure, I get you."

"Still a long way off. I haven't told anyone in the campaign yet because I want to see if it has a chance first. And it may be dead anyway now… Hey, no more work talk. Let's go to the Sheep Meadow."

The two rose and strolled hand in hand.

"Hey Gary, I've been meaning to ask you something for a while now."

"Yeah?"

"What's your real name? I mean, your parents couldn't have really named you Gary, right? I'm sure that's a common name in Hong Kong… Not!"

Gary chuckled. "No, that's really my name. And actually, it's not an uncommon name in China. My mom used to say Gary originated from an ancient Mandarin word for 'mighty with spear.' But my mom made up a lot of stuff."

"But it's kinda funny because Gary sounds so all-American," Manny said.

"It's pronounced different though in China," Gary said. "The G is sounded like a J. More of an accent on the first syllable."

"JAR-Y?"

"Yeah, but you know us yellow people have a hard time saying our 'r's, so it sounds more like Jolly."

Manny smiled. Jolly was not exactly how she would have described his demeanor. Subdued and placid on the surface, not easily ruffled, somewhat laid-back. She wondered often what he was thinking. But she liked that about him. She had dealt with too many guys in the past who were bullshit artists, only talked about themselves, were all bluster and braggadocio, insecure cads. Gary was secure within himself. His voice was low and calm. She found his quiet intellect sexy.

She grew up in a household with an alcoholic father. After downing a bottle of Jamaican rum, the sweet daddy who always sent her off to school with a morning kiss would turn into a darkly bitter man who could never get traction in the Great Land of Opportunity. He would hurl thunderous curses at her and her little brother, Winston Jr. Her mother got the worst of it. Annabel would position herself between Manny's father and her children, prepared to receive whatever slap or punch they could see rearing up. When Manny got old enough, she was the one who stood before her father and talked him down or planted her feet and balled her fists, ready to fight back if she had to, for the sake of her mother and brother. So she was perfectly okay with calm and quiet. She would take all the low-key she could get.

Once they reached the Sheep Meadow, Manny and Gary plopped down and joined scores of others lying out on the expansive cushy lawn. The grass had such a shiny green sheen that it almost looked plastic.

"I bet it was hard for your family to leave Hong Kong for the US back then." Manny stretched her legs out.

"I dunno. My parents left the mainland for Hong Kong when the Cultural Revolution hit. Even though Dad was officially a member of the Communist Party, he was also a grad student in applied physics and so was considered part of the 'degenerate bourgeoisie elite.'" He made air quotation marks. "When the Brits decided to hand Hong Kong back to China in 1997, my parents were smart enough to see what would come. So, I think they were kinda glad to get the hell out of there, even though Hong Kong was a pretty swell place back then."

"But it had to have affected you. You were just a little kid."

"I was seven. We moved to LA after Dad got a job teaching at UCLA. Nothing wrong with Westwood, that's for sure. My brother was five years older than me. I think it weighed on him a lot more."

"Why don't you ever talk about your brother? What's his name again?"

"His given name was Jai-Guo. People started calling him Joe when we moved to the states."

"And what's his story?"

Gary inhaled deeply, then exhaled. "Well, if you went to Chinatown and asked someone on the street about Smokey Joe, that person would probably shake his head and move on from you as quick as he could."

"Like he's a bad dude of some type?"

"You know, Manny, I'm just not ready to talk about all that right now. What happened with Joe has been painful for my parents and me. Give me some time before—"

At that moment, his phone with the ringtone "Tchaikovsky 1812 Overture" sounded, saving him from any more talk about his brother.

"Hey, long time no talk, dude!" Gary said after answering his phone. "Damn, has it been that long? So, you're in town? Great. Where you staying? Sure, let's get together…yeah, restaurants are open, but it's all outdoors, which is okay since the weather has been so good. Okay, I'll make a reservation at some place near your hotel and buzz you back. Cool. I look forward to it too. Talk later."

"So, who was that?" Manny asked.

"What a coincidence. A Brit who was also at the Academy with me happens to be in town. Going to meet for drinks and dinner tonight."

"What's his name?"

"Danny. Danny Copper."

"Just think about what Viagra, Cialis and all these dick

drugs have done to our culture, our society, goddamn fucking Western Civilization," Danny Copper said, slightly stumbling over pronouncing civilization. After two martinis and now on a second bottle of 2000 Chateau Margaux, Copper was frequently mangling words with more than two syllables.

Gary and Copper were dining al fresco at La Vie En Rose in Soho. Gary did not select La Vie En Rose as the place to meet Danny because it was a celebrated celebrity hotspot but because it was not far from the Soho Grand where Danny said he was staying. Gary wouldn't have thought less of Copper if he had told him the truth, namely that he was staying at a Hamptons Inn off a side pocket of Times Square, a room which he procured with the help of a fifty-dollar Coronavirus coupon. Anyway, Gary did think it was cool to see Jared Leto and his retinue taking a large table three down from where Gary and Copper sat.

"Loved you in *Dallas Buyers Club,"* Copper shouted to Leto as he took his seat.

Leto, who wore a custom-made mask encrusted with emeralds, nodded to his inebriated fan boy.

"So, I'm talking with my father a couple of weeks ago," Copper said, continuing his lecture on the topic of drugs like Viagra and Cialis undermining Western Civilization, "and he's telling me how he and his other seventy-plus-year-old chums hang out at Rude Gentlemen's Club—this is back in February before Covid mind you—and how he's getting hand jobs back in the VIP Champagne Room. The idea that Pops is getting his todger yanked really turns my stomach."

"Yeah, I hear you man." The martini slurred Gary's words. "You kinda like to think at that age, you're not so much about getting your rocks off. Maybe thinking some about your mind and soul."

"Exactly," Copper said. "When you got no lead in the pencil or crank in the crane, old dogs have to learn new tricks. Right?"

"Become wise, you mean?"

"Yes. Who wants to walk around at eighty, you know, with your cock as hard as your walking cane? I pity the poor woman in the twilight of her years whose husband discovered Levitra."

"True marketing genius to come up with that name: Levitra as in levitate."

Copper broke into laughter.

"Let's change the subject, mate." Copper wiped the laugh tears from his eyes. "So, how's the campaign going?"

Gary noticed Copper reach into his inside pocket and finger with something, but he paid it no mind.

"Good. I'm a volunteer, but Biden has actually asked my advice on China policy a couple of times, which was kinda neat. We're still in buildup mode but getting there fast. Gushers of money pouring in."

"Hmmm…speaking of money," Copper said, "I've been hearing some rather alarming things."

Gary took another sip of wine as he looked at Copper, "You mean the Chinese money?"

Copper raised an eyebrow and paused before saying anything. "Why yes. So, you know all about it?"

"Of course, I do. I knew about it a couple of weeks ago."

"Really?"

"And what exactly are you hearing?"

"That the Chinese government is funneling twenty million into your campaign."

Gary frowned and shook his head. "Damn!"

Copper noted Gary's displeasure that the word was out.

Being drunker than he had been in a long time, Gary misunderstood the gist of Copper's questioning. Gary thought he talked about the rumor, but Copper talked about the funding, as if it were in fact true. In Copper's alcohol-soaked mind, Gary confirmed the campaign was receiving funds from Chinese sources and that he knew all about it.

"And do you think this grows?" Copper asked.

"Of course," Gary replied, "once this thing is out of the bottle, it's hard to put the stopper back in."

"I can imagine that's a gargantuan bottle with a lot to pour out," Copper said, referring to Chinese funding capacity.

"You're damn right. And next thing you know, it'll be fifty million instead of twenty," Gary said, talking about the rumor spreading and getting more and more outlandish.

"Whoaaa!" Copper exclaimed. "And you think it gets to that?"

"Of course, and probably much more." Churchill's quote, "A lie gets halfway around the world before the truth has a chance to get its pants on," briefly crossed his mind.

Copper was struck by Gary's nonchalance in tossing about this bombshell. He glanced up to thank his lucky stars for this unexpected coup, and re-filled Gary's glass, hoping the drunker he got the more he would spill.

"And when do you think this fifty million will happen?"

"Give it a week or so. You know how these things develop."

"Indeed. Aren't you worried about the FBI catching wind of this?" Copper asked.

Gary laughed. "Those Keystone Cops will never figure out where all this is coming from, the source of it all." The source of the rumor he meant. Gary held a lot of respect for the FBI, but the wine spoke with its usual wise-guy impudence.

Just as Copper was going to ask Gary if he feared that he might go to jail over this, a raucous shouting broke out a couple of blocks down from the restaurant on West Broadway. A crowd of angry young men came marching down the avenue, blocking traffic, setting trash cans on fire, smashing parked car windows with steel batons.

"Oh shit, here come the Proud Boys," Gary said.

Many in the protest march wore camouflage outfits or black attire. A lot of yellow colors also, the organization's semi-official color. Also popular were bulletproof vests, a variety of helmets such as baseball, motorcycle, US Army infantry. Tight t-shirts displayed biceps all swollen up. Trump banners and American flags mixed with a couple of Confederate battle flags and "Don't Tread on Me" banners.

"White lives matter!" they shouted. "Fuck Antifa!" "White rights...White rights!" "USA! USA!"

A lot of beards and caps turned backward, most not wearing masks. Twisted Sister's "We're Not Gonna Take It" boomed over the throng. NYPD officers, positioned on the fringe of the crowd and dressed in riot gear, followed the march, braced for action.

The nation's major cities had suffered all summer alt-right marches turning into riots and looting. The media in general seemed to have a hard time denouncing the movement. "Whether you disagree with them or not, Proud Boys have a First Amendment right to express their political views" was the common refrain voiced by many news commentators. "The white working class is in a lot of trouble, so we should listen to what they have to say and try to understand their anger and worries."

One marcher spotted Gary. He and a couple of his buddies rushed over to the table where he and Copper sat. The guy leaned over the white linen-covered table and yelled directly into Gary's face. "Hey, you wanna apologize for you people spreading the Kung Fu Flu?"

Copper stood. "Settle down boys. We're not looking for a squabble."

"Squabble?" one of the Proud Boys said with dripping sarcasm. "Look fellas, we got a Brit fag here."

He had what Copper thought was a Southern accent. A lot of the Boys must have gleefully traveled a long way for a weekend of protests in Sodom and Gomorrah New York City.

"The slang for queer in Britain is poofter, not fag," Copper casually said.

Another one pointed at Danny's white blazer jacket with the polka dotted hanky square in its front pocket and his salmon pink shorts decorated with tiny whale emblems. He looked like he had just returned from a vacation in Bermuda.

"What the fuck is that get-up?" the Proud Boy said with a guffaw. "Looks like a poofter suit."

"You know what we do to boys down in Oklahoma dressed like that?" one of the protesting trio asked.

"Pray tell," Copper said, holding his temper in check.

"We fuck 'em, that's what," the intruder said. With that, he lifted the wine glass that was sitting on the table and guzzled it down.

"I'll have you know that wine you just slurped down like a common Philistine cost over $1,000 per bottle." Copper was expecting the Biden campaign to pick up the tab, of course.

"Well then, I don't mind if I do have another," the wine connoisseur said as he reached for the bottle.

"But I do mind," Copper said as he forcefully knocked the guy's hand away. Copper's adrenaline gland squirted like a lemon being squeezed as he savored the chance to use for the first time in years the martial arts he learned decades ago as a MI5 special ops guy.

With that, the Proud Boy took a swing at Copper, who grabbed the fist in mid-air, took hold of the guy's wrist with his other hand, and snapped it back. The guy screamed like an old lady who just witnessed her dear Petite Basset Griffon Vendeen run over by a bus.

"Goddamn, you broke my wrist, dude!"

One of his partners then charged Copper, who flattened his hand like a blade, drew it back, and with deadly force and aim thrust it into the guy's esophagus. The guy stopped in the middle of his sally and clutched his throat, gagging violently, his eyes bulging.

The third guy then made his move toward Copper, throwing a wild punch that missed his target completely but exposed him to a straight right from Copper, not with his fist but with the butt of his hand, a karate blow, which burst his attacker's nose as if it were an overripe tomato. The blow completely disabled any further threats from that joker, however proud he may have been.

At that moment a squad of police officers in riot gear stormed onto the scene. They immediately took hold of Copper, whom they treated as the aggressor.

"Hey, he wasn't doing anything but protecting himself," Gary shouted to the arresting officers.

"Sit down and shut the fuck up," one of the officers said to Gary. "We observed what he did."

Meanwhile the three Proud Boy accosters stumbled back into the crowd.

The officers handcuffed Copper and bum-rushed him away.

"I'll put up bail for you," Gary shouted to Danny.

"Thanks mate," Copper said. Little did Gary know that the thanks was for a lot more than bail.

Chapter Four

FOLLOW THE FACTS

Director Cummings sat at his imposing desk, while in the two chairs in front of it sat Deputy Director Fisherwood and independent contractor secret agent man, Danny Copper. Since the chairs were six feet apart and six feet from his desk, Cummings figured no need to wear masks, even if that was a technical breach of CDC guidance.

"So, Mr. Copper, I'm glad we finally got to meet. I've heard good things about your work from my cousins over in the CIA." Cummings couldn't help but notice Copper's bluish Scottish Shaw plaid suit, white shirt with horizontal blue stripes, solid blue tie, pink pocket hanky.

"And uncovering the Chinese money flow was a real catch," Fisherwood said. "We're going to dig deep into the Biden campaign. I got a feeling we'll find a lot of other 'irregularities.'"

"But let's keep in mind that we still don't have conclusive proof," Cummings said. He found himself constantly reining in Fisherwood's Trumpian fervor.

"Exactly," Copper said. "And that's why I asked for this emergency meeting because I've come across further evidence to support the Chinese involvement in the presidential election."

"I hope you appreciate that it's highly outside the norm for someone to ask for a meeting just with the Director and Deputy Director," Cummings said. "But we acquiesced because of your reputation."

"So, we're expecting more good stuff." Fisherwood sounded eager.

"I do have information that I classify as 'good stuff,' as you put it. First, I need to give full disclosure about an incident that occurred while I was in the process of obtaining said information."

"Okay, shoot."

"Well, while dining with my source in New York last night, a mob of Proud Boys marched down the street past the restaurant where we were. A group of them assaulted our table for no other reason than that my dinner companion was of Chinese extraction and hence, in their small minds at least, responsible for Covid-19. Long story short, a scuffle ensued, NYPD officers intervened and arrested me for some inexplicable reason, seeing how I was the victim and not the aggressor in this fray, and hauled me off to the Sixth Precinct cooler. Luckily, I was able to quickly escape with a summons to appear in Court on August 21 for the charge of assault in the third degree, which fortunately the State of New York has recently changed to a misdemeanor requiring no bail."

"For sure, the Proud Boys might not be saints and angels," Fisherwood said, "but that's what you get when the elites devastate the blue-collar working class. Read *Hillbilly Elegy* if you want to see what I'm talking about."

"Okay, so you got arrested for a misdemeanor." Cummings wished to quickly get back on point. "Duly noted. Tell us why you asked for this meeting that you said was urgent."

"Just some background: I dined last night with a gentleman named Gary Wang, who is a Chinese specialist, having graduated from Columbia University with a degree in Sino Studies. Both his parents were formerly Chinese nationals before becoming US citizens. I should note that his father was once a member of the Chinese Communist Party.

"Wang was a fellow for two years at the Hong Kong based Confucius Academy of International Understanding. I believe your cousins at the CIA will tell you that the Academy is a notorious hotbed and recruiting ground for Chinese intelligence operations. My affiliation as a guest lecturer with the Academy has proven to be a great source of intelligence and contacts for me. Wang now works for the Biden campaign and has the informal title of advisor for Chinese affairs."

"Interesting." Cummings put his fingers up like a tent. "So, what were you able to get out of this guy?"

"Rather than my telling you second hand, let's hear it from the horse's mouth." Copper retrieved the recording device from his jacket pocket. He placed it on Cummings' desk and turned up the volume. When the recording got to Gary's Keystone Cops remark, Cumming's finger tent had not only collapsed, but his two hands had separated and balled into fists. Fisherwood shifted in his chair and emanated something between a cough and a guttural groan.

"Karl, I think we need to call a meeting about this. And Danny, we want you to stay on this case."

"Certainly," Copper said. "But there is a little matter that I need to bring up."

"Yes?" Cummings asked.

"Well, my work, including the work that I've already done for the FBI, which you yourself described as a real catch, all this requires a good deal of expense on my part and continuing—"

"How much you want, Danny?"

Copper looked at the ceiling as if calculating in his head. "I would say $100,000 should cover it."

Cummings and Fisherwood glanced at each other.

"Okay, we can handle that."

"But we want to make this look like reimbursement of expenses incurred by you doing your work for us," Fisherwood said. "So, any and everything that you spend money on, like airfare, your meal last night, everything including the kitchen sink, keep a receipt so we can justify it."

"Most certainly." Copper shifted in his chair.

His smile just then reminded Cummings of the Cheshire Cat's, not knowing that Copper smiled so because he had finagled a double dip, getting paid by both Global Fission and the FBI for the same work.

As he rose to leave, Copper reached to retrieve his recording device.

"No, sorry, you need to leave that with us. Buy a new one. Send us the receipt. We'll get a copy of all the recordings on it back to you."

"Okay, but just so you know, that little machine

was custom made for me and cost $1,500."

"No sweat. Just send us the receipt. Keep your ear to the ground and report back to us when you get anything new."

"I do have a couple of operations in process that I hope will generate benefits." Copper turned and walked to the door.

After Fisherwood sat down, Cummings said, "We need to call a meeting with the 2020 election task force pronto, Peckerwood."

"I'm on it, Boss."

The next day, Cummings, Fisherwood, four senior agents from the Counterintelligence Election Monitoring Task Force, and Department of Justice assistant attorney Anita Frankenforth, gathered in an electronically secured conference room where nothing came in and nothing went out.

Cummings stood while addressing those gathered around the large conference table. "You've read the reports, you've heard the recording, what do you think we should do with this?"

A few seconds of silence until Agent Sylvia Books spoke up. "I think it's obvious what we should do with this Wang character. We get a warrant and surveil his ass."

"I agree one hundred percent." Fisherwood sat up straighter.

Cummings expected Sylvia to be the first to strongly state an opinion. Others in the organization had expressed their annoyance to Cummings about Ms. Books: she constantly interrupts those she disagrees with; she undermines whoever speaks contrarily to her opinion, with eye rolls and loud exhaling.

"She's a flat-out bitch," one of her colleagues—a female agent, said.

"I think that's rushing in too quickly," Ms. Frankenforth said. "I think the right approach would be to gain access to the Biden campaign bank accounts first."

"The problem with that is if they were in fact receiving Chinese money, they'd make sure it was well disguised," Fisherwood said. "We'd probably spend weeks scouring the records and likely come up with nothing."

Ms. Books directed her glare at Ms. Frankenworth. "Look, Anita, what is it you want? We have the smoking gun, but you want the silver bullet too?"

"Biden has raised eyebrows with his friendly comments about China," one of the other agents said. "'China's gonna eat our lunch? C'mon man!'" The agent's decent imitation of Biden caused some light laughter at the conference table.

"And look at how he freaked out when the President put a travel ban on China," Fisherwood said. "Xenophobic! Racist! And don't forget about that billion dollar deal that Hunter scored with some Bank of China subsidiary. Given all that, is it so far–fetched that the same people might be pumping a measly twenty million into Uncle Joe's campaign?"

"Hey, Karl…" Cummings said, raising his hand to Fisherwood as if to say, "Tone it down."

"Danny Copper is a professional," Fisherwood said. "The recording speaks for itself. I agree with Sylvia that we should keep tabs on this guy."

Cummings rubbed the back of his head and let out a labored sigh. He then remembered Wang's Keystone

Cops comment. "I think you're right. But if we're going down that path, we need to get a warrant from the FISA court. Mr. Wang is a US citizen and resides inside the US, right? So, we must apply to FISA for approval of surveillance warrants. Anita, you think you can put something together to present to the court? Shouldn't be a problem, should it?"

"Give me a couple of days. As far as a problem, you know a case FISA ever turned down?"

Cummings smirked. "I believe the record is 18,742 approved, four rejected. I like our odds. Okay all, that does it for now."

As everyone rose from the table, Cummings asked Sylvia to stay.

Cummings sat down. "I wanted to speak to you before this meeting. In fact, I was going to tell you not to come but couldn't get to you in time."

Books looked bewildered. "What?"

"Sylvia, are you not aware that we monitor texts on all FBI issued phones? Not only that, but we also preserve them. You didn't know that?"

Books gulped. "Uh, I guess I did."

"Then why were you sending emails like this to Agent Peter Strop: 'Biden will never become president, right? Right?' And then Strop answers, 'No. No, we'll stop it.'"

Books blushed and looked down.

"And then Strop texts to you, 'We got an insurance policy to keep Sleepy Joe from ever becoming president.' And you answer, 'Yep, China!'"

"Here's another one from you to Strop: 'OMG, did you see Biden at the presser yesterday? He kept losing his train of thought. A ghost train! LOL! I thought he was going to start drooling on himself.'

"I'm not even going to get into all the romantic goo-goo talk between you two, like favorite sex positions." Cummings cleared his throat. "Am I not mistaken, but aren't both you and Strop married?"

Speechless, perhaps for the first time, Books didn't answer.

"Sylvia, how could you be so frickin' careless?" Cumming's residue Southern manners kept him from saying fucking to a lady.

"I'm taking you out of this election task force. You will be removed from all email chains. You understand? And as far as your future here, we'll discuss that at your quarterly review in a couple of weeks." Cummings would have fired her right then and there if he could have, but he knew it was almost easier to climb Mt. Everest than fire a federal government employee.

Books abashedly nodded.

Cummings rose and walked out of the room as Books remained seated, evidently too stunned to stand.

The telephone intercom buzzed.

"Yes, Sheila?"

"The President's office called, Director Cummings. The President would like to meet with you at two thirty this afternoon in the Oval Office."

Ah, here we go, I wonder what's taken him so long. The President's tweet at 2 a.m. that morning left no doubt that he would be called to the Oval Office carpet shortly: "Hearing that Biden getting more than a kiss from his lover boy Xi. Hear that sound? Cha Ching Cha Ching China! China! Stay tuned!"

"I guess I won't be getting in my afternoon meditation exercise, Sheila." Afternoon meditation exercise was code for nap.

"Duty calls, Director Cummings."

Later that day, Cummings crossed Pennsylvania Avenue and walked a few blocks to the White House. The Director of the FBI walking alone in broad daylight instead of being ushered in an armor-plated black SUV would be considered a serious breach of protocol. But Cummings wanted to get a breath of fresh air on this summer day and a little exercise before the dreaded meeting.

The FBI Director meeting in person with POTUS was not routine, or not supposed to be routine anyway. The traditional understanding, however quaint, was that the Director should keep some distance from the office of the President. But President Trump was not one to follow rules, conventions, or protocol. Each time the President called him for a meeting, Cummings once again wondered why he had accepted Trump's offer to move up from US Attorney for the Southern Alabama District to FBI Directorship. Maybe he had bitten off more than he could swallow. No doubt, his prior position had less pressure and a slower pace. Maybe he would have been better off if Trump had known the truth, namely that he hadn't voted for him but instead had written in John McCain's name on the ballot.

Cummings entered the White House through a side door and a steward led him to the Oval Office. Trump rose from his ponderous, ornate desk. He wore the usual blue suite, white shirt, and extra-long red tie to compensate for something.

"Good to see you again, Director Barney." President Trump rose from his chair.

Cummings suppressed the urge to cringe at being addressed as Director Barney. He figured Trump had heard that Cummings' friends called him Barney, and the President appeared to earnestly desire a friendly relationship with him, only because he was the Director of the FBI. The Director was sure that Trump thought he would deem such a friendship as a privilege and honor.

Trump reached out to shake his hand, even though everyone and his five-year-old kid knew that was against CDC guidance. Cummings smiled and shook the president's hand anyway.

Cummings sat in a chair in front of the desk. He knew the desk had been made from oak timbers of the H.M.S. Resolute and given by Queen Victoria to President Rutherford B. Hayes. Hence the name "Resolute Desk." He couldn't avoid seeing something incongruous between the stately history of that desk and its present occupant.

He took a few seconds to appraise the president's appearance. His skin didn't glow with so much bronze since the last time he saw him. More yellowish. But the white half-moons under his eyes from where he kept his tanning goggles were still there. *Where in the White House do they keep that tanning bed*?

"So, how's 'Bama football looking for next season?" the President asked.

Before Cummings could respond, Trump continued.

"Coach Saban's a good guy. A good friend of mine. We played Trump National Briarcliff Manor together. Good guy. I should get you up there sometime. You're a scratch golfer, right?"

Cummings smiled. "Ha, yeah, maybe twenty years

ago."

"We'll get you out at Trump National down in NOVA someday. Best golf course in the world. Beautiful greens. I got a special hybrid of Bermuda custom made just for the greens. From a horticultural research lab at Texas A&M. Just for me. Beautiful greens. Jack Nicklaus told me they were the prettiest greens he'd ever seen. Jack Nicklaus. Been friends since…I don't know when. Long time."

During this monologue, Cummings' mind began to wander. He couldn't help but marvel at Trump's hair. *A little blonder since last time we met. But damn, what an engineering feat! What an ingenious cantilever over the brow! How does he do that* do? *And how much time every morning does it take to construct?*

Trump leaned over his desk, staring intently at Cummings, and abruptly changed the subject. "What's this about the Chinese?"

"Sorry, Mr. President. Been a long day. You're asking about the Chinese."

"Of course, I'm asking about the Chinese, Barney. It's all over town that they're bankrolling Biden's campaign. Please don't tell me you haven't heard about this. I know Xi personally. I even like the guy. He likes me. We're good friends. But don't tell me you don't know about this. FBI Director and all. Xi's not a bad guy, but he's gotta do what he's gotta do. But we can't let him do what he's gotta do. You got me? Don't tell me you don't know about this? FBI director and all."

The whole while he spoke, the president held his hands aloft from his desk and kept moving them in and out, like he was playing an invisible old-timey accordion. The thought that he might be the monkey dancing to the street accordion music briefly crossed the Director's mind. He sometimes wondered if Trump took him as a patsy and that was why he surprised everyone and appointed him head of the FBI.

"So, I want you on Sleazy Joe's case. He and that son of his, Hunter. Going around all over the world doing sleazy deals. On Air Force Two. All kinds of sleazy deals. It's terrible."

The president leaned over the desk again, like that cantilevered bouffant was a weapon threatening Director Barney to stay on Sleazy Joe's case.

"Mr. President, I can assure you that we are aware of the rumors about the Chinese government supporting the Biden campaign. We are investigating the matter fully."

"Let me tell you, Director Barney, there are plenty of people who would like to be Director of the FBI. They're lined out the door. Plenty of people. Excellent people. So, I want results. I don't want President Xi laughing at me. He's a good guy. We're friends, but I don't want him laughing at me. So, I want results."

"I understand your concern, Mr. President. We are presently looking into this, and I will keep you and the Attorney General apprised of any developments that come from our investigation."

President Trump remained silent, a contemplative expression on his face. "I just wonder, Director Barney, if I should contact President Xi. Talk man-to-man. He's a good guy. We're friends. And ask why he's doing this to me."

"Mr. President, I would strongly, strongly advise you to not do that. Nothing good will result from that."

The president considered for a few moments. "Yeah, you're probably right," he said sullenly. "Okay, Director Barney, that's all I needed from you. Be on your way."

"Thank you, sir." Cummings rose and got out of there as quickly as he could, lest the President wanted to talk more about Alabama football or putting greens.

Sylvia Books stood on the corner of Madison and 49th street, holding a black umbrella up against the light summer shower. A few moments later, another woman holding an umbrella approached Ms. Books.

"Sylvia?" she asked.

"Yes."

"I'm Gale Sturmstrom with CNN news. Good to meet you and thanks for coming up from DC."

"Same here." Books flashed her FBI badge for Sturmstrom's perusal, so she would be sure that Books was who she said she was. Sturmstrom nodded her acknowledgement.

"Shall we walk?" Books asked.

"I would have preferred a sunny day for a stroll, but let's go. Can you hear me okay through this mask?"

"I hear you fine. I do like that paisley print."

"Ha, thanks." Sturmstrom tightened the mask. "Who in the world would have ever thought that face masks would become some kind of fashion statement?"

The two walked past windows covered with plywood boarding. Scraps of paper turned in the damp gentle breeze like the souls of dead commerce.

"So, Sylvia, you said in your phone call that you had something to tell me regarding the election."

"Yes, I do." Books paused. "The Chinese are illegally injecting money into the Biden campaign."

"Okay." Sturmstrom kept any hint of acknowledgement off her face. Of course, Books didn't know that Sturmstrom had already been tipped off about this by Aliasione.

"And you know this firsthand?" Sturmstrom asked.

"Yes. I sat in on an FBI briefing three days ago."

"And how much are we talking, as far as what the Chinese are funding?"

"Twenty million dollars to start." Books cleared her throat, as if the idea was stuck there.

"Do you have a name in the Biden organization associated with this?"

"I do, but I don't feel comfortable disclosing that right now. I'm checking the legal consequences before I do so.

"That's understandable."

"I can tell you that he's a young guy, Chinese-American," Books added after seeing an inkling of doubt flicker across Sturmstrom' s expression.

"Good. Whenever you are ready to talk, text 'Hello' to me, and we will meet here again. And make sure that you do not use your FBI issued phone. A burner is best."

"I know not to use my company phone, believe me," Books said.

"You do know that we can't pay you for this tip, right?" Sturmstrom asked, glancing at Sylvia.

Staring straight ahead, Books said, "I'm not doing this for money."

Ah, revenge, Sturmstrom thought. *Hell hath no fury...*

Chapter Five

HOLLYWOOD SQUARES

Director Cummings logged onto the virtual meeting. Half a dozen squares showed up on his computer screen: himself, Fisherwood, Frankenforth, a court recorder, an assistant deputy from the Department of Justice, and The Honorable Alicia Townsend, the judge presiding over this matter and the only African American woman currently on the Foreign Intelligence Surveillance Court, commonly known as the FISA court.

Despite this being a virtual hearing, the judge had donned a black robe. Cummings felt uneasy when he saw that Townsend would be presiding, as she was known to be a no-nonsense judge who was hypersensitive to violations of privacy and civil liberties. Unlike the other eleven judges assigned to the FISA court, she wielded a gavel but no rubber stamp.

All the squares caused Cummings to remember when as a kid he used to watch the game show *Hollywood Squares*. *"I'll take Charles Nelson Reilly to block, Gene,* and his uneasiness eased.

Judge Townsend began the meeting. "Thank you all for joining this hearing regarding the FBI application to surveil a Mr. Gary Wang. I appreciate all your patience in conducting this virtual meeting. As you know, the Federal courthouse in DC has been locked down due to Covid-19. I have been told by the IT people at the DOJ that communication lines to this meeting are contained within the DOJ secured network, so we don't have to worry about any of those pesky hackers. Also, I don't know about y'all, but I'm happy to forgo wearing a mask. I appreciate that the FBI has submitted its application and supporting material to this court seven days before this hearing, as FISA rules require. Okay, now let's get down to business. I have a question for you gentlepersons."

"Yes, your honor," Cummings, Fisherwood, and Frankenforth said simultaneously

"You are asking this court to approve a warrant allowing this administration to surveil—okay, let's just call it what is, to spy on—an individual who works for the campaign of the apparent presidential nominee of the party out of power in the middle of an election. Really?"

Again, Cummings, Fisherwood and Frankenforth all spoke simultaneously: "Your Honor, we at the FBI..." Cummings said.

"I understand, your Honor," Fisherwood said.

"May it please the court..." Frankenforth said.

Cummings and the others paused for a second when they realized they were Zoom trampling each other. Two seconds later, after each said, "Go ahead" to the other two, they each pounced again to give their answers to the judge's somewhat rhetorical query. Another pause and again the trinity of voices.

"Stop it! Now!" the judge shouted. "Jeezus," she muttered under her breath. "Director Cummings, will you please go first."

"Your Honor, we appreciate that this request is somewhat unprecedented, but given the voice evidence you heard on the tape, we at the FBI believe the gravity of the situation requires that we surveil Wang for the next thirty days."

"Frankly, Director Cummings, I did not find what Mr. Wang said on the tape one hundred percent convincing. He never directly stated he personally knew firsthand that funds had been sent to the campaign by Chinese nationals. I did not hear eyewitness testimony but what sounded like secondhand information at best. I did happen to notice he slurred his words once or twice and evidently there was some significant imbibing going on."

Cummings continued. "I understand that your Honor, however—"

He paused at the sound of a toilet flushing.

"Tommy, I told you not to use my bathroom," Frankenforth said.

"I couldn't use the upstairs cause Jenny used it and stunk up the whole room."

"Anita! You're open," shouted Cummings. "Mute it!"

"Fuck!" Chief Counsel Frankenforth said, that being the last thing she said during the call.

Judge Townsend looked up to the ceiling or perhaps heaven and moaned, "Oh, my God.

"Gentlepersons, I'm going to mercifully cut this hearing short," she said after re-composing herself. "I and my staff thoroughly reviewed your presentation and have not found enough evidence to justify a warrant to surveil Mr. Wang. I understand how serious this matter is, and I encourage you to come back to this court with whatever supporting evidence you may henceforth discover. I am now adjourning this meeting. Good luck people."

"Thank you, your Honor," Cummings mumbled as the judge's square turned black. He prayed that his team would find enough evidence to convince Judge Townsend before the Great Orange Turd learned they struck out.

"Robert De Niro is a moron," Gale Sturmstrom said with confidence. "And I should know because I interviewed him once. It was all 'Fuck that guy Trump… Fuck Trump… Dat fat fuckin' guy.'"

Sturmstrom lounged in her silk kimono-style robe with her legs curled up on her chintz couch. She lived in a one-bedroom apartment in the newly built and three quarters empty Parc Flamboyante apartment building on 63rd and Lex. With occupancy rates having plummeted during the plague, she was able to get a sweet deal on a 750-square-foot pad. At that moment, she was sharing a bottle of wine with her friend, Manny Carleton.

"Why do you say that?" Manny asked. "He's a great actor."

"My dear, no less a director than Alfred Hitchcock called actors cattle, and Otto Preminger infamously said that the dumber they are the better." Sturmstrom lifted her wine glass and savored a slurp of Provencal Rose.

"You just don't like them because a lot of them are progressive." Manny crossed and uncrossed his legs.

"Oh please. What do they do? They do what children do, which is make-believe, pretend, play act. Don't you see that a developed intellect hinders that child-like ability? The greater your comprehension of reality, the less you're able to imagine being someone else or in another place like, say, a pirate in the Caribbean. Johnny Dep, ugh, speaking of another numbskull knucklehead."

"Geez, you're being a little angry over nothing, aren't you." Manny shifted again.

"No, you just told me you saw De Niro interviewed about the election, and you, for some reason, seemed impressed. Look, I allow entertainers into my consciousness not to educate or edify, but to entertain me. And that's it. When they start pontificating about something that has nothing to do with why I, their patron, granted them entry into my brain, I get pissed and feel like I've been taken advantage of." Sturmstrom paused to catch her breath.

"They have a right to have political opinions."

"You're missing my point, dear," Sturmstrom said as she flipped back her shoulder-length, chestnut-colored hair. "Of course, an actor can have political opinions. All I'm saying is I just don't want to hear them, any more than I want to hear my doorman's opinion on the Iran nuclear deal. They make pronouncements on politics because they think that makes them look smart. I'm mean, it's not like you must know anything to make a political pronouncement, like say, a scientific one. And so, politics is their favorite thing to do when not acting or engaging in one of their usual narcissistic, hedonistic, conspicuously consuming activities. I just don't give a rat's ass to hear what they think."

Manny rolled her eyes. "Wow, speaking of pontificating. I'm sorry I brought up Robert De Niro."

Manny tolerated Sturmstrom's right-wing opinions because she owed so much to her. Sturmstrom entered her life when Manny's mother's cleaning business, consisting of Annabel Carleton and three undocumented Jamaican ladies, got hired to tidy up her Queens flat twice a month, before she landed the CNN gig that tripled her pay and enabled her to move to Parc Flamboyante.

Manny's mother had mentioned to Sturmstrom that Manny was about to graduate from St. John's University and had her sights on a career in journalism. Sturmstrom, who was fond of Manny's mother, made a few calls and, before you could say Rupert Murdock, had gotten Manny an entry level job at Fox News, that "news clown car" as Sturmstrom called the network. "But hey, Manny dear, a job's a job.'"

Loyalty was one of Manny's innate virtues, and she met with Gale once a month or so for drinks or dinner, even if that meant suffering what she regarded as benighted rants. But Sturmstrom did occasionally have good color about happenings in the business as well as career guidance. In short, Gale was Manny's mentor, and she Gale's protégé.

"I'm sorry you brought up De Niro, too."

Sturmstrom languidly stretched her full length out on the couch and propped her head on a satin-covered pillow. She cut a fine figure, thanks to five days a week at LA Fitness. Makeup, both cosmetic and genetic, helped her look ten years younger than her forty-five years. Manny felt some sympathy for her because she needed that cut body and almost flawless skin to compete with on-air talent increasingly younger and invariably attractive.

"You sound like a true Trumper." Two glasses of wine emboldened Manny to voice her opinion, even if it annoyed her host. "How can you support that pig, by the way?"

"Yes, he is admittedly a pig."

"And he lies all the time, right?"

"True, he often doesn't tell the truth." Sturmstrom's words were calm, controlled.

"And he's pathologically narcissistic too."

"Yes, you can check that box. He's just as narcissistic as Obama but more blatantly and boorishly so."

"So how can you vote for a lying, narcissistic pig?"

Sturmstrom sighed. "Oh my, where do I begin... Do you understand what authentic means, Manny?"

"Of course."

"An authentic person says what he means and means what he says, however cliché that sounds. An authentic person means it when she promises something and does her damnedest to live up to that promise. We haven't had an authentic president since Reagan…until Donald J. weirdly descended that escalator in Trump Tower. At least in my humble opinion."

Humble Gale made Manny do a mind laugh. "I guess you could say Hitler was authentic too," Manny said.

"Oh, stop it with that Hitler stuff." Sturmstrom sat

up straight. "Trump didn't murder millions of people and turn most of Europe into rubble. You're too young to appreciate the low regard that most Americans have toward these inauthentic career politicians. Trump is the antithesis to them, the anti-Christ."

"Which do you think is lower in the public's regard, politicians or journalists?" Manny asked.

"Very cheeky, Manny… But these politicians, all they've managed to do to the middle class and blue-collar workers is fuck them over twenty different ways. You see how these folks are constantly mocked at movies, on TV, in college classrooms. Deplorables clinging to their guns and religion. And HRC, Her Royal Clinton, epitomized that disdain more than anybody."

"She's smart and experienced compared to that jackass Trump."

"True and true. But here's an analogy that sums it for me: Trump is a greasy diner cheeseburger with fries and Hilary a cup of zero fat Greek yogurt. And Jeb Bush is decaf espresso. And Biden a loaf of whitebread way past its shelf life, all stale and covered with mold spots. Do you call any of them authentic, much less exciting?"

"Yeah well, eating too many greasy cheeseburgers can do a lot of damage to you, and you end up with a heart attack. And Trump has done a lot of damage to this country."

"Really? Do this thought experiment for me: Imagine you went into a coma October 2016 and came out of the coma February 2020. And then someone showed you videos and tweets of Trump and told you that he was the President of the United States. You'd go, 'No fucking way. You've got to be kidding me!'

But next, you're given information about the economy and the state of the US and the world, you'd probably say, 'Damn, things are pretty good.' Intelligence is the ability to hold two opposing ideas in your head at the same time and not go crazy, to paraphrase F. Scott. I judge Trump not by his lying, narcissistic, piggish behavior but by what he's done."

"Covid-19 showed that the emperor wasn't wearing any clothes, Gale. Ugh, the thought of Trump naked."

"You think Hilary would have or could have done anything much different? She might have done worse. If you're going to blame anybody for Coronavirus, blame Xi."

"Okay, Gale, I've heard all this before. I blame him for all the stupid shit he said and the fountain of disinformation that he constantly spouted. The Bully Pulpit takes on a whole new meaning when he's using it. Anyway, let's talk about something else."

"Speaking of Xi, um, I do think I've come across a big story. A bombshell. I know I don't even have to ask if I can confide in you."

"Of course, you can. I know loose lips sink ships."

"I've heard through a reliable source, a first-hand source, that the Chinese are supporting Biden with a lot of money."

Manny's eyes widened, and she jerked straight up in her chair. "Really?" She didn't let on that she had heard this rumor already because she wanted to hear Sturmstrom's version.

"The question is what did the Biden people know about this and when did they know it?"

"But you don't even know if it's true or not."

"I believe this source is reliable. I've heard that

there's a connection in the campaign to the Chinese. That person might be the key to this whole thing."

"And you don't know anything about this person?" Manny asked.

"Nothing much. Except he's a guy, a young guy. A Chinese guy."

If Gale had been paying attention, she would have noticed the sudden alarm in Manny's eyes. She had not told Gale about her budding romance with Gary since they had started dating after the last time she and Gale had met. Besides, she was somewhat wary of telling Gale too much about her personal life.

"Manny, you have got to promise, promise me that this conversation does not leave this room."

Sturmstrom held her pinky finger up for Manny to wrap her pinky around.

"I pinky promise," she said as their pinkies entwined.

Sturmstrom couldn't see that Manny had crossed her fingers on the other hand she held behind her back.

"So, what you think?" Manny asked Gary as he bit into the red snapper.

"Hmm, interesting." He looked down and wiped his mouth with his napkin.

Manny sat back from the table and crossed her arms. "As my mama used to say. 'Tain't nutin inturestin' wid food. 'Tis either gut or bad."

Manny had prepared a fish dish that was her effort at fusion cuisine. A combination of Jamaican jerk and Szechuan. Bold but risky. Gary had come over to her studio apartment in Harlem to be her guinea pig.

"Don't get pissed. It's okay, Manny. It's just, you know, interesting…"

Manny slammed down the rest of her Cuba Libre cocktail and sat silent. She stared glumly at the scented candle on the small kitchen table even though the summer sun still peered into the small kitchen window.

"Hey Manny, what's up?" Gary reached out and touched her hand. "You've been kinda moody since I got here. What gives?".

Manny put her hand to her face, where tears welled. "I had drinks with Gale last night."

Gary smiled sympathetically. "Don't tell me all her Trump ravings sent you in a spiral. That could make me cry too."

Manny wiped at her eyes with the back of her hand and sort of laughed. "No, that wasn't it. I'm used to that. It's just that…she said some things, about all this Chinese stuff."

Gary's smile disappeared. "Like what?"

"She told me word is the Chinese have some inside guy with the Biden campaign. I guess like a mole, who's doing all this money stuff. Putting money into the campaign."

"Okay, we already heard that. So what?" Gary squeezed Manny's hand.

"She said she heard the guy's young, you know, a young Chinese male. And I…I couldn't help but think…that they might think it's you."

"C'mon Manny, how could they think that person is me? Really."

"I know. I know."

"You think I'm the only young Chinese guy who works in the campaign? There must be dozens. And besides, what Gale is saying is probably all baloney anyway."

Manny met Gary's gaze. "It's just that I'm so worried that they might, like, think that for some crazy reason, you know…"

"Manny, stop. There's nothing there, nothing to it."

"I've been worried sick about it, so worried that…that I realize that I'm in love with you." She gave Gary a tentative look.

The concern in Gary's expression softened. "Guess what, Amancia, I'm in love with you too."

Manny half-smiled. "So, I guess we're really in trouble now."

"A little trouble never hurt anyone," Gary leaned over and kissed Manny until all the fear inside her melted away.

"Let's go back to the bedroom and make some trouble there," she murmured into his ear.

Chapter Six

TEENAGE HOOKERS! WHAT?

July 2020

Danny Copper was driving his black BMW 530xi with the bumper barely held to the car's body by black duct tape, the damage the result of his recently rear-ending another car. He planned to spend $5,000 of the $50,000 that Global Fission had recently deposited into his Cayman account to make the necessary repairs. But other monetary exigencies had gotten in the way, like the demand letter from his dear ex's attorney for three months owed alimony. Meanwhile, Coronavirus claustrophobia had become intolerable, so he decided to take a leisurely Sunday drive along the Alaskan Way, the sparkling Elliot Bay in full view.

A phone call interrupted his singing along to the

Eagles "Hotel California" playing through his ear buds. *Ah drat, it's a bright beautiful morning and the ferries are gliding in, and the sailboats are tilting into the wind and the damn phone rings.* When he saw it was Meng calling, he uttered "Shit!" and switched from the music to the call.

"Meng, good morning, or I mean good afternoon where you are."

"Yes, Professor Copper, good whatever to you also."

"I hope you are back at your job."

"Yes, Professor, probation over. They take me back. They never find someone in my instead."

"Excellent. So, what's going on?"

"I have some super-duper plausible rumors to tell you. A cornucopia of rumors. Cornucopia, I learned that word yesterday. So much joy to say that word."

"Yes, yes, but what's in your cornucopia besides fruit and such?"

"You know Hunter, son of Joe Biden?"

"Yes, I know of him but not personally."

"You know he fly on Air Force Two plane to China in 2013. And an investment firm that he's partner in made big deal with Bank of China."

"I heard about it," Copper said, his interest piqued. "Supposedly $1.5 billion."

"My source telling me that the money that goes into campaign came out of bank account that Hunter's investment firm has at Bank of China."

"Wow, that could be huge." Copper knew his way around money laundering well enough to see that once Chinese money entered Hunter's investment vehicle, it could go anywhere and everywhere before it ended up in a Biden campaign bank account. A forensic accountant would get lost in a labyrinth of money transfers in any effort to get to the original source of the funds. *How you like them cornucopia apples, Director Cummings?*

"Sorry, Professor, but I could not get the number of that bank account the US dollars went into. My friend at Bank of China too nervous to tell me more. I had to pay him some of the money you sent me to get him to say that."

"That's okay, Meng. Remember, all we want is plausibility." Copper knew, though, that Meng paying her source money put into doubt anything he told her. He decided that little no-no would stay just between her and him.

"Let others work their legs to dig out facts, right Professor?"

"Exactly. Your metaphor is a bit mixed, but you got the right idea. What else you got in that nasty cornucopia of yours?"

Meng giggled. "I am not nasty girl, Professor. But I do have some nasty rumors for you."

"Like what?"

"Joe Biden likes teenage whores."

"What? Meng, what on earth are you talking about?"

"On that same trip when Vice President and son of Vice President flew on Air Force Two."

"Yes."

"They stayed at the Mandarin Oriental Hotel. I have girlfriend who worked there when that happened. She tells me that after he and son check in, three little prostitutes go into hotel."

"Meng. I know Beijing well enough to know that prostitutes going into the Mandarin Oriental is not exactly uncommon."

"Maybe. My person at hotel has phone video of the little whores going into the hotel. She thinks she saw girl push elevator button to same floor that Biden father and son staying on. That is not on video though, but she says that anyway."

"My dear Meng, an entourage of aids and security and press accompany the Vice President wherever he goes. He might not be the brightest bulb in the chandelier, but he's not that dumb. Really, we can do better than this nonsense."

"But Professor, you said you want plausible rumors to make money. News media in US tells the world that Trump likes Russian prostitutes. Makes them money. Did they prove he did? Did he prove he didn't? What is truth? Where did it come from? Came from people like us."

People like us. That stung Copper a bit. But then he considered how much fun Aliasione could have with this, however impossible it might be. Bismarck said politics is the art of the possible. Politics in 2020 had become the art of the impossible. Yes, Aliasione and company might have enough fun with this to pay him a nice bonus. Still, he wondered how low he could go. But he knew he would ultimately dismiss any qualms he may have and throw in the prostitutes to add some extra Cayenne pepper to the info gumbo. And so, what if he knew it was ridiculous? Aliasione would use it as chum to attract one of the internet shark tabloids like Buzzsaw since the New York Times wouldn't deem it fit to print (although nowadays you never could tell).

"You think your friend can get a copy of that video?"

"I give her ten US dollars; she gives me video."

"Okay." Copper knew what kind of people he was. He would hand it off to Aliasione and let him do his magic with it.

"Just one more thing, Professor Copper."

"Shoot."

"Ha, okay. This good bullet… You know my friend Wei who works at what you call the Ministry of State Security?"

"Ah, yes…the guy who snores like a hog."

"Yes, that is one. He did some work for me in exchange for a month free rent at my apartment. His friend tells him that some Biden person made several calls to government people. Calls intercepted."

Copper tensed up. "Does he know the nature of the calls? I mean what the calls were about?"

"No, sorry. But he does know the name of Biden person who made calls."

"Yes, and…"

"His name Gary Wang."

"Jolly Wang?" Copper said, puzzled.

"No, Professor. G-A-R-Y Wang."

Oh my God, Copper thought, the Copper File just turned to gold.

"I have to sign off now and focus on driving. You've done great, Meng. Five thousand dollars will be wired to your account first thing tomorrow."

"Wa! Da! Hip, hip, hooray!"

"Teenage hookers? What!" Peter Aliasione shouted into his smart phone. Now, he lay prone and naked on a chaise lounge, aboard his 80-foot Hatteras somewhere off the Florida Keys. Across the stern of his yacht, stenciled in teal cursive letters were the words,

"The Gaslighter," with a flame dotting the "i" and Southampton, NY in large black letters. Aliasione's "Little J. Edgar" was in the middle of administering sunscreen to his backside.

"Correct. My source at the Mandarin Oriental witnessed three females, who she estimated to be of nubile years and dressed in attire too alluring to allow entrance through the main door, entering a side entrance and from there proceeding to the floor secured for the use of Vice President Biden and his son, Hunter."

"Truly incredible," Aliasione said. "But I guess anything is plausible in this day and age."

"Plausible, yes exactly," Copper said.

"But back to Gary Wang. So he's the Chinese bag man, huh?

"Without a doubt."

"Wow, you've gone beyond the call of duty on this one, Danny. But by the way, whatever happened to the file you were supposed to send me? Been two weeks now."

"Certainly, I'm cleaning up some things, but it should be ready to go tomorrow."

"Okay, make sure you have this hooker stuff in there."

"And, uh, the matter of the fee that we discussed?" Copper asked delicately.

"Oh, the hundred grand. Sure, that'll be coming your way as soon as I get comfortable with what you send. I mean, talk about a real bombshell."

"Peter, you don't sound like you trust my work completely."

"Hey Danny, like my hero Ronnie use to say, 'Trust but verify.' Don't worry, you'll be taken care of.

Talk to you after I review it."

After Aliasione hung up, Little J. Edgar asked, "Teenage what?"

"On a need-to-know basis. Keep rubbing." The last thing he wanted was Little J. Edgar seeking to win some brownie points with his higher ups at the FBI by springing this on them. He would make sure the FBI knew in due course.

"Teenage what?!" Director Cummings exclaimed.

Copper was sitting in front of Cummings' desk after giving the download of his latest and maybe greatest intelligence scoop. He never had complete faith in the Federal Government IT and its so-called secured communications, and so he felt he needed to deliver his findings in person to Cummings. Plus, he liked to see the pleased expression on a customer's face when he delivered the goods.

He had toned down his attire for this meeting, wearing a lavender blazer, with a bolo tie fastened with a turquoise brooch. The purple alligator loafers seemed to have caught Cumming's attention though.

"Can't be too surprised, Boss," said Fisherwood, sitting next to Copper. "Biden is known to get a little too close for comfort around young ladies. Whispering in their ears, stroking their hair, breathing on their necks."

"Okay, okay, we get the picture Karl. Hunter I can see. That's par for the course with him. But the former Vice President of the United States?

"But the main thing we have to do is focus on this Gary Wang character," Cummings said to Fisherwood. "Let's get the counterintelligence gang back together and prepare another submission to Judge Townsend for a warrant to keep tabs on this guy."

"Got it, Boss," Fisherwood said.

"Great work, Danny," Cummings said, "we'll be following up with you on this."

"That's fine, Director Cummings, but there is the little matter of my fee, the $100,000. Remember?" Copper cracked a playful but awkward smile.

"Send up expenses that you've rung up so far, Danny. Load it up. And we'll get a wire right to you. Don't worry, we'll take care of you."

"But don't include any expenses for wardrobe, Danny boy," Fisherwood said.

Cummings had to pinch his lips to suppress the chuckles. Copper, however, was none too amused.

"Teenage prostitutes? What?" Gale Sturmstrom said over her phone to Peter Aliasione. Sturmstrom rose from her desk on the noisy CNN New York newsroom floor, her mouth agape. She had been in the middle of editing a report for *The Situation Room* that she entitled "Biden's Addiction to Plagiarizing" when Aliasione had called.

"I know. Unbelievable, right?" Aliasone said. Sturmstrom could tell from his voice that he certainly didn't believe it. "We got some evidence, video, an eyewitness, sort of. But the main thing is we've established a connection between the Chinese and Biden. We got bank accounts and a Chinese guy in the Biden campaign."

"And you say this connection's name is Gary Wang?"

"Yeah. But Gale, let's hold off broadcasting his name out to the world. Keep that off record for the time being."

"Why?"

"Because I don't want to ruin this guy's life just yet. A couple of things I have to check off first."

"Since when did you grow a heart, Peter darling?"

"Look, you got enough to go out with the story that the FBI is investigating the Biden campaign. We got enough background now to know there's plenty to investigate."

"I could have done that weeks ago, Peter, after I met with agent Page. But I want to load it up with as much crap as I can. Like this Wang kid."

"Didn't I just give you enough? What my source told me? We don't need to sacrifice Gary Wang...at least not yet."

Gale did like the idea of letting the crap flow out to the public evenly over the next few weeks rather than in just one big dump. Best to string her audience along, right up to the Democratic convention.

"Speaking of your source, you haven't even given me his name yet."

"No, Gale, you know I can't do that. I told you before he's ex-MI5. Done a lot of work for the CIA. Isn't that enough for you?"

"No. Look, I've got First Amendment protection, Peter. They can come after me, but they can't ever force me to reveal my sources."

"Ha, tell that to Judith Miller. The Nobel Peace Prize winner Obama locked her up for just that. And she worked for the friendly *New York Times*. But okay, the guy's name is Daniel Copper."

"I dunno Peter. I never heard of this guy. And I'm

supposed to put a story together about Biden and Chinese bank accounts without giving up the name of the main actor, Gary Wang?"

"How long have we known each other, Gale?"

"Oh, let me think." Gale stood in the middle of the hustle and bustle of news in the making. "When was it that time you hit on me at the piano bar in the Carlyle hotel…1992?"

"Funny Gale. You're a lovely woman, but you know homey don't play that bi-sexual game."

"Peter, I would call you tri-sexual. You'll *try* anything and lick any flavor of ice cream to get what you want."

"Oh, sweetie, you should do stand-up. Look, what I'm saying is we've known each other long enough and been through many a shit storm that you should be able to grant me a modicum of trust."

Sturmstrom sighed and walked back to her desk, dodging an eager beaver assistant producer scrambling to get a story out about oral sex causing cancer.

"Okay. I'll get with my producer and an editor and talk about it."

"You go girl," Aliasione said.

"Is this how Woodward and Bernstein did it, Pete ole pal?"

"I'm going to make you a star, baby!" Aliasione said with a facetious tone.

"Oh God, last thing I want," Sturmstrom said, lying through her bleached, capped teeth.

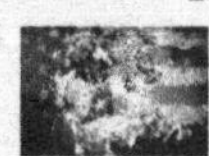

Director Cummings rose from his chair at the conference table in the nothing in, nothing out secured conference room. He addressed the same assembled members of the Counterintelligence Election Monitoring Task Force as at the last group meeting, minus Sylvia Books.

"Now that Deputy Director Fisherwood has debriefed everyone, I'm informing you that we're officially launching a counterintelligence operation whose mandate is to investigate any connections between the People's Republic of China and the Biden campaign. You all have the raw intelligence, including the Copper File. The Attorney General and I believe that we have enough to justify a preliminary investigation. Any questions?"

No questions asked.

"We're calling this operation Jumpin' Jack Flash. Why? Because Fisherwood is a Stones junkie."

The remark broke through the seriousness of the matter at hand and most everyone at the table chuckled or smiled at Fisherwood who said, "Let it bleed, baby."

"The focus of this investigation will be Gary Wang, whose profile is in the presentations you all received. He will be code referenced in all internal communications as Jack Flash. First order of business will be to re-submit our request for a warrant to surveil Jack Flash to the FISA court. And then we'll see where that leads us. Everyone follow?"

Everyone around the table nodded.

"Deputy Director Fisherwood will follow up over the next couple of days with your assigned duties in this investigation. Needless to say, all information in the presentation that has been given to you and everything stated in this meeting has been classified." Cummings paused. "So no leaks to the media! I'll have the head of anyone who does put on a pike and planted on the

Memorial Bridge!"

Cummings' raised voice caused some eyes to suddenly open much wider.

"Okay, gang, you got it, now get on it," he said in closing.

Next day…

"Dang it!"

Cummings hurled his coffee mug/pin cup at the flat screen television.

"Dang it!"

He dropped onto his chair.

"Dang it!" He bowed his head, clutched at his hair, and pulled.

Sheila burst into his office. "Director Cummings? Are you all right?"

He raised his head just enough to see her shocked expression as her eyes moved from him to the spider web of cracked LCD glass defacing Gale Sturmstrom as she gave a news report outside presidential candidate Joe Biden's house/bunker in Delaware. At the bottom of the fractured screen scrolled the headline: BOMBSHELL REPORT THAT FBI INVESTIGATING BIDEN CAMPAIGN FOR ILLEGAL CHINESE CONTRIBUTIONS.

Cummings collected himself and said to Sheila. "Tell Fisherwood to get his ass in here ASAP."

Five minutes later, Deputy Director Fisherwood sat like a chastened flunky before the director's desk.

"Boss, I have no clue who would have leaked. There were eight people in the room yesterday besides you and me. You know none of them would ever leak. They're as a dependable as—"

"A pair of my Daddy's Depend diapers," Cummings said, finishing his sentence with some gallows humor.

"The only other person outside that room yesterday who knows about this is Danny Copper."

Cummings looked at Fisherwood for a few seconds, his raised fingers pressing together as if he were praying. He hit the line on his desk phone that connected to Sheila's.

"Sheila, see if you can get Danny Copper on the line. A secured line."

Two minutes later, Sheila transferred Copper to Cummings' phone.

"Hey Danny. I've got Deputy Director Fisherwood with me in my office on the speaker phone.

"Hey there, Danny," Fisherwood said.

"Hello," Copper said flatly. Cummings guessed that he was still smarting from Fisherwood's wardrobe crack after their last meeting.

"So how in the heck do you think CNN got a hold of this story?" Cummings asked.

"I have no earthly idea."

"Let me ask you a question, Danny," Fisherwood said. "Has anyone else that you know of seen this file besides us?"

After seconds of silence on the other end of the line, Cummings added, "And please keep in mind, Danny, that there are serious repercussions for lying to the FBI, even if you're not under oath."

Copper's long exhale was clearly audible over the phone. "I did deliver the file to another party. I had to because they paid for it."

"What!" Fisherwood said. "We paid for it. What do you think that hundred grand was for?"

"Yes, I understand, and I appreciate your contribution to my efforts," Copper said. "But another party also contracted for my services. I never promised you an exclusive regarding my work."

"Exclusive? We're the fucking FBI, Danny," Fisherwood shouted.

"Indeed, you are," Copper said. "But you have to appreciate that the client list requesting my services is rather lengthy. And this other party had already engaged me for research before I met with you gentlemen."

"But you did sign an agreement not to talk to the media," Fisherwood said.

"Again, Deputy Director, I have not spoken to anyone in the media. I am prepared to sign an affidavit swearing so under oath."

"Research you said… Opposition research, right?" Cummings asked. "And so, who is this third party, Danny? And don't give me that lame excuse that you can't tell me because of client confidentiality agreement or some nonsense like that. If you do that, we'll get before a judge and have a subpoena in a New York minute."

"The firm to whom I delivered the report, which they helped pay for, was Global Fission."

"Oh Lord." Fisherwood looked up to the ceiling.

"Global Fission? You mean Peter Aliasione Global Fission?" Cummings asked.

"Yes."

"Aliasione is an operative for the Republican Party, Danny."

"And a sleaze ball," Fisherwood mumbled.

"Which means that the money he gave you for that report likely came directly or indirectly from Trump campaign funds. Right?"

"I can't answer to that, Director," Copper said.

"Jesus, now this thing has more taint on it than those hookers in your report," Fisherwood said.

Cummings frowned and raised his hand to Fisherwood. "C'mon Karl, let's keep this professional," he said sotto voce.

"Let me be clear about this, Danny," Cummings continued with a more official tone. "Your actions are way out of bounds and raise all kinds of possible legal issues and complications. Given that, we will henceforth cease all communications with you whether by phone, email, or text."

"Nice work, Danny. You better lawyer up real quick." Fisherwood groaned in disgust.

"Bollocks," Copper muttered.

"You can say that again, whatever it means." Cummings ended the call.

After head shaking and gnashing of teeth, Cummings said to Fisherwood, "We need to get a FISA warrant to follow this Gary Wang guy before Sturmstrom finds out who he is and he becomes thoroughly compromised."

"We've already set up a re-submit for this Thursday."

"That's good, Karl." Cummings pressed his lips together and looked straight ahead.

"What you thinking, Boss?"

"Question is, do we tell Judge Townsend the new information we're submitting to her was paid for by the Trump campaign?"

Fisherwood didn't hesitate to respond. "We don't

know for sure if that's the case. And even if it is true, that doesn't—you know—necessarily negate the integrity of the report. If we tell her, then you know for sure she'll shoot us down again because I don't think Townsend likes us spying on anybody period. And then we might have missed the chance to expose the Chinese trying to get their man elected President of the United States. Can we afford to take that chance?"

Fisherwood leaned toward Cummings, staring him in the eyes.

Cummings glanced out the window at the Washington Monument. "We'll leave it at a third party paid for the research. If she asks who, we tell her. If not, we just leave it alone."

"Sounds good to me." Fisherwood leaned back into his seat.

Chapter Seven

JACK FLASH

"Okay, gentlepeople, I have received and reviewed the resubmission of your request for a warrant to surveil Mr. Gary Wang with the new supporting information," Judge Townsend said to the assembled Zoom faces, the same faces that were at the last hearing, except this time Frankenforth's audio was intentionally disabled.

"But I must say, as I did last time, that I am somewhat chary to approve of the incumbent administration spying on the opposition party's presidential nominee's campaign in the middle of the election. But this new evidence justifies granting you a warrant for thirty days."

"Thank you, your Honor." Relief spread across Cummings' face.

"But Director Cummings, please be advised that

there is no guarantee that this court will renew this warrant after thirty days expires. As you should know by now, nothing's automatic with me."

"We at the FBI understand that Judge Townsend."

"One question for you, Director Cummings. I've seen several media outlets reporting this story about Chinese involvement in the election. How do you think Gale Sturmstrom et al. discovered this?"

Cummings swallowed a couple of times before answering. "Your Honor, the primary source of the information supporting this warrant, recently informed my office that he had previously contracted with another firm to supply this file to them, since they had paid for it. For opposition research or something like that. My supposition is that this third party may have leaked the story to CNN and others."

"Hmm…and what's the name of this firm?"

"Global Fission."

"Never heard of them." The judge's expression changed. "But don't you think you should have disclosed this to the court up front?"

"Perhaps, looking back on it, we should have. But we are fully confident that this third-party involvement has in no way debased the intelligence that Mr. Copper provided us, and that's why we didn't inform the court of what we consider an incidental issue."

"Well, I'm not sure that's incidental, Director. Just make sure that doesn't happen again."

"Yes, your Honor."

"Thirty-day warrant as requested in the re-submission is hereby granted. This hearing is adjourned. Have a good day people."

After Cummings logged off, his body relaxed with relief that the judge didn't delve any further into the source of the money Global Fission used to pay for the Copper file. Sure, he felt a tinge of guilt about that omission; but he figured they would learn enough over the next thirty days to move on Wang or shut the case, regardless of Peter Aliasione's involvement. Why needlessly complicate the situation with that impertinent fact? At least that was what he told himself, without admitting that he also didn't want to risk having the President find out that the FISA court blocked them from following the Chinese-Biden money trail. The last thing he needed was Mango Mussolini breathing down his neck.

"I guess this story is more real than we thought," Manny said to Gary as they sat on his couch in his apartment. She was still in her lingerie and he in his boxers and t-shirt. She had her legs propped on his lap while they sipped their Saturday morning coffees.

"You think because CNN reports something that makes it real?" Gary asked.

"I know Gale. She's surely capable of slanting something but she doesn't just make stuff up."

"I can tell you one thing for sure: it's got everybody in the campaign freaked out. I mean no one really believes it, you know, but it's like three months before the election, and we have to deal with this crap."

"Maybe it'll blow over soon," Manny said. *Here I am, once again hoping a storm will pass.*

So many storms had passed through her life when she was a kid. Usually, the center of those storms had been her father. Many nights the swirling black clouds billowed up as he slumped in his beat-up La-Z-Boy and drank down a bottle of Appleton Rum while watching a Yankees game on the tube but not really following it. Manny had cried her eyes out when he died, not only because she loved him dearly despite everything, but also because she always saw the man and father he could have been, if he had only gotten a lucky break or two.

And now, just when her life had attained a calm and even flow with Gary, another threatening storm brewed on the horizon.

She sat quietly with Gary and sipped her coffee. She knew that Gary was right, being his usual rational self, but still she worried. Maybe the skies were tranquil, even sunny, but still a foreboding wind ruffled the treetops. Her intuition, like a barometer, sensed the pressure of some future disaster looming over the horizon. She knew that she could do nothing but wait for it, wait for it like she used to wait for her father's eruptions, wait for it to hit.

Sheila walked to the Director's open office door. "Director Cummings, the President's office called, and President Trump would like to meet with you in the Oval Office. The President's assistant said ASAP."

Cummings scrunched his mouth up into a glum expression. "Thanks Sheila," he said, adding, "I guess…" as she walked out the door.

Ten minutes later, Cummings was once again sitting in front of the Resolute Desk in the Oval

Office.

"Glad to see you again, Director Barney. So, this China thing is all over the news. I got five TVs in my bedroom on all the time. All they're talking about is this China thing. Except those know-nothings at Fox. They're the worst. I hear Murdock's losing his shirt on Fox News. They'll be history in a year. Failing Fox News. But Sturmstrom at CNN, she's a pro. She was the first to jump on it. You know, there's something kind of, what's the word? Alluring, that's it. Something alluring about her too."

Cummings sort of smiled, not sure how to respond to that last comment.

"Director Barney, you're on this China thing, right? Like a duck on a June bug. Your people in Alabama say that, right?" The President repeated "Like a duck on a June bug" with a hokey Southern accent that sounded like a New Yorker who had never been to Alabama. "I love Alabama. I won by twenty-three points in '16. They love me. Hated Hilary. She's terrible. But you're all over the Chinese pouring money into Biden, right?"

"Yes, Mr. President, we have launched a counterintelligence operation to investigate this matter."

"These Chinese, they hate me because I put tariffs on them. The tariffs are beautiful. No president ever did that before. None. They hate me, but they respect me, and that's all that matters to me. Xi likes me. He respects me. He's an okay guy. But I had to get tough with him. Had to. All the bullshit they've gotten away with. Obama was their little pussycat. Bush not any better. Not the brightest guy Bush. His cell phone's a few bars short of a full charge. Do cell phones still show those bars? Good guy though. We played Trump National out in Bedminster a couple of times. Not a good golfer. Didn't break a hundred. But he doesn't drink either, so we get along great."

While Trump talked, Cummings noticed once again the President's hands playing the accordion, the rest of his body totally stiff and still, not moving, only his hands and his mouth moved. And his facial expression stayed the same while he spoke, a willful, earnest expression, his head slightly tilted forward. No smile, no frown, all intention only. He reminded Cummings of those turbaned automatons that he used to see as a kid at fairs and amusement parks, with unblinking eyes and mechanical hand movements. Put a quarter in their mouth slot and they would tell you your future. Sometimes though, the President seemed to be just now awakening to the truth of whatever he was saying. Like, "Can you believe it? Crazy!" His eyes would widen, go a little wild, and shift back and forth with disbelief.

"But you got my back on this, right Director Barney? You're gonna help me?"

Once again, Cummings was at a loss to respond to one of Trump's queries. The President didn't seem to understand that as the FBI Director, his purview didn't include White House politics. His job was not to help the President like some kind of election consultant or personal attorney. He worked for the Justice Department, and the DOJ was supposed to be politically independent of the White House, at least in theory.

"Mr. President," Cummings said, "one thing for sure that I can promise you is that this investigation will go deep and far and take us wherever we need to go. We take foreign interference in our elections with utmost seriousness."

"There's something here, Director Barney. You can smell it. Let's face it, those Chinese can be sneaky bastards. Not all of them, but there's like, what, a billion of them, right? So even a small percentage comes to a lot of sneaky bastards." Again, the President's eyes went a little wild and crazy and his hands pulled on the accordion. "But the Chinese, they're smart, sneaky smart. Invented lots of stuff. Like firecrackers, laundry detergent, I think. So, you get to the bottom of this."

"Yes, Mr. President."

"One last thing, Director Barney."

"Yes, Mr. President?"

"What's this I hear about teenage hookers? I heard that on TMZ or some show like that."

"We don't have conclusive evidence of that, but that has been reported to our source. Frankly the story seems to be totally apocryphal."

"Apocryphal? That means made up? You know there's some nasty rumors about me out there. Something about Russian call girls peeing in my bed or on me, golden showers or whatever you call it. Nasty lame stream media stuff."

Again, his eyes did that dance of disbelief, and he raised his hands as if presenting himself.

"You think a guy like me needs to pay for sex? The worst thing was Melania. She wasn't too happy when that got to her. I had to sleep in the Lincoln Bedroom for a few nights."

And for the first time since they had been conversing, the lower half of the President's face lifted into a quick, wide grin, dimples and all.

"Why you holding out on me? Not giving me what I want?" Avi Silverman whined while sitting up in bed with no clothes on.

Referenced bed belonged to Gale Sturmstrom, who, also naked, reclined behind Avi while caressing his back. "Oh, don't be grouchy, sweetie. Doesn't Mama always give you what you want?"

"I know you know more than you're telling me about the China-Biden connection."

"I told you what I can, my circumcised Adonis," Sturmstrom said playfully.

Avi turned and faced his sugar mama. "Why are you always making a big deal about me being circumcised? It's weird."

"Because my last lover—a Guatemalan who worked for Telemundo—wasn't, and it was like looking at an ant-eater when we got down to biz. So, I gained a new appreciation for the skills of a good moil."

"Look, McClintock is crawling all over me to get some info to follow up what you last told me. Which I do appreciate by the way. But I need to give him more. Like, I heard something about a Copper File. You know anything about that?"

Sturmstrom groaned. "Slade McClintock, gross. Could you imagine that guy crawling all over you?"

"I'm not a woman and consequently could not imagine having sex with Senator McClintock to get what I want. The only reason I put up with the guy is that he knows everybody and can help me move up to the next incarnation of whatever it is I hope to be.

That's all I want from him."

"Oh, you silly fool, that's what women want from powerful men too. We just have a few more tricks in our bag than you guys do."

"That I grant you."

"And that is the same thing that a young man like you wants from a powerful woman like me, correct?" Sturmstrom asked slyly.

Avi fell back into the bed and cuddled next to Sturmstrom. "Don't be so cynical. I like being with you. I can't say the same thing about ole Slade. Besides, your breath doesn't stink like a tiger's asshole like his does."

Sturmstrom tilted her head back against the pillow, laughing with her eyes shut.

"C'mon, give me some crap that I can feed to the monster," Avi sweetly pleaded as he stroked her hair.

Sturmstrom sighed and considered for a few seconds while looking up at the ceiling. "Okay, I've already told you and the world that the FBI has officially launched a counterintelligence operation to explore connections between the Biden campaign and the Chinese."

"Yeah. Old news. So what?"

"Let me finish please." She looked at Avi with mock irritation. "There's a guy who works for Biden campaign who's at the center of it, Gary Wang. And that's all the crapola I got."

"You're the best," Avi said with a grin. "How can I ever repay you?"

"Hmm...I'll think of something," Sturmstrom said as she reached under the sheets down to where the moil had done such good work.

"Director Cummings, Senator McClintock's office is on the line," Sheila said.

Oh man, first the Great Orange Turd and now Senator McFlapJowls. Cummings lifted the receiver. "Hello."

"Director Cummings, Senator McClintock would like a few moments with you," the pleasant female voice said.

"Sure." *Of course, it's beneath the senator to just call me direct.*

"Director Cummings, my man, how are you this sweltering July afternoon?" a booming voice asked.

"Fine, Senator. And how are you?"

"I'm doing okay, even though it's hotter than a three-balled billy goat in a pepper patch."

Cummings couldn't help but chuckle.

"But you and me, Cummings, we're Southern boys so we can take the heat. But these Yankees, they wilt in this humidity like the Wicked Witch when Dorothy threw some water on her."

"And don't you just know it," Cummings said, unwittingly falling into McClintock's folksy manner of speaking. "So, what can I do for you, Senator?"

"I'm calling you about all this chirping going on about the Chinese and Biden. Something called the Copper File. "

"Yes sir."

"And I'm wondering how much is true and how much is the usual media mountain out of a molehill stuff. Do you have this so-called Copper File?

"Yes sir."

"And what do you think about all this hullabaloo?"

"We have started an investigation into this matter in an effort to verify whether the allegations in the file are true."

"CNN's already let that kitty out of that bag."

Cummings suppressed a growl rising within him at the mention of that report.

"Cut through the bullshit, Director. Do you think anything will come out of this or not?"

"I don't know. That's why we're delving into it."

"Well, lemme tell you, as head of the Senate Intelligence Committee, I'm considering requesting you to debrief the committee on what you have found in the Copper File."

"Senator, as you know, I'm happy to provide your committee with whatever information it thinks it needs. However, in this case, it's much too early because, really, I don't have a good handle yet on the situation. When I do, I will inform you so, and then you can consider whether it's worth your committee's time to hear what I have to say about it."

"Hmm. I see. Would you do me the courtesy of providing me with a copy of the Copper File?"

"I can't do that right now, Senator. It's all just too preliminary. It could turn out that its contents aren't worth the paper it's written on."

"Okay, I'll take that as a No. But you will give me a heads up on any developments, won't you, Director?"

"Of course, Senator."

"Thank you kindly, sir. And by the way, I'm hosting a quail hunt down in Culpepper this coming Saturday. Gonna be the usual gaggle of politicians, lobbyists, and media types. You're welcome to join us. I'll send you an invite."

"I haven't been quail hunting in ages. But unfortunately, I'm dropping my son and daughter off at Bible camp, Senator, and so will have to regretfully decline your kind invitation."

"Oh, there's nothing unfortunate about dropping your kids off at Bible camp, Barney," the Senator said, suddenly getting informal in his address.

"I agree with you, Slade." Cummings returned the informality. "It never hurts for the kids to receive instruction in the Good Book."

Senator McClintock laughed. "That's not what I meant, Barney. What I meant is that you get the rug rats out of your way for a couple of weeks. Gives you and Mrs. Cummings some fun time."

McClintock mentioning fun time with his wife made Cummings a tad queasy. "Ha, right you are."

"Now you keep me up on any Chinese shenanigans, Barney. With the election coming up, this could be a real bombshell."

God, I'm beginning to hate that word—bombshell. You can count on it."

"Well then, have yourself a good day, Barney."

"Same to you, Slade."

After the Senator hung up the phone, he looked intently at Avi Silverman standing in front of his desk. Avi looked intently back at the senator.

"Get one of the committee's legal monkeys to draft up a subpoena for the Copper File," McClintock said. "And send me what you dug up on this Gary Wang guy."

Chapter Eight

A PERSON OF INTEREST

August 2020

"Hey, Peter. Gale here."

"Hello, Gale honey," Aliasione said. "I was just thinking about you. Seems like the China story is dying down. Puffington Post hasn't mentioned it in over a week."

"Yes, that's exactly why I'm calling you, Peter. We need to squirt some lighter fluid on the fire before it burns out."

"How do you propose we do that?"

"I need to release the name of the Biden campaign worker. Gary Wang, you said, right?"

Peter emitted a low half groan.

"Peter, my producer is all over my case. Saying we

need some follow through on the story. I mean, you told me you had a hundred percent confidence in your source who gave you Gary Wang."

"Yep," Aliasione said glumly.

"So, what's the big deal? I'm going out with the name. Taking too much heat. I don't want to drop the ball on this."

Aliasione, usually so articulate, couldn't clearly say why he wanted to hold up releasing Wang's name. If he did trust Copper's report, then Wang was clearly up to no good. Since 2016, foreign interference in US elections had become a cardinal sin. So, what *exactly* was the big deal?

Maybe I'm getting soft. Or just finally appreciating after twenty years that dirty politics is, well, really dirty. Take no prisoners! Do whatever it takes! March forward and trample whatever is in the way.

He, the master of those dark arts, had seen so many trampled. Not because they deserved it but because they were obstructing the path to victory. He had seen so many of the accused hounded into bankruptcy, divorce, and once even suicide by politicians, media, bureaucrats. Even worse, none of the accusers' consciences ever once blinked with considerations of right and wrong, truth or falsity. They never saw the accused as real individuals of flesh bone blood, mind and memory, as walking, breathing mosaics constructed from millions of experiences.

No, they, he, only saw them as inanimate objects to be removed or used or trampled. Getting Trump or Biden elected served a greater purpose than those little desperate lives, made more desperate by people like him. Maybe Gale was right, and he had grown a heart, or just discovered it. Or maybe something in his gut told him that Copper's evidence was circumstantial at best, even though that had never stopped him before. Whatever it was, he wanted to hold off as long as possible before releasing the name and plucking a young man's life that was just now blossoming like it was a boutonniere for his lapel.

"Okay, Gale. Go ahead. It doesn't matter what I say anyway, does it? So run with it."

"Thanks, Peter."

Aliasione clicked the call off, not bothering to say, "You're welcome."

Manny detected a different buzz on the Fox News floor that afternoon. It was frenetic as usual, but a kind of inaudible growl underlied it. Some of the senior people looked concerned about something. She noticed a group of producers and editors huddled in the conference room with the glass walls. They appeared agitated, definitely not happy. A lot of scowls and arm waving.

"Something going on?" Manny asked a friend as she hurriedly walked by her desk.

The friend stopped. "Supposedly CNN got some big story on the Biden-China connection. Sturmstrom's about to break it. Muckety-mucks are pissed off that CNN out-scooped us again." The friend scurried away.

Manny looked around and then surreptitiously got CNN live on her laptop. And sure enough, Sturmstrom appeared a few minutes later after a "Breaking Story" alert appeared with dramatic fanfare on the screen.

"And now we have Gale Sturmstrom outside Biden's New York campaign headquarters with a breaking story… Gale?" The screen then went from the stony face news anchor with his lip makeup a little too pink to Sturmstrom.

"Thanks, Dan," Sturmstrom said. "We have a significant update to our prior report that the FBI has begun a counterintelligence operation to investigate connections between the Biden campaign and The People's Republic of China. That investigation concerns efforts by the Chinese government to influence the 2020 election results and more specifically the possibility that funds were transferred to the Biden campaign from the Chinese government as part of that effort.

"Under US election laws, accepting campaign contributions from a foreign government is a criminal offense. As the foreign government making these suspected contributions is China, the political implications for the Biden campaign could be extremely damaging. A reliable anonymous source has identified for CNN an individual who is the focus of this investigation and who works as a China analyst for the campaign in New York. That individual, according to our source, is Mr. Gary Wang. We expect—"

Manny slammed her laptop shut. She stared straight ahead. She dialed Gary's number from her cell phone but got his voice mail. She then rose from her desk with her bag and laptop.

"I have an urgent matter to attend to," she said to a co-worker in her group. "I won't be back this afternoon." She ran to the elevator. Once outside the building, she hurried to the subway stop right around the corner. There she caught the No. 7 line that took her to Times Square, where she caught the N train. She called Gary again while on the subway platform and again got no answer. Thirty minutes later, she flew out of the subway station at Astoria Boulevard and dashed with her arm high in the air to hail a taxi. In the taxi, she told the driver Gary's address. "Hurry please."

When the taxi hit a traffic jam on Ditmars Boulevard, she told the driver she would exit the taxi, paid the fare, not bothering to take the five dollars in change, dashed out of the cab and began running the remaining half mile to Gary's apartment.

When she finally got there, she punched in the code she knew by heart and was granted entry to the building housing his third-floor walk-up apartment. Huffing and puffing through her mask for breath, sweat beading on her brow, she inserted the key that Gary had given her and entered his one-bedroom apartment.

Manny barged into the room and threw her bag and laptop on the couch where she and Gary had spent so much time talking about everything. Gary sat at the kitchen table. Around him stood half a dozen masked strangers. Manny ran to Gary and gave him a tearful hug. She then looked at the masked congregation. "Who the fuck are you, the FBI?" she said while wiping the tears from her eyes.

"Manny, take it easy," Gary said. "These are Biden people. We're just trying to figure out what the hell happened and what we need to do."

"Okay, Gary," a woman in the group said. "We'll get you down to Wilmington as soon as possible, and you can debrief the Vice President on everything you know."

Gary rose from the kitchen table. "Okay, that sounds good. I'll tell him what I'm telling you: this is all complete and total bullshit."

The Biden people all nodded and proceeded out

the door. Manny sat in the one other chair that constituted Gary's dining room. She stared at him with wide-eyed bewilderment. She didn't know what to say, where to start.

"Manny, listen to me." Gary took her hands and looked directly into her eyes. "This is utter nonsense. I have no earthly idea where Sturmstrom is getting this misinformation."

Manny nodded.

"You and Sturmstrom are friends, right? Can you find out where she's getting this?"

"I'll call her now," Manny said. "I'll meet with her. I'll find out." Manny had forsaken her tears and her voice was now resolute.

"Anything you can find out before I meet with Biden would be great."

Manny rose from her chair, went to her bag, and got her phone. "Yo, Gale," she said after hitting Strumstrom's number. "Wazup? I saw your big scoop today. Kudos..." The whole while she talked, she looked intently at Gary. "Hey, let's get out for a drink or two or three on me tonight to celebrate... Okay, I get you're busy after dropping this bombshell. You got a few minutes now? I can swing by your place or your office, whatever. Something I need to talk with you about... Okay, I'll see you at your apartment in a few."

Gary walked over and put his arms around her. "You are one fierce lady," he whispered to her.

Manny pulled away from him. "I have to go."

When Manny left the apartment building, she encountered a murder of ravenous reporters with accompanying video cameras already stationed on the sidewalk in front of the building. "Holy shit," she said to herself as she wended her way through them.

Forty-five minutes later, Manny was again sitting in Sturmstrom's apartment.

"Four-thirty-six in the afternoon is not too early for a little Rose, is it?" Sturmstrom asked rhetorically as she emerged from the kitchen with a chilled bottle of wine. She was wearing satin sweatpants and a t-shirt bearing that iconic photo of John Lennon in his sleeveless "New York City" t-shirt.

"I didn't come here to sip wine," Manny said.

"Oh, okay," Sturmstrom said. "I'll save it for this evening. It's been such a crazy week breaking that story and all, I think I'll just have the whole bottle to myself." She laughed. "So, what brings you here then, Manny? You look like you mean business."

"I came here to tell you that the story you put out this afternoon is wrong."

"Really? And how's that?"

"Gary Wang is not a Chinese connection or spy or whatever it was you were claiming."

"Is that so? And how did you arrive at that conclusion?"

"He's my boyfriend."

Shock briefly passed over Sturmstom's face. "Hmm…" she said.

She opened the bottle of Rose after all. It was a screw-off cap, and she was able to open it quickly. She poured herself a full glass and downed about half of it in one gulp.

"I didn't know. I'm surprised you hadn't told me before."

"We met after you and I got together in May. And when we met again last month, I dunno, I just didn't feel like bringing it up. All I can tell you, Gale, is that I've been with him almost every day since we met at a

Biden campaign function weeks ago. He's either the greatest con artist of all time or you got your story wrong. I'm one hundred percent sure it's the latter."

"Oh Manny, Manny…"

Sturmstrom seemed to say that at least once every time they met, and she never liked the patronizing *I'm going to have to school you girl* way it sounded.

"Can you prove that he isn't what I, or rather my source, says he is?" Sturmstrom asked.

"How am I supposed to prove a negative, Gale? Isn't he supposed to be considered innocent until proven guilty?"

Sturmstrom flashed an ironic smile. "Maybe in a court of law, but you should know by now that doesn't apply to our business. In fact, it's quite the opposite."

She emphasized *our*.

"All I can tell you, dear," Sturmstrom said, "is that we have an individual who was told by Gary Wang that he knew all about the Chinese money going to Biden and expected it to increase. We also have phone records that your boyfriend made to some people in the Chinese government. There's more to tell, but I'm not at liberty to do so."

"Who is this person who says Gary told him that? You must tell me Gale. He's either lying or misunderstanding."

"I can't Manny. That would be a cardinal sin for me to give up my source to anyone. You know that."

Manny looked away and shook her head in frustration. "Gale, I love this person. I can see spending the rest of my life with him. You destroy him, you destroy me."

"Well, maybe you better find someone else to spend the rest of your life with."

Manny's eyes narrowed and her teeth clenched. "That's really fucking snide, Gale. You don't sound like a friend looking to help me."

"What if I interviewed him? You think he would be up for that?" Sturmstrom asked.

"Uh, I'm not sure. I'll ask him. He would probably have to get some legal advice for that." Manny hadn't become cynical enough to see that Sturmstrom saw an opportunity to make some lemonade for herself from Manny's lemons.

"Then that's more than likely a No since any lawyer worth the degree mounted on his wall will tell him that's too risky."

"I'll ask him anyway. I have to go."

Manny rose, and Sturmstrom walked her to the door.

"Manny, you're so young." Sturmstrom put her hand on the doorknob. "Whatever happens with this, it won't be the last thing that happens that changes your life. Everything passes, like a kidney stone. It hurts so bad you think you can't survive it. But then the next morning, you see that little black evil looking pellet at the bottom of your toilet basin. All you have to do is flush it away."

Manny flinched when Sturmstrom gave her a goodbye hug.

"Hello, Meng," Danny Copper said when her secret number showed on his phone ID.

"And a wonderful hello to you, Professor. I hope the sun is shining today."

"Unfortunately, no. Overcast and gray here in Seattle."

"Sun shining here but too bad too much pollution not good for its shine."

"Sorry to hear. So, what's up, Meng?"

"Long time, no talk. I wonder if your clients look for more rumors, so we get more pay."

Copper sighed. "Ah, one of them I think has gotten all he needs for the time being. And the other one, well, I believe is not happy with me. Thinks I was too aggressive in disseminating our rumors."

"Too aggressive, Professor?"

"You know, spreading it around too much. Letting others in on it."

"Oh, I see. Well, like Redman says, 'If you gonna be a monkey, be a gorilla.'"

"Redman? I'm not familiar with that philosopher."

Meng laughed. "Redman not a philosopher. He's a rapper. My fav."

"How amusing. You know Meng, there's a question I asked you once, and you said you couldn't give me the full and complete answer."

"Okay, what question?"

"When we put out that initial story that the Chinese were funding Biden's campaign, where exactly did you get that information? You mentioned the MSS, but I was careless in not seeking more specifics. I guess I was so excited to get it that I never asked that simple question."

"Simple question, but answer not so simple, Professor."

"Yeah, and so…"

"I used to have intelligence relations with this Russian man. Later became sexual relations I confess. But he knows many people everywhere and had some super dope."

"What? A Russian man!"

"Yes, he works in GRU."

"You're kidding?"

"No kidding. He knows people in Chinese higher ups. In the MSS. People I don't know, so he's good person to know and exchange with. So yes, did come from MSS, I believed."

Copper shook his head in disbelief. "You ever think he might be using you to spread what we call rumors? In other words, using you for disinformation?"

"Maybe so. But I got paid and you got paid. So, what is big deal?"

"Meng, I have to go. I don't think it's good that we talk anymore. Bye."

After Copper clicked off the call, he muttered to himself, "Russians… Russians..." He then burst out laughing and kept laughing until tears rolled down his face.

Chapter Nine

YOU'RE FIRED!

A half dozen Adirondack chairs had been placed in a semi-circle in Joe Biden's back yard at his home/bunker in Wilmington, Delaware. Beside each chair was a small table upon which a sweating cold-water bottle was placed. Occupying those chairs and accompanying the presumptive Democratic presidential nominee were four higher-ups in the Biden campaign, and Gary Wang. The chairs were placed six feet apart from one another. Everyone was wearing a blue mask with Go Joe! lettering and casually dressed, except Gary in his beige cotton suit and cloth tie. Three secret service agents took their stations in the near distance. Clusters of hydrangea bushes surrounding the chairs had burst into explosions of lavender. Birds chirped and bees buzzed.

But Gary's mind was not taken with this idyllic summer afternoon. He focused on one thing only: nip this crazy accusation against him in the bud. He was counting on the Biden campaign brain trust to formulate a strategy to do that.

Earlier that day, a chauffeured black SUV had picked him up at his apartment and driven him for two hours to the Biden abode. He was ushered directly from the SUV to his appointed Adirondack chair by one of the campaign people. Shortly thereafter, Biden had emerged through a door from his house with the other three campaign aides. Biden nodded at Gary. "Hi, I'm Joe Biden. Gary, right?" He exchanged an elbow bump with Gary and took a seat in the next chair over.

"Okay gang," Biden said to the summoned group, "I brought you all here because we have to rapidly respond to all this Russian malarkey that's being spread around like shit on a shingle. The convention is coming up and we're balls to the wall trying to pick a VP candidate, so none of us have time for this nonsense."

"Sir, that's Chinese not Russian malarkey," Glenn Turbot, head of the campaign said to the former VP.

"What's that Glenn? I can't hear you through the mask."

"I said, sir, that it's Chinese not Russians that we're talking about," Turbot said, his raised voice tinged with annoyance.

"Oh, did I say Russian? You guys know what I meant. Anyway, Jerry, you seem to be the guy in the eye of the storm, unfortunately—"

"Excuse me, Mr. Vice President, but it's Gary, not Jerry."

"Who's Gary?" Biden asked as he looked around at the masked faces, not noticing a couple of eye rolls.

"I am, sir."

"Oh, I messed up there. Okay, Gary. But you are the guy this report mentioned. So, we need to ask you some questions so we can get to the bottom of this crock of horse manure."

Gary didn't feel the need to remind the Vice-President that he advised him a couple of times about Chinese foreign policy issues.

"Karen, you want to start with the questions?"

Biden was addressing Karen Quigley, the person in the campaign responsible for crafting responses to Republican attacks.

"Certainly," said Darren Lichterman, the campaign official running opposition research. "Gary, can you tell us—"

"No, I said Karen, not you Darren," Biden said.

"Ah, I thought you said me, through the mask you know. You're kinda stifled."

Biden pulled his mask below his chin. "Look everybody, this is ridiculous. When you wanna speak, pull your mask down. There are no snoopy reporters around here to bust us for not keeping our masks on. At least I don't think so. Karen, go ahead with questions for Gary here." He took a swig from his water bottle.

"Hi there, Gary," Ms. Quigley began. "I was wondering—

Biden broke in, blurting, "And by the way, everybody, I wanted to just have glasses and pitchers of water out here and not plastic bottles because I know they can be bad for the ocean and other environmental things. But Jill's had like ten cases of Evian lying around, so we need to use them up, so they don't go to waste. Sorry, Karen, go ahead with questions for Jerry."

"So, Gary," Quigley resumed, not bothering to correct Mr. Biden about the name, "the news report implicated you in this story about us receiving money from the Chinese government. We all know that's not true, but do you have any idea where that absurd claim originated?"

Gary shook his head. "I have no earthly idea. It's so preposterous, I just can't conceive of where it could come from."

"Have you talked with anyone outside the campaign about the campaign, whether about funding or anything else?" Ms. Quigley asked.

Gary took a few seconds to consider. "I did recently have dinner with a friend, or acquaintance from when I had a fellowship at the Confucius Academy of Global Understanding. He asked me about the campaign. I didn't tell him much except things were going well. We talked about all these rumors about Chinese money."

"And what is the name of this friend of yours?" Turbot asked.

"Danny Copper."

Turbot and Quigley exchanged knowing glances.

"And what is Mr. Copper's present occupation?" Quigley asked.

"Um, he told me that he's still affiliated with the Academy as a senior research fellow. Writing papers and giving lectures occasionally, at least before Covid hit."

"And we're also hearing that CNN has some records of phone calls that you made to Chinese officials," Alex Gristmill, senior director of media relations said. "Is that true, and if so, can you elaborate?"

Gary sighed and let his head drop. "Yeah, I was trying to set up a meeting between Mr. Biden and President Xi. I kinda took the initiative to explore the possibility. So, I, like uh, called some people I knew from the Academy and who hold positions in the government. You know, not real high up but people who could at least get the wheels turning."

"C'mon Gary," Biden said. "You never told anyone about that? You didn't run that by any of us first?"

Gary was at a loss for words.

"You wanted to score some points, be a hero who was able to set up a summit between Joe and Xi, right?' Darren asked.

Gary nodded. "Yep…that's pretty accurate."

No one spoke for several seconds, until Biden held up the Evian water bottle and said, "Look Gary, you see the label on this water bottle? Evian. You know what that spells backwards?"

Gary looked at the bottle. "Naïve," he muttered.

"That's right, son. I know you meant well, but I don't need you to be a back channel to the Chinese. I already have enough of those. That was truly naïve of you to make those calls because they're incriminating to both you and me. You see that?"

"Yes sir."

"You have to understand, Gary," Quigley said, "that you can no longer be associated with the campaign. It doesn't matter that you're innocent of what this news report alleges. We all know this story is totally false, but until we can clear it up, we have to keep our distance."

"We will stay in contact with you as we try to clear both your name and our campaign of these scurrilous charges," Turbot said. "In the meantime, we can suggest a few law firms you should consider engaging."

"Law firms?"

"Son, I'm sorry to tell you, but this circus just got started, and you're the first one they're planning to shoot out of a cannon," the former vice president said.

"So, what are we going to do about Wang, Boss?" Fisherwood asked Director Cummings as they sat in the latter's office.

"Sturmstrom strikes again," Cummings said as he glanced at the television with the cracked screen.

Fisherwood sighed. "Yeah, that hurt. You think it's Global Fission deep throating her?"

"Well, if you believe Danny Copper, Aliasione is the only guy outside the loop who's seen his intel," Cummings said.

"And the worst thing about it is that now that Wang's been out-ed," Fisherwood said, "that FISA warrant to surveil him is pointless. He's gotta figure that he's being watched now."

"You're right, Karl. Which means we must get to him fast, before he destroys evidence or absconds back to China or wherever. Our FISA warrant's purview allows us to interview him and search his apartment, right?"

"Yes, it's pretty open-ended," Fisherwood said.

"Good then. You get a couple of agents and pay Wang a visit. I want you leading the charge, Peckerwood."

"You got it, Boss."

Gary sat in the waiting room of a small office in a building next to the Bronx County Courthouse. The saving grace of this architecturally obsolete 1940s building was that it had windows that opened. With the Big C stalking the city, an office building with open windows that gave exit to the virus was ironically something of a luxury.

He sat on the leather sofa, enjoying the summer breeze coming through the open tenth-floor window. The receptionist/secretary, who had put on her light blue mask as soon as he entered the office, told him that Ramon Aruba, esquire, would be arriving any moment. He passed the time perusing a coffee-table book entitled *Puerto Rico, The American Eden!*

As promised, Mr. Aruba showed up a few minutes later. He came bounding into the office, carrying a large satchel filled with documents. Short and stocky, he wore beige shorts and a blue pullover shirt. Sandals with white socks adorned his feet. His clip-on shades kept him from noticing Gary in the corner.

The secretary nodded toward him and said, "Mr. Wang is waiting to meet with you."

Mr. Aruba turned and smiled. "Oh, Mr. Wang, how are you, sir?"

He wrestled the large satchel under his arm so that he could slip on the mask dangling from his ear. He had a well-trimmed gray beard that blended in perfectly with his short-cropped gray hair and eyeglasses with gray metal frames. All this gray against his caramel-colored complexion was pleasing to the eye. Gary imagined that pleasing the eye, a juror's eye, was an important attribute for a defense attorney.

"Please excuse my attire, Mr. Wang. With the courtrooms closed means I thankfully don't have to wear a suit, and the weather being what it is," he stopped, smiled bashfully and pointed out the window, "I just had to put on my shorts and sandals."

"No problem," Gary said. "And call me Gary, please."

"Fine. And you call me Mr. Aruba, please."

Gary looked puzzled.

"Just kidding, call me Ramon," he said with a robust laugh. "C'mon into my office and let's get down to business."

Gary had come to Aruba by way of Glenn Turbot, who had taken Gary aside after the Wilmington meeting. "Look Gary, I'm probably not supposed to be doing this, being that you're sort of," Glenn paused, trying to think of the right phrase but ended up saying the wrong one, "persona non grata, if you know what I mean. But I can recommend an attorney for you. I'm guessing you don't have a lot of dollars to blow on a lawyer, but this guy is good for the price. And let's hope you don't even need one, but you ought to get in touch with this guy and be ready just in case. The problem with big firms is that you might get lost in the shuffle. This guy is a bit too maverick for a big firm. But he's damn good. Does both civil and criminal work."

Gary winced when Turbot said criminal. He couldn't believe that he was the subject of such a conversation.

Gary and Aruba sat down at a little seating arrangement Aruba had set up in a corner, a space cleared of the mounds of documents that occupied much of the office. This consultation area consisted of a couple of red molded plastic chairs around a glass-topped table.

"So..." Aruba said after they took their seats. "Do you believe that you are innocent, Gary?"

The question startled Gary. "I thought lawyers were never supposed to ask their clients if they did it or not," he said.

"I didn't ask you if you are innocent," he said. "I asked you if you *believe* that you are innocent. I saw all the news reports about you. A Chinese agent. Making illegal campaign contributions. So, I have to ask you if you believe you are innocent of these allegations."

"Don't all the people who sit in this chair believe they are innocent?"

"No. I've had cases where the guy is as guilty as O.J. Simpson. He tells me everything that happened in tedious detail and justifies why he did it. He expects me to pull a rabbit out of the hat and get him off."

"Do you take those cases?" Gary asked.

"Of course not. I'm a lawyer, not a magician. Take Johnnie Cochran, God bless him, but he was more a flim-flam artist than a lawyer. That's not my shtick.

"And then there are a few cases where the guy is innocent but thinks he's guilty," Aruba continued. "His wife's lover slits her throat, but he thinks he's guilty because his inability to satisfy her drove her to her killer."

"And so, you're willing to represent him?"

"No."

"Why not?"

Aruba paused for a moment of reflection. "You have to understand that there's much psychic energy that is transmitted between a lawyer and his client...not to sound too New Age. And if that energy is positive, then it amplifies itself as it's reflected back and forth between lawyer and client. But if the energy is negative, if the guy for whatever reason believes he's guilty, then that energy weakens. However innocent he might be, my defense of him is undermined, you see."

"Okay, and what about the guilty who believe they are innocent?" Gary asked, enjoying this little repartee.

"Ah, now they are the most interesting," Aruba said as he sat up in his chair. "Ultimately it comes down to how you define guilt and innocence. The law might be clear, but the situations hardly ever are. The difference between innocence and guilt is sometimes not a fine line but more of, let's say, a squiggle. It's up to me to get the jury or judge to see that my client is on the right side of that squiggle." Aruba paused to smile knowingly.

Gary nodded.

"And then we have you, Gary. The innocent who believes he is innocent."

"How can you tell that about me? Just from the summary that I emailed you?"

"After doing this for twenty-five years, I know how to read people."

"Yes, I am innocent." His eyes latched onto Aruba's. "I believe it because I know it."

Aruba crossed his arms over his chest. "There's just one thing that bothers me."

"What's that?" Gary asked.

"So where are these news reports coming from? CNN certainly believes you are guilty. And the court of public opinion can be just as important as the court of law."

"I have no idea what they have or think they have,"

Gary said.

Aruba then went over with Gary a few of the cases he had taken in the past that pertained to Gary's situation. In most of these cases, his clients got off; the worst outcomes were usually settlements whereby a pound of flesh had been paid without any admission of guilt.

"You have to have some help, don't you?" Gary asked. "You don't handle all this by yourself?"

Aruba smiled. "Yes, I have my little elves. Three associates and five paralegals. They work out of my office at 250 Park in Manhattan."

Gary felt relieved. There was something irrationally reassuring about a Park Avenue address. "So, this is not your main office?"

"I've had this office since I passed the bar exam. I guess it's nostalgia that makes me keep it. I feel more relaxed here than I do there."

Aruba then outlined the terms and conditions of his retainer, in the event Gary needed his services. Yes, Aruba charged a cut-rate fee compared to the big firms, but, damn, he was going to have to empty his brokerage account to pay for it.

Aruba walked Gary out of the office and to the elevators.

"So, do you think the Feds are coming after me, Ramon?"

Aruba shrugged. "Maybe yes, maybe no. And if it's yes, then it's probably going to be very serious."

Gary took a deep, anxious breath and stared at the old-fashioned dial over the elevator door showing which floor the car was passing. The door opened.

"Hopefully, for your sake, this will be the first and last time we ever meet," said Aruba as he ushered him into the elevator.

Riding in the Lex Express subway from Aruba's office to his apartment, Gary heard a beep on his phone notifying him that he had received an email. He pulled up his email and read a Gmail notification: "**WARNING:** We believe state-sponsored attackers may be attempting to compromise your phone account." His whole body blinked. He stared at the warning long after he had read it. State sponsored…what else could that mean but that his own government was spying on him? Or could it be the Chinese, wondering what was behind this story? But he figured the Chinese would be too hacker savvy to be detected. No doubt, he was in the US government's crosshairs. He felt lightheaded, like his head was full of cotton balls.

Chapter Ten

TIE THE NOOSE

"What the hell," Gary said as he sat up in bed. Did someone just knock on his front door or was he dreaming? He looked at the alarm clock. Six in the morning.

He donned a bathrobe and bedroom slippers and walked half asleep to the front door. He looked through the peephole and saw a balding head with ruddy cheeks and a double chin. The guy looked innocuous enough for Gary to open the door.

"Good morning, Mr. Wang." The gentleman held up his badge. "My name is Karl Fisherwood, and I'm with the FBI, as are these three agents with me." He nodded at the woman and two men accompanying him. One agent carried a silver metal suitcase.

Gary shook his head, as if to knock off what he

hoped was a dream, or nightmare.

"We have a court-ordered warrant to seize any electronic devices you may have in your apartment, including computers and cell phones. Here's a copy for your perusal."

Fisherwood handed Gary the warrant and then brusquely pushed past him into his apartment, the other three agents in tow. Gary detected something almost personal in Fisherwood's grudging demeanor toward him.

After the agents entered his apartment, shock still disabled him from uttering a word, until he saw one of the agents pull a compact MP5 submachine gun from his black jacket with FBI in large block yellow letters on the back.

"C'mon, is that really necessary?" Gary asked Fisherwood as he pointed at the weapon.

"This is a SWAT operation." Fisherwood looked around the apartment. "Perfectly okay when conducting operations that may involve foreign intelligence assets. You never know what might happen."

Gary felt completely discombobulated. "Foreign intelligence assets? You're not really serious, are you?"

"Do I look like I'm not serious?" Fisherwood asked. "Please lead us to any computers that you have in your apartment."

"The only one I have is that one on the desk there," Gary pointed to his computer. An agent walked to the desk, unplugged the computer, and put the drive into the silver case. Meanwhile, the lady agent had stealthily moseyed her way into Gary's bedroom.

"What's she doing?"

"Properly executing the search warrant,"

Fisherwood said. "What cell phones do you have? Hand them over."

Gary went to his bedroom to find the agent rifling through his drawers. He retrieved his phone and walked back to Fisherwood and presented it to him.

"This the only one you have?" Fisherwood asked as he surveyed the room.

"Yes."

"You know lying to the FBI is a felony, right?"

"Yes, it's the only phone I have," Gary said.

"Everything's clean in there," the female agent said to Fisherwood as she exited Gary's bedroom.

"And do you have any other electronic devices that you communicate with?"

"No."

"You sure?" Fisherwood asked.

"Of course, I'm sure. You think I'm a liar?"

"You better not be, or else your dead meat."

"Let's go, guys," he said to his colleagues. They walked to the door, Gary's possessions in hand, and left the apartment.

Before Fisherwood completely exited, he nodded and gave Gary a knowing, almost sinister smile.

Gary stared at the apartment door, barely able to think, his consciousness as thick as clay. Pounding that clay were the last words that Aruba had said to him when he asked if the Feds would be coming after him, 'And if it's yes, then it's probably going to be very serious.'

Once he had gotten his bearings back, the first thing he did was call Aruba and set up a meeting at his Bronx office for later that day.

"And the lead agent didn't give you his card?" Aruba asked Gary once they had settled in his office.

"Nope, just flashed his badge."

"Well, that's the first no-no. You remember what he said his name was?"

"Fisherwood. That's a name easy to remember. And he was an A-one asshole."

"Okay, let's Google this guy." Aruba lifted his chin and peered through his eyeglasses at the computer screen on his desk. "Fisherwood… FBI," he muttered as he typed.

Anxious, Gary rubbed his hands together.

"Hijole!"

"I don't know what that means but it doesn't sound good, Ramon."

Aruba turned and looked at Gary with an incredulous expression. "Fisherwood is Deputy Director of the FBI. What the hell was he doing on an evidence raid?"

"Shit." Gary shook his head.

"Gary, I have to tell you man, that even though we think they have nothing on you, they obviously think otherwise."

"What do we do?"

"First thing is I'm going to try to have a conversation with Fisherwood. Reach out to him and try to discern what they're thinking. That may mean that we have to meet with him. You okay with that?"

"I'll do anything or go anywhere if it helps make this go away."

"We need to get this story out tonight, so it's not buried

by the Democratic convention going prime time two days from now," Gale Sturmstrom said to Tom Dailey, her senior news editor, and Burt Schwartzman, a CNN producer. The three had secluded themselves in a side conference room off the newsroom floor. "The timing is perfect."

"So, you're sure about this story, Gale?" Dailey asked.

"Yes, it came from Peter Aliasione, and he's been one hundred percent right so far. He spoke to one of six people at the meeting where they fired Wang."

"It's still second hand," Schwartzman said. "Guys upstairs are getting a little tired of the constant use of 'If true…' to start a story with."

"We don't need to qualify this story, guys." Sturmstrom looked challengingly at her two cohorts. "I wanna start out with 'We can report that Gary Wang, who is suspected of being the subject of an FBI counterintelligence investigation into Chinese interference in the presidential election, has been fired from the Biden campaign.'"

"We asked Alex Gristmill for a comment from the Biden campaign, but he wouldn't give us anything," Dailey said.

"Yeah, so fuck them then," Sturmstrom said. "They don't want to say anything because they know firing Wang gives credence to the story."

Schwartzman rested his chin on his hand and looked sideways at Dailey. "Okay, we can probably slide it in after the lead about the wildfires in California," Schwartzman said.

"Oh c'mon, Burt!" Sturmstrom said as she slapped her hand against the conference table. "Everyone keeps telling me to put some legs on this story. Well, here's a new development about the main character. I mean, who really gives a shit about another wildfire in California."

"Those wildfires have killed five people, Gale," Dailey said. "Is this kid getting fired more important than that?"

Sturmstrom leaned over the conference table and looked hard at Dailey. "For God's sake, Tom, don't you know who decides what's important and what isn't? We do! They eat what we feed them."

"Alright, alright, we'll lead with it," Schwartzman said.

Sturmstrom eased back into her chair. *About time these guys figure out who's the queen bee and who are the drones.*

"And Tom, when you write it up, use this as a good time to summarize everything I've brought to light so far about Wang and the Biden-China collusion." *Like a greatest hits collection.*

"Yes ma'am."

"Okay, you ready?" Gary asked Manny as they stood inside the small foyer at the entrance to his apartment building later that day.

"Yep," she said. "So, you go out first and when they chase after you, then I'll dash out. And we'll meet at the café. First one there gets a table." They both pulled their masks up over their faces.

"Okay, ready, one, two, three," Gary said. He lowered his head, took a deep breath, and pushed the door open to face the lowing mob eagerly awaiting his appearance, like a gang of masked bandits. The clicking cameras sounded like a hailstorm. He shoved his way through the crush of reporters and cameramen. Questions from reporters armed with microphones flew at him like arrows.

"Hey Wang, I hear you're Xi's little bitch," a photographer shouted.

Gary glared at him. Perfect—the photographer clicked rapid fire—mission accomplished. The crowd collapsed around him, encasing him, stabbing him with leading questions.

"Is Biden aware of what you're doing?

Has the FBI contacted you?

Are you a spy too?"

He maneuvered into the street to hail a cab, the news people moving with him, like they all constituted a twenty-four-legged braying beast. He literally jumped in front of an unoccupied taxi to bring it to a stop. A guy holding a video camera tripped and fell in front of the taxi, barely avoiding being run over. Gary scrambled into the taxi. He saw Manny exiting the building as the taxi sped away. He hyperventilated for a few seconds before telling the driver where to go.

A few minutes later, he saw Manny sitting at a table outside the appointed café on the Upper Eastside. Her Panamanian hat and mask with the Jamaican yellow, green, black colors made her easy to spot on the crowded sidewalk outside the café.

"Isn't it great being a celebrity," Manny said as he sat down.

Gary put his hands on the table, leaned back, tilted his head up, pulled his mask down, and let out a long "Shhhoooo."

"Let's order a couple of drinks," Manny said.

"Make it a double for me." The stress was gradually releasing the headlock it had on him.

Halfway through the drinks, Manny's phone blurted a beep. "Who is this," she said as she squinted at her phone and read the text.

"What?" Gary asked, seeing concern weigh on her face as she read the text. Gale Sturmstrom's voice then emanated from the phone. "We can report that Gary Wang, rumored to be at the center of an FBI investigation into involvement by the Chinese government in the presidential election, has been fired from the Biden campaign."

The two stayed silent during the next couple of minutes of Sturmstrom's reporting, except when Manny held up her phone screen to Gary and said, "Well, at least they used a nice photo of you."

"That was the photo from my Columbia student ID. I wonder how they got that. I mean, in this day and age it's like everybody's life is just a book waiting for the government or media to open it."

"A colleague of mine at Fox sent that video to me. Said it was the opening story on CNN this evening. Just aired."

"Dog days of summer. Not much else going on I guess, until the convention starts," Gary said sourly.

He and Manny didn't talk much after the news report. Not only did tension knot their tongues but Gary's phone, the new one he bought after the FBI confiscated his, started sounding nonstop. He didn't answer any of the calls, even the ones from friends who were calling after seeing CNN evening news. Other calls were unidentified and probably people from the press, making Gary wonder how they got his cell phone number. After the tenth 1812 Overture, Gary turned his phone off.

"You wanna move in with me for a while?" Manny

asked. “So you don’t have to face that mob every time you come in and go out of your apartment?”

Gary’s downcast eyes moved up to meet hers. “Sure. I already have a lot of my stuff there.”

“But I’m not sharing my toothbrush with you,” Manny said with a laugh, drawing out a half chuckle from Gary.

“I got this,” Manny said, when the waitress brought the bill after they had finished a light supper. She didn’t have to say anything, but Gary appreciated that she paid for dinner because she knew he would probably soon be facing a cascade of legal bills from Aruba.

While waiting for the waitress to return, Gary eyed a guy sitting by himself at a table diagonal from theirs. He noticed earlier the guy paying too close attention to Manny and him. Nothing stood out about the man, an unprepossessing middle-aged white guy, except that he kept his sunglasses on even though the sun had sunk behind the trees and his table was ensconced in shadows.

No, he didn’t think too much about it at first, but after the news report he did. For the first time, it occurred to him that maybe he was being tailed. The FBI most likely. Or was he being paranoid? But then he remembered that his phone had been hacked by a state-sponsored entity.

When the waitress brought Manny’s credit card back, she stopped and looked at Gary.

“I saw you on the news tonight, didn’t I?”

Neither Gary nor Manny said anything.

“You’re the Biden guy in cahoots with the Chinese, right?”

Again, no response from Gary and Manny.

"Lemme tell you something, dude, if you ever decide to come here again while I'm on shift, I hope you'll enjoy the snotty loogie I'm gonna hock into your food."

The waitress spun on her heels and stomped away.

"Let's get outta here," Gary said. He and Manny hastened to the street to grab a cab. Gary was in such a hurry that he didn't notice the gentleman at the table diagonal from theirs also rose and made his exit.

Hi Mama," Gary said to the face on his smartphone screen. Her gray hair was styled in such a way as to indicate modest affluence. The face overwhelmed the screen with worry.

"Gary, what on earth is going on? I called you because I saw that woman on CNN talking about a Gary Wang who worked for Biden and was doing something like money laundering."

"Not money laundering, Mama. Illegal campaign contributions."

"I thought no, oh my god, no that can't be you, but then how many Gary Wang's work for the campaign? Then they showed your photo…

Gary stared at the face on the screen, not sure where to start. He gained consolation that his sixty-eight-year-old mother looked fine and fit, notwithstanding the stress lines that Sturmstrom's report had caused.

"Where's Baba? I want you both to hear this."

"He's right here," his mom said as she pulled the phone back so his father could be seen sitting next to her. "Say hi to Gary, Bo."

"Hi Gary."

He wore a white shirt, top buttoned, and a confused smile. His father was several years older than his mother, and his mind was gradually turning into something analogous to the black holes that he once spent so much time studying as a physics professor at UCLA. No light escaped.

Gary spent the next few minutes trying to explain what was inexplicable. What could he say other than the story was utter and complete *fai waa,* the closest thing in Cantonese to bullshit.

"I've hired a good lawyer, Mama. We're going to get this straight. Just some gigantic misunderstanding. The truth always comes out. Might take some time but it will."

Gary gazed at his mother gazing at her son. Neither said anything for a few seconds, two faces suspended in the air at arm's length. He hated to see the downturned lines on her face, her eyes watering up with worry. He had seen her face that way so many times when his brother Joe had done something to make her cry.

The memory flashed through his mind of the time when Joe got arrested for dealing coke. Gary walked by his parent's bedroom and heard her crying. He was fifteen and didn't know what to do or say. He stood by the door listening to her soft sobs, and then walked away. He never forgave Joe for making his mother cry, even though he got off on the charges that might have sent him to prison. He never forgave himself for walking away. Now she feared he too would go the way of Joe.

"Mama, don't cry…please...everything is going to be okay. I have to go now. I love you. Tell Baba goodbye."

"Bo, tell Gary goodbye."

His father looked up from wherever he had gone and back into the visage of Gary in the tiny little box.

"Goodbye, Gary. We are so proud of you, son."

John Phillip Sousa's "The Stars and Stripes Forever" sounded from Peter Aliasione's phone as he sat in British Airway's exclusive The Concorde Room at JFK airport, waiting to catch the next flight to London.

"Hello, Peter speaking."

"Peter Aliasione, you fucking asshole!"

"Gale, is this you?"

"Fuck yes, it's me. I wish I was wherever you are so I could wrap my hands around that neck of yours and choke you to death."

"Dear me, seems like someone got up on the wrong side of the bed this morning. Are you off your meds, my lady friend?" Aliasione rose from his cushy chair and walked to the floor-to-ceiling windows overlooking a runway so the few people in the lounge wouldn't overhear what he knew was going to be a sensitive conversation.

"Did you see Buzzsaw this morning?"

"Buzzsaw, are you kidding me? If I'm going to read an online tabloid, I'll read your former employer the *New York Post*, although it's never been the same without you."

"Cut the crap, Peter. Buzzsaw this morning posted The Copper Files, the whole goddamned thing. And you're the only person who had it, so you must have put it in their greasy grubby little paws, you asshole."

"You might be a tad presumptuous saying I'm the only one who had possession of it."

"That's what you told me. And I begged you to let me have it. To let me put it out there. But you always said no, it wouldn't be proper or appropriate. Since when did you become proper and appropriate?"

"Gale, you know I couldn't do that because I didn't know what was true, or let's say credible or not. A lot of shit in that report wasn't going to pass the smell test. Like Biden and hookers."

"What did those Buzzsaw pimps pay you, you little homo whore? You know I should have gotten the first look. I've been exclusive on this story from the get-go. It's my story. There's even talk about me being up for a duPont-Columbia award for journalistic excellence. And now you go and pull the red carpet out from under me. And just two days after I broke the news that Wang had been fired from the campaign."

Aliasione smiled to himself, thinking, *and yes, darling, your reports jived nicely with what I had to give to Buzzsaw and why they paid extra for it.* He didn't tell Sturmstom that one of the reasons that he had given the Copper File to Buzzsaw instead of her, besides the money, was that he resented the way she bulldozed over him to throw Gary Wang's name into the shark tank known as the public realm.

"Listen, Gale gal, like that great statesman, Bill Clinton, once said, 'Sometimes, you gotta do what you gotta do.' I have to go now. Time to board my flight. Adieu mon amour."

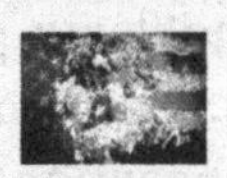

Danny Copper sat on his faux leather sofa on a bright August morning in Seattle. He was attired in a blue, light wool, double-breasted blazer and white linen pants with saddle oxford shoes, even though he had nowhere special to go that day. Abhorring the recent mass descent into sweatpants and collarless shirts, he was determined to maintain his sartorial standards. Someone had to hold the line.

He witnessed a pandemic of slovenly dress everywhere he went, and such degeneracy had slowly begun to crush his spirit. One of the worst things about the plague was people losing all sense of not only smell and taste but also savoir-faire. For Copper, how society dressed itself indicated the degree by which it was removed from barbarism. Churchill or somebody said that you could judge whether a man was a gentleman or not by his table manners when he ate alone. The same thing with how one clothed oneself even if one were sitting in one's shabby little den all by oneself. Besides, he had spent a small fortune over the years on his wardrobe, so he was going to dress elegantly come hell or high water.

Copper's rumination on American shabbiness was interrupted by his landline ringing. He glanced at the caller ID and saw that it was Gary Wang calling. No fucking way he'd answer that call. Voicemail could pick it up.

"Hello, Danny here. I'm out and about at the moment, but please be so kind as to leave a message, and I'll call you back when I return from whatever adventure I might be on. Toot-a-loo."

"Danny, pick up the damn phone. This is Gary. I know you're there. Pick up the phone! Okay, you coward. I read some concoction of yours on Buzzsaw. The Copper File they're calling it. You set me up, you motherfucker. Why, I don't know. Has to do with money, I'm sure. My lawyer is going to get to the bottom of this. They got something called libel and slander laws in this country. I know you don't have much except for a bunch of silly looking outfits; but whatever it is I'm coming for it and for you too."

Hmm, unlike Gary to lose his cool like that, and threatening too. If he had the courage to pick up the phone, Copper would have told him that to survive, a man sometimes has gotta do what he's gotta do. That's just the way the cookie crumbles, the eggs break to make the omelet, and don't cry over spilt milk because it could have been scotch. And, for the record, nothing he said about Gary was a lie, or at least a lie per se. Sorry my young erstwhile friend, he might have said, but sometimes you're da bomb, and sometimes you're collateral damage.

Biden and his inner circle, including newly admitted Kamala Harris, gathered via an emergency video conferencing to discuss the Copper File and consider if any damage control was needed.

"Who is this Cooper guy putting out all this horse hockey," the former VP asked the assorted people assembled on his sixty-five-inch TV screen. He was wearing a newly manufactured Biden/Harris 2020 mask, which had been made in China ironically enough.

"It's Copper not Cooper, Joe," Glenn Turbot said.

"Whatever the jasper's name is, he's full of it," Biden said. "Messed up our convention good. Threw a turd into the party punch bowl."

"And Joe, by the way, I don't think there is any need to wear a mask since there's no one there with you," Turbot added. "It's hard to hear you."

"Oh yeah, you're right. Kinda forgot I was wearing it. Jill makes me keep one on 24/7." He removed the mask. "Ah, that's better."

"Copper worked for MI5 years ago. Now an independent contractor."

"You mean a gun for hire?" Biden asked.

"Yep, and adding insult to injury, I'm hearing that Global Fission funded the report," Turbot said. "Opposition research."

"Peter Aliasione, you're talking about?" Biden asked. "That sleazy operator is a Trump guy all the way. Dyed-in-the wool Republican. His pockets are stuffed with Trump campaign money. Oh man, this is outrageous."

"Shouldn't we release a statement pointing that out?" Harris asked.

"I don't know that for sure," Turbot said. "What a contact at CNN told me."

Karen Quigley jumped in. "First of all, I don't think we need to publicly make a statement of any sort."

"Yes, let's not dignify this with any kind of official response," Harris said, abandoning the suggestion that she had just made. She followed that with her weird nervous cackle.

"Of course not," Biden said. "I mean, c'mon, teenage hookers, you gotta be kidding me. Guy claims he has video of some strumpets entering the hotel and pushing the elevator button to the floor Hunter and me were staying on. Look, I've learned not to rule out anything when it comes to Hunter, but me? C'mon man!"

All the square people nodded in assent; the notion

that the former Vice President would do something as reckless as call up an escort to his hotel room was inconceivable. But as he said, Hunter on the other hand...

"We don't make any statement about Global Fission paying for this crap, but we leak it to some friendlies, like Fox," Gristmill said. "We can count on Sean and Tucker to do the heavy lifting for us."

"But what about all this stuff about that Gary Wang fellow that's in there?" Biden asked.

"Just more garbage," Turbot said. "I think we feel pretty confident that Wang wasn't doing some rogue fund-raising stuff on his own. I thought he was one hundred percent credible when we met with him."

"I hear you, Glenn," Biden said. "But this Copper fellow says in his report that Wang told him face-to-face that he was involved in some dirty pool. Wasn't that in the report, or am I imagining things again?"

"And supposedly there's a bunch of phone calls that Wang made to some people in the Chinese government," Darren Lichterman said. "I mean, let's not forget that he's being investigated by the FBI for Pete's sake."

"That's a rumor, Darren," Quigley said. "The FBI hasn't confirmed that."

"They never do, Karen," Lichterman said.

"Yeah, but Wang explained those calls. He was just trying to be a hero and set up a meeting with Joe and Xi," Turbot said. "Guy was being a little too gung-ho is all. Besides, he's no longer associated with us."

"If any of us believed there was even a modicum of truth to this, then we would have kept him close instead of firing him," Quigley said.

"So, what does our presidential candidate Harris

think?" Joe beamed to the box encapsulating Kamala Harris.

"Vice-president," Harris said while smiling uncomfortably.

"Yes, of course, and what a great one you're gonna be," Biden said.

Harris continued. "But yes, let's make no official campaign response and just issue a blanket full-throated denial if asked about it. Just a pack of lies."

"Yeah, let's just let this pass like a rat through a python," Biden said. "We'll be okay."

"Back to Wang," Lichterman said. "You don't think the FBI is basing its counterintelligence operation on this Copper File, do you?"

Biden harrumphed. "C'mon Darren, this is the US of A, not some banana republic with sham elections. You think the FBI is going to spy on the campaign of the presidential nominee of the other party in the middle of an election, and based on opposition research paid for by the party of the sitting administration? No fucking way."

"Yeah, of course not," Lichterman said sheepishly. "What was I thinking?"

Chapter Eleven

SLIP THE NOOSE AROUND THE NECK

September 2020

The taxi stopped at 935 Pennsylvania Avenue. Gary looked out the window at the J. Edgar Hoover Building, home of the FBI. The building didn't much impress Gary. The main part of the building looked to be six stories high. A cantilever section of another three stories was set perpendicular atop the building,

"Here we are," Aruba said as counted the money to give to the driver.

"That's one ugly building," Aruba said as he and Gary stood outside the brown concrete structure. "Looks like a fort or maybe a prison."

Gary didn't like hearing the word prison, given the circumstances.

"It's a type of architecture popular back in the

sixties called Brutalism," Gary said.

"Brutalism…as in brutal, huh?" Aruba asked.

"Yep."

"Alrighty then," Aruba said. "Let's go in and see how brutal it's going to be." He and Gary donned their facemasks.

Large concrete barriers lined the front of the building. Soldiers with M-16s stood at their posts. Once inside, one of several armed security guards in the lobby approached the two.

"Gentlemen, you need to come this way for security clearance," he said.

After Gary and Aruba presented identification, they were led to a security set-up much like that in an airport. A hollow, unsettling feeling expanded inside Gary as a guard scanned his body with a metal detector wand.

"You know, you look almost distinguished in a suit and tie, Ramon," Gary said to break the tension as they entered the elevator. "And that "RICAN AND RICH!" mask really adds some flair."

"Hey, my young friend, I know sarcasm when I hear it," Aruba said with a smile. "And you look snazzy in blue pinstripe."

"Yeah, it's better than prison stripes, that's for sure."

"Nice sense of humor, Gary. Kind of dry, but I like it."

"I think I've worn this suit once in the past year." Gary remembered that one time, at the Biden campaign fundraiser when he met Manny. That seemed like years ago, not months. What he wouldn't give to have Manny here with him now.

They exited the elevator and checked in with the

receptionist. Another armed security guard escorted them to a conference room. The room was small, windowless, and contained a conference table and chairs. A plastic ficha plant collected dust in the corner. They sat under the watchful eyes of the big guy with the big gun. A couple of tense minutes passed with no words exchanged between Gary and Aruba.

Fisherwood and a convoy of eight other people filed into the room, all wearing black masks adorned with the FBI seal and logo: Fidelity, Bravery, Integrity. Gary found it eerie that no one said a word to Aruba and him or even acknowledged their presence.

After everyone had taken their seats, Fisherwood addressed Gary and Aruba. "I'm Deputy Director, Karl Fisherwood. I'll be conducting this inquiry. Thank you, gentlemen, for coming."

He didn't bother to introduce his factotums.

The incongruence of Fisherwood's middle-aged cherubic features combined with his barely latent hostility disturbed Gary. *This guy is out to get me.*

"I'm Daniel Aruba, counsel to Mr. Wang here," Aruba said as he lifted his hand toward Gary, who sat up straight, his face expressionless. He nodded to Fisherwood.

Fisherwood continued. "Before we begin, I need to make certain, Mr. Wang, that you are fully aware that any statement made by you to an FBI agent or representative that is false or not completely true will constitute a federal crime and felony punishable by up to five years in prison. Do you understand me, Mr. Wang?"

"Of course, my client understands, Deputy Director," Aruba said.

Gary noticed a stenographer typing on her laptop

every word that was being uttered in this room. He wondered why that was needed since he could see the surveillance cameras in each corner of the ceiling, recording the meeting.

Fisherwood confronted Aruba with an irritable expression, "Excuse me, but I was asking Mr. Wang, not you sir."

"I understand," Gary said impassively.

"Good, so let's begin. We have some questions that we would like you to answer, Mr. Wang. Please keep your answers as brief as possible."

"Whatever." Gary could barely conceal his anger and disbelief that he had to suffer the indignity of this inquisition, or rather inquiry.

"Whatever?" Fisherwood asked, eyes narrowing.

Aruba kicked Gary's ankle under the table. Gary almost laughed; he thought people only did that in sit-coms.

Fisherwood glared at Gary. "I strongly urge you, Mr. Wang, to undertake these proceedings with the utmost seriousness," he said.

"We do, Deputy Director," Aruba said.

Fisherwood didn't say anything but continued to look hard at Gary.

"I do take these proceedings with the utmost seriousness," Gary said. "This..." Gary struggled for the words to describe *this,* "has totally turned my life upside down."

"Okay, let's get these questions answered as quickly as we can, and we'll let you get back to your upturned life." Fisherwood placed a sheet of paper before him. "Have you ever been to the People's Republic of China, Mr. Wang?"

"No."

"Have you ever been to Hong Kong?"

"Of course, I was born there."

"Yeah, we know, Wang." Fisherwood's formality melted into insolence. "Other than that, have you ever been to Hong Kong? And if so, when was the last time?"

"Several times. The most recent a year or so ago."

"And the purpose of that trip?"

"I had a fellowship at the Confucius Academy of Global Understanding that lasted two years."

"Yeah, we know all about the Academy, if that's what you want to call it."

Gary let that cryptic remark slide for the sake of getting out of there ASAP. The room was making him feel claustrophobic and the agents' vacant stares reminded him of the zombies in *Night of the Living Dead*.

"Has any person in your immediate family ever been a member of the Chinese Communist Party?"

"My dad was. Back in the 60s. He and my mother fled from there after the Cultural Revolution and have been ardent—"

"A yes or no answer is all we need," Fisherwood said. "How would you describe your role with the Biden campaign?"

"I'm a volunteer. I do whatever they ask me to do, including answering phones."

Fisherwood sneered. "C'mon Gary. We know your resume. You're better than that."

Gary wondered what they *didn't* know about him, "I have advised the Vice President two or three times on matters that involved Hong Kong and the PRC."

Fisherwood took a few seconds to pause and look at Gary. "Have you advised the campaign on any financial matters?"

"Of course not. Why would they ask me anything about that? I barely know the difference between a bond and a stock." Gary hoped his answer would make it clear that the line of inquiry would end in a cul-de-sac.

"Have you had any communications with anyone working in the PRC government?"

Gary took a deep breath. "Yes, I have." He then listed the friends whom he had called and the dates as best as he could remember. He figured the FBI already had the records showing the date and time of the calls.

"And what was the purpose of those calls?"

Gary looked down at the table to compose his answer. "I was hoping to set up a meeting between Mr. Biden and President Xi."

"Really?"

Gary thought Fisherwood was suppressing a guffaw.

"And did anyone in the Biden campaign authorize you to do that? Did anyone else know about your um, diplomatic outreach, I guess we can call it?"

"No and no."

"Huh, that's really interesting. Kinda hard to believe, don't you think, Gary?"

"It is what it is," Gary said with a dash of insouciance.

"Oh, we're going to find out what *it* is, don't you worry about that."

"I'm sure you will, and I hope you do."

"One last question for you, Gary. You know Danny Copper, correct?"

"Yes, unfortunately."

"Did you tell Danny Copper that you knew about

money being transferred from PRC into the Biden campaign? Did you tell him the amount and you expected that amount would grow to fifty million dollars?"

Before Gary could answer, Aruba interjected. "Deputy Director, do you mind if I have a short conversation with my client in the hallway?"

"I guess not," Fisherwood said in an annoyed tone.

Once they exited the room, Aruba suggested that they walk to the end of the hallway. "No telling how many bugs they got out here."

Aruba appeared agitated, pacing the hall.

"Gary, we need to be careful here,"

"Why's that?"

Aruba stopped pacing and looked directly at Gary. "Because they obviously think you said something about Chinese money to Copper. He might have been wired."

"I'm telling you the truth, Ramon. I couldn't have told Copper that because I didn't know that. And I didn't know that because that never happened."

Aruba considered a few seconds. "Okay, let's go back in and you can tell them that. And let's just pray that the truth really will set you free."

The two re-entered the room and sat down.

"The answer to your last question about my conversation with Danny Copper is, no, I did not tell him I knew about money being funded by China into the campaign. I could not have told him that because that never happened."

As if on cue, Fisherwood and his team all rose from their seats and began filing out of the room. No one uttered a word, except Fisherwood, who was the last to leave.

Before exiting the room, he turned and said to Gary, "We'll be in touch."

The next evening at 6:32 eastern standard time, Gail Sturmstrom stood on the White House South Lawn to open CNN News Room with some breaking news.

"President Trump confirmed a few minutes ago what we recently reported, namely that the FBI has opened a counterintelligence operation to investigate reports that the Biden campaign has knowingly received money from the People's Republic of China. Here are the President's earlier comments."

President Trump appeared on screen striding across the White House lawn to the waiting Marine 1 helicopter that would take him to Andrews Air Force Base, where Air Force One awaited him. He was going to spend a few days at Mar-a-Lago, the "summer White House," where he planned to do some work and play a lot of golf. As always, the blue suit, white shirt, red tie. He stopped to take some questions from the gathered reporters. Trump wouldn't be the first president to take pleasure in the fact that reporters had to shout their questions above the drone of the helicopter, which also presented a convenient excuse to say that he couldn't hear the question.

The roped off herd of reporters shouted their questions to the president in a pathetic, pleading cacophony. He pointed to Sturmstom to ask the first question.

"Mr. President, can you comment on reports that the FBI has officially opened an investigation into the Biden-China money connection."

Trump raised his hands to play the accordion.

"Yes, I can. Everybody's known about this for weeks. I think they're calling it China-gate, right? Maybe not, not yet anyway. I don't know why Cummings can't come out and let everybody know. Everybody knows it already. Is he trying to protect Biden? I don't think so, but I don't know. Ridiculous. Everybody knows it. It's a disgrace Biden taking money from communist China. And this Wang kid, I don't know if he's a bad guy or done anything wrong, but the FBI must think so. Anyway, we'll see what dirt the investigation turns up."

"Fuck!" said Joe Biden at the flat screen mounted on a basement wall in his bunker.

"Fuck!" shouted Gary Wang as he gawked at the television in Manny's apartment.

"Dang it!" said Director Cummings as he stared at the brand-new TV monitor set in his office credenza.

"Ooooh yeah," murmured Senator Slade McClintock as he savored his cocktail hour Manhattan in his Dupont Circle apartment penthouse while watching Sturmstrom.

"Ah damn it, who now?" Gary said to Manny snuggled next to him on her couch as he glanced at caller ID on his phone. When he saw Senator McClintock's name, he said "Whoa!" and hit the green accept button.

"Hello."

"Gary Wang?"

"Yes."

"Hi, I'm Avi Silverman. Assistant chief of staff to Senator McClintock. How are you this evening?"

"Good. I think."

"Ha… I hear you. I'm calling you because the

senator would like you to testify before the Senate Intelligence Committee."

"What? Testify about what?"

"Uh, well, about Chinese involvement in this election. The President yesterday confirmed that you are the subject of an FBI investigation, right? We'd like to hear your side of the story."

"I'm sure a staunch Trump supporter like McClintock really cares about my side of the story. Sounds like a PR stunt to me. What if I don't care to participate in this show trial?"

"Look Gary—okay if I call you Gary?—the committee will subpoena you if it has to. That's a hassle for you and the committee both, so let's don't go down that road."

"I got nothing to hide, so really I have no problem telling you and your committee the truth, which is that this is a lot of unimaginable and utter bullshit."

"Hey, be my guest. I got no dog in this fight, as my boss might say."

"I'll talk to my lawyer. I don't want to walk into a trap."

"He'll probably tell you to testify but just plead the fifth. Hey, that's cool with me."

"Send me a subpoena if you have to. Frankly, at this point I don't give a fuck. Goodbye."

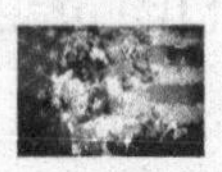

After Gary hung up on him, Avi looked at Senator McClintock sitting next to him in a limousine cruising along Route One, with the Tidal Basin and the Jefferson Memorial in view on the left. Avi was hoping for a sign of approval from the senator.

"You did good, Avi. That whippersnapper is going

to realize real quick that he doesn't have any choice but to testify. And if he wants to plead the fifth at every question, that's even better. That's always good entertainment. That's got guilt written all over it." McClintock grinned at Avi.

"Now, next thing you do is call your girlfriend Sturmstrom and tell her that we're dragging Wang before our committee. And you'll be letting her know what comes out of it, classified or not. I'm sure she'll reward you with a nice blowjob for that."

Besides feeling somewhat nauseated by McClintock referencing fellatio, Avi had qualms about leaking classified information coming out of the Intelligence Committee to a reporter. Not only was that against the law, but it was also a felony. He thought about pointing that out to the senator. But wouldn't he seem like a naïf doing that? He could already hear Slade McClintock's snarky laugh at such scruples. Maybe there was a time when passing along classified information was considered criminal, treacherous, even treasonous. But Avi had been in D.C. long enough to know that leaking classified stuff was par for the course, just another weapon used to advance the cause. Besides, getting a blowjob from Gale wasn't such a bad result either.

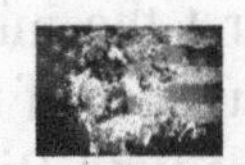

Manny waited for Gary to say something after he finished the call from Avi Silverman, but he sat silent. He stared at nothing, a hundred-foot stare in a ten-foot-long room.

"What happened, Gary? What was that call about?"

"I just can't believe this," he finally uttered.

His face compressed and reddened with anguish and frustration. He pounded his fist on the glass tabletop table in front of the sofa, causing Manny to flinch. When he flung his fist against the table a second time, the glass shattered, and shards rained down onto the rug.

"Gary, what's wrong!"

He put his head in his hands as blood streamed from his wrist.

"Gary, you cut yourself!"

Manny ran to the first aid cabinet and returned with medicine and bandages.

He sat slumped on the sofa, his hands still covering his face. His head trembled. His chest heaved in and out. The space between his fingers turned wet with tears.

"Gary, give me your hand. Tell me what happened."

His hands fell. Manny took the one that was cut. He looked down, his eyelids red and moist. "That was Senator McClintock's office. They want me to testify to the Senate Intelligence Committee."

Seeing Gary like this made Manny's heart sink. She had never seen him cry before. He had been so stalwart up to now. First the initial rumors, then the news that he was the subject of an FBI investigation, the meeting in Delaware with Biden and getting fired from the campaign, the FBI raid on his apartment, family and friends calling non-stop asking what in God's name was going on...and he was going to be grilled by a senate committee about something he didn't do. But now he looked more than down, he looked defeated.

"Manny, I just can't get out from under this. No matter what I do, no matter how innocent I am." He wiped at his eyes with his other hand, obviously embarrassed by his tears.

She calmly wrapped the bandage around his wrist. "We have to be strong, Gary."

Gary sniffled, nodded his head, and sat up straight.

"We know this is coming from Danny Copper, that bogus Copper File. Ramon needs to get hold of the primary source of what Copper says you told him that night you went to dinner. He was probably recording you, so we need to get that recording, the raw recording, not some transcript. As far as the phone calls to your friends in China, Ramon will have to find some way to depose them, so they can say what the calls were about." She smiled at Gary. "So see, we got better than a fighting chance."

He nodded and smiled weakly. "I guess we need to go find you a new coffee table."

That calm, steady voice that she loved so much was returning. "We probably need to get you some stitches first." She lifted his wounded hand and kissed it.

Chapter Twelve

UPEKKHA LOST

October 2020

Gary whiled away the afternoon as he had done so many afternoons since getting fired: lying on the sofa in Manny's apartment. Of course, looking for a job was out of the question, since nobody was going to hire someone with such a dark cloud hanging over him. He couldn't leave the apartment anyway lest reporters or rabid Trumpeters accosted him.

So instead, he watched the television tuned to CNN so he could see what Sturmstrom might come up with next, what bombshell. God, how he had come to hate that word. Just another one of those shibboleths that politicians and media latch onto from a dearth of imagination, like Kumbaya, nothing-burger, dog whistle, sausage making, existential. America's so-called intelligentsia were like parrots trained to mimic whatever they heard. And now the words that they had tagged him with were money man, bag boy, traitor, and colluder.

And he couldn't help but think that it had all come down to this, lying on a couch at 2:35 p.m. on a Tuesday afternoon. After the emigration from Hong Kong, the slant-eyed jokes and Asian geek taunts, the assimilation, high school valedictorian, Columbia…rising expectations, upward mobility, infinite promise, deserved reward. Now this, a futureless future…tin cans tied to the tail of a dog.

His phone's ringtone saved him from sinking into self-pity. He was glad when he saw it was Manny calling. "Hey there, what's up?"

"Gary, you can't believe what just happened. You just can't."

She sounded frantic. "Calm down, Manny. What happened?"

"I'm at work and two guys come into the newsroom. The security guard leads them straight over to my desk. And one of the guys pulls out a badge or whatever and says he's with the FBI. Like, right in front of everybody. I was so humiliated…" She paused and began crying uncontrollably.

"Manny, please calm down. What happened next?"

"They said they wanted to ask me some questions. We went into a side room off the floor. Everybody saw me. And they sat me down and started asking me all these questions about you, like how much money do you have, do you spend a lot, do you talk to people in China regularly. They just left a few minutes ago. I haven't left this room yet. I just can't go back out there because I can't stop crying. And my boss came in ten seconds ago and said she wants to see me tomorrow morning."

"Don't worry, they can't fire you over this. You haven't done anything."

"It's not me I'm worried about, it's you, Gary. They are out to get you. I can tell by the questions. I'm so afraid for you."

"Manny, remember what you told me the other day, when you were bandaging my hand? Remember?"

"Yes."

"You told me to be strong. Now you have to be strong. Like you said, we got better than a fighting chance because none of this is real. You need to come home. Do you want me to come get you?"

"No, that's okay. I'm going to leave now and meet you at the apartment. I'm okay."

Gary was happy to see that she had gained some semblance of composure. "I'll call Ramon. We'll meet with him tomorrow as soon as we can. Stay calm."

"I will. I love you."

"I love you too."

"I was able to finally get in touch with Fisherwood," Aruba said to Gary and Manny who sat in his Bronx office. "Took about ten damn calls."

"And what did he say about letting us have copies of any recordings they might have of Copper and me talking that night?" Gary asked.

"He said he wasn't at liberty to discuss that. And any recordings the FBI may or may not have would be classified anyway, which is total nonsense since any such recording that was done privately and released to the public as it was to Buzzsaw could not be classified. He knows that was ridiculous, but it's like he wanted to insult my intelligence on purpose."

"And what about them harassing Manny, did he have anything to say about that?"

"No comment was all I got on that one," Aruba said. "That was probably just to soften you up, Gary. A common tactic for these guys is to go after a loved one or somebody close to the target. Gives them leverage over you."

"Leverage for what?" Manny asked.

"Gary is not the end and be all of what these guys are up to. They're trying to put together a daisy chain, and Gary, you're the first daisy on the chain. They're hoping that you'll rat on someone the next level above you. And they'll do the same to that person what they're doing to you now. And that person will rat on the person at the next level, and so on and so forth until they get the big Kahuna they've been after all along."

"And that would be who?" Gary asked.

"Biden of course," Aruba said.

"Jesus, no way," Gary said. "Trump is the one sic'ing them on Biden?"

"Nah, I don't think necessarily so. These guys hate Biden. FBI is full of Trumpeters. They got enough ill will to motivate them without Trump egging them on. You've seen some of those FBI emails that Fox News released. Agents talking about Biden being a patsy for the soft-on-crime woke progressives. How they'll not only defund the police but the FBI too. Biden has to be stopped at all costs, all that junk."

"Really pissed me off how the rest of the media totally ignored that FBI bias, didn't think it was worthy of reporting, even suppressed it," Manny said. "Wasn't there a time when the press fought to expose the establishment and authorities instead of being its lackeys?"

"Nowadays it's all about The Cause, Manny," Ramon said. "The media is all too willing to be a dumb tool for whatever they deem to be The Cause."

"So, what's next, Ramon?" Gary asked.

"I'm guessing the harassment will intensify. You will probably be getting another visit from the G-men. So be ready."

"Great… I can hardly wait," Gary said.

Gary sat cross-legged on Manny's den floor. He had assumed the lotus position: back straight, hands resting on thighs, head up. His eyes were open but focused on nothing really.

After having spent one afternoon after another on Manny's couch, which had become the boundaries of the hell he'd fallen into, he knew he had to escape this depressing routine. He couldn't spend his waking hours wondering when the next shoe was going to drop, or more like wondering when the next Paul Bunyan size hobnail boot was going to crash on his head. All he could think about was what would the Feds do to him next.

One day the thought occurred to him: why not meditate to rid his mind of all this tension and angst, to get his Zen back? His family had converted to Buddhism after they fled the mainland, or actually returned to Buddhism since both his parents had practiced it in their youths. He had often joined them in the exercise. But he was a bit rusty after not having practiced it in decades. So, he eagerly watched a video on the Internet to relearn the right technique.

He breathed in five seconds, breathed out five seconds. One Mississippi, two Mississippi… He focused on breathing only.

In out, in out.

What time did Manny say she would be home from work?

Breathe in, breathe out.

Eight o'clock, was it? I'll whip up some dinner tonight.

"Upekkha," he murmured, the Buddhist word for equanimity, to bring him back to his breathing. Three Mississippi, four Mississippi, five Mississippi.

Breathe out.

The phone inside the kitchen trilled, trilled, trilled. The message machine picked up the call and loudly replayed: *This is Pam from Discover Card calling about your delinquent account...*

Upekkha!

In and out, surge and subside…he felt his forehead skin loosen. One Mississippi, two Mississippi. A wave of relaxation moved from his forehead to around his eye sockets…Breathe in, breathe out…flowed down his jawline. His tongue moved slightly up against the roof of his mouth. His counting stopped and his breathing fell into a natural flow. He noticed the natural flow. He felt the natural flow down into his shoulders, into his palms. *How am I going to get out of testifying? Subpoena will probably be here any day.*

Upekkha. Upekkha. *Hopefully Aruba can at least get it put off.* Breathe in, breathe out. "Upekkha," he said. In, out…suuussss, seeessss…surge, subside.

This was not working the way the YouTube video

presented it. The first two times he meditated for fifteen minutes or so, but could never quite get to Upekkha. He couldn't erase from his mind the FBI circling, McClintock threatening, no job, no money to help Manny pay the bills, his name associated with treachery, crime, treason. He remembered the old Buddhist proverb: Meditation is like trying to tie a rope to a monkey and making it dance. He told himself to concentrate harder.

The phone rang again, but this time it was his cell phone. He glanced at the phone on the floor in front of him and saw that it was Aruba calling. So long Upekkha.

"Hey Ramon."

"Where are you?"

"I'm at Manny's. Trying to get away without getting out."

"You need to stay put. I got a tip from a friendly agent that the FBI is on its way there."

"Shit, how many times do I have to give these guys an interview? Haven't they've gotten enough already?"

"They're not coming to interview you, Gary."

"What do they want then?"

"They're coming to arrest you."

Chapter Thirteen

HIGHTAILIN' IT

Gary paid little attention to Aruba as he told Gary he would meet him at the courthouse and post bail if needed, and that he had to remain calm, that the charge was lying to FBI and they could beat that no doubt, and don't say anything to the agents once they got there, tell them you want your lawyer present before answering any questions, and…Aruba's words were like raindrops falling on the puddle that was Gary's mind at that moment. All he could think was, *my life is over*.

He rose from the floor, but his knees weakened, and he had to steady himself. Panic coursed through his nervous system like an electric current. *This is really happening.* He paced from one wall of the apartment to the other, both hands pressed against his forehead. He couldn't let them arrest him. His first thought was to run. His second thought was to run. His third thought was to run.

Gary ran from the apartment, down the three flights of steps and burst out the building's front door. He raced past two guys in suits outside the door.

"Hey, that's Wang isn't it, Kaminsky?" one of the guys in a suit asked the other guy.

"Sure is. Let's go!" Kaminsky said.

"Hey Wang, stop. FBI. Stop!

The agents chased after him. Fortunately, he was at least ten years younger than his pursers, one of whom, Kaminsky, was about twenty pounds overweight, and so managed to put some distance between them. He made his way to the nearest subway stop. He hurdled the turnstile. A train was at the station, filling up fast when the chime sounded, signaling that the door would soon close. Gary almost knocked over two tourists studying a map as he lunged toward the train's door just as it closed shut.

Gary banged on the door. "Open up! This is an emergency!" he yelled, discomfiting the by-standers waiting for the next train. The conductor sat in his booth and looked straight ahead, pretending he didn't hear or see Gary. Gary looked over his shoulder and saw the two agents at the turnstile. They struggled to heave themselves over the metal bar. Fortunately for Gary, there was no easy access door for the handicapped at this station. In the meantime, the train was rolling away from the station.

He darted along the train platform, trapped. The other agent had gotten over the turnstile and was helping Kaminsky do the same. He saw no choice but to jump off the platform and onto the tracks.

Gary sprinted along the tracks, tripped and almost

fell onto the third rail, the rail charged with the electric current powering the trains. If he touched that, he knew he would have sizzled like a beetle on one of those bug grillers people hang over the patio in the summer. Into the inky darkness of the tunnel he headed, as his two pursuers stood on the platform, bending over and peering into the tunnel.

"Wang, come back! You're gonna get yourself killed!" Kaminsky slapped his thigh in frustration. Apparently, neither agent had any intention of leaping into that rat-infested, dark, dank, stinking hole with a dormant lightning bolt running down the middle of it.

Gary ran, not bothering to look over his shoulder to see if he were still being chased. The tunnel grew darker and narrower as the uptown and downtown lines diverged into separate tubes. The only light was the small blue light bulbs spaced every thirty yards or so along the wall. But then he stopped in wonder as a glimmer of gold appeared on the rails in front of him. A light rose above the tracks, then another light...two unblinking eyes coming toward him. A rumbling noise began to build. The subway train was turning a corner and coming full speed at him.

The motorman sounded his horn, not because he saw Gary, but because regulations required that he do so as the train approached the station. Coming around the bend, the motorman would not be able to stop the train in time even if he did espy Gary.

Gary quickly looked back toward the station. He was at least a hundred yards away, with no chance to make it all the way back there. The train would be on him in a matter of seconds. So, he did the only thing that he could do, and that was immediately fall flat between the rails. He pulled his arms as tight as he could against his sides and scrunched his body against the rail bed. In a flash and with a roar, the train descended upon him like an angry dragon ready to gobble him in one bite.

Gary shut his eyes and held his breath, sucking his body into itself as much as he could. The train's hot, greasy, iron underbelly rushed over him…*clack, clack, clack, clack.* The dragon's fifty round, metal teeth chattered less than a foot on each side of his head, so loud that he thought his eardrums might burst.

He lay as still as a corpse in a coffin, expecting some low-hanging piece of metal to plow into him, tearing his body straight down the middle. Then suddenly the train was gone. He gasped with relief—the dragon had spat him back out. He ran a hand over his body to make sure it was still in one piece. He rose and staggered off the tracks only to fall against the near-by wall. The small blue bulbs cast just enough light for him to see a railing running along the wall. Amazed to find a catwalk there, he lifted himself up and rolled over onto it.

After resting until his heartbeat had gotten somewhat back to normal, he stood and walked along the catwalk. The tunnel was now dead quiet except for the occasional rat that squeaked in surprise and scurried away.

Finally, he came to a metal ladder. In the darkness he couldn't see exactly where the ladder ended but climbed it anyway. After going up a few rungs, he reached and pushed hard with both hands against a round cover. Suddenly he left the pitch black of the subway and entered the bright Manhattan afternoon. He poked his head through the aperture and realized that the opening was in the middle of Seventh Avenue.

Luckily traffic was nothing like it used to be thanks to Covid-19, and he was able to extract himself from the manhole without getting run over.

Stumbling onto the street, he inhaled the city's pungent air. Urine, days old trash spilling onto the sidewalks, dog poop, or was it human, had never smelled better to him. He stood there a moment and looked in each direction to make sure the coast was clear of the two agents. He guessed that they were waiting for him at the next subway stop.

He walked to a bank branch across the street and withdrew the $356 from his checking account. He figured that the FBI would alert his bank and want to know whenever he withdrew money so they could track his location, so he emptied his account.

He then went over to the grand marbled entrance of a boarded-up department store, which gave him cover from the street. *Goldsmiths* was inscribed in large golden block letters over the broad bronze doors. *Established 1946.* The store was once a flourishing emporium, recently closed due to the plague and riots.

Once he got his bearings, his first thought was Manny. He called her cell phone.

"Hey babe. How's the meditation going?" Manny answered when she saw Gary calling. "It takes a while to really get it going you know."

"Manny, I'm leaving."

"Gary, you shouldn't leave the apartment. You're a recognized face now. Some MAGA maniac might jump you."

"You don't understand, Manny. I'm leaving… leaving for good."

"Huh?"

"The FBI came to arrest me today."

"Oh my God! Are you in jail now?"

"I ran away from them."

"What? Gary, you can't do that. Why on earth would you do that? You're a fugitive now!"

Gary sighed. He looked down and shut his eyes as he spoke. "If they arrested me, my life would be over. And that's because...because there's something that happened a long time ago, something I've never told you about. Something I've never told anyone. But if they arrested me, they would know about it, and I might as well be dead then."

"What? Tell me. What could be so bad that you can't tell me?"

"I can't right now. It's a long story. I have to go. I just called to tell you that I'm leaving, and I don't know when—

"When what?"

"When I'll see you again."

Manny didn't say anything for a few seconds. "Gary, please don't leave. We can face this. Ramon can fix whatever it is that's making you," she paused, "leave me."

"I don't think so. We'll see each other again someday. I know we will. But not now, not for a—" He stopped.

"A long time? Is that what you were going to say?"

"And this is the last time I'll be able to call you, at least from this phone. They can track my phone and find my location. I have to destroy it. This is my last call."

Neither said anything.

"I have to go, Manny," he said, breaking the silence. "Just know that wherever I am and whatever happens to me, I love you."

"Oh Gary…"

He couldn't stand to hear her sobbing. "Goodbye, Manny."

He clicked off the call, looked at the phone, and threw it against the marble wall with as much force as he could, once, twice, three times until it shattered into pieces. He fell against the wall and would have wailed but didn't lest he attract attention.

"C'mon again, Karl. Repeat what you just told me. I'm hoping I misheard you." Director Cummings leaned over his desk and glared at Fisherwood.

Cowering in the seat with his head bowed, Fisherwood raised his hands in the air. "I don't know what to tell you, Boss. Just when Stout and Kaminsky got to the apartment building where we found out Wang's been hanging out, Wang burst from the door like a bat outta hell and hauled ass to a nearby subway station. Stout and Kaminsky lost him."

"Jesus Christ, Peckerwood!"

Fisherwood had heard the Director and deacon cuss before, but never using his Lord and Savior's name in vain like that. He knew he was really in hot water now, boiling hot water.

"Wang was right," Cummings continued, "we really are a bunch of Keystone Cops."

"Somebody must have tipped him off that we were coming, Boss."

"Of course, he was tipped off. Next thing you know that news hound Sturmstrom will be blasting it on CNN."

"That news bitch," Fisherwood mumbled angrily.

"That's not appropriate language in this office, Karl."

"I was just playing off news hound. She's a woman, so, you know, female hound..."

"I get it but I'm in no mood for puns. Nor will the Great Orange Turd be when he gets wind of it."

Speaking of appropriate language, Fisherwood wished the Director would not refer to the President with such disrespect. But now was certainly not the time to raise that objection.

"We got the dragnet out, Boss. We're checking any associations or friends that Wang might have in the area. Got bulletins out with all the airlines and rental car companies. Agents posted at Penn Station, Grand Central, La Guardia, JFK, Newark airports. Fugitive alerts across the Northeast. He's going on the FBI Most Wanted list today."

"We should probably check in again with that girlfriend of his," Cummings said. "See what she knows."

"Got it, Boss. That all for now?"

"Yeah, Karl, that's all for now." Cummings leaned his head back against the chair and wearily shut his eyes.

Fisherwood exited the office thinking, *I'm going to catch that fucker if I have to chase him all the way back to China.*

Gary Wang was still at the Goldsmith's entrance. For over two hours he had sat against the cool marble wall, his arms resting on his knees, his head down. Where could he go? In his panicky haste to escape arrest, he hadn't thought about that.

With nothing else to do, he wondered how he would have explained to Manny why he had to run, what had happened over five years before when he was a student at Columbia. The memory was so vivid, that knock on his dorm room door. When he opened it, he at first thought he was seeing things, an apparition. Standing before him was his brother, Joe.

"What are you doing here?" Gary asked Joe with a flat tone.

"Is that any way to speak to your *gege*," Joe replied. "You going to let me in?"

Joe was wearing tan light wool slacks, a red golf shirt, and a navy-blue jacket. His hair was slicked back and as a black as his wrap-around designer sunglasses. He could have been the latest matinee idol in the burgeoning China movie business. He did have the looks: high cheekbones, eyes limned with lashes as pronounced as mascara, endowing his face with fierceness even when he laughed.

Gary moved out of the doorway so Joe could enter. He hadn't seen Joe since he first arrived at Columbia, three years before. His parents had never given up on rehabilitating Joe and urged Gary to reach out to him now that they were both in the same city. So, he met Joe and some of his buddies at a restaurant downtown. In between bites of crispy Peking duck pancakes with oyster sauce, his dinner companions mostly talked in Cantonese amongst themselves, largely ignoring Gary. He knew enough Cantonese to know that the few times they mentioned him, it was only to crudely make fun of him. "Hey Joe, your little brother looks as soft as a virgin's pussy."

"How did you get in this building without the entry door passcode?" Gary asked.

"You ever hear of a Bluetooth sniffer?" Joe pulled his phone from his inside jacket pocket which had a small rectangular box with an antenna attached to it. "Everything flying around in public Wi-Fi can be snatched, including pass codes to electronic locks."

"Ah, that's really neat," Gary said sarcastically. "I bet it comes in handy when you want to unlock car doors too."

"Yep, it certainly does."

"So, what do you want?" Gary asked, annoyed.

"I need to meet someone here. An associate."

"An associate?"

"Yeah, someone who works for me. Shouldn't last long, assuming things go right. Here, this should make it worth your time." Joe fished out a C-note from his wallet and handed it to Gary. Being a student without a job, he was not exactly rolling in cash and was tempted to take the money. But before he had time to tell Joe to take his dirty money and shove it, Joe's phone rang.

"Yeah, come on up," Joe said to the person on the other end of the line. "Pass code is 458639. Room 312, up on the third floor. Yeah, I got my money. See you then."

Gary noticed that Joe talked differently while on his phone with this person. Was he trying to disguise his voice?

"Gary, get in the closet. Now!" Joe said.

"What are you talking about, damn it?"

Joe looked him straight in the face. "Get in the fucking closet. For your own good. There might be some trouble."

Just then, a knock sounded against the door. "Go!" Joe commanded in a low, stern tone. Gary did what Joe told him to do, as he usually had done growing up as Joe's little brother. The fact that Joe was six foot one, about three inches taller than Gary also had a subliminal effect on him. He went into the closet and left the door slightly ajar so he could see what the hell was about to happen.

Joe opened the door. The visitor's mouth dropped when he saw it was Joe. Before the kid had time to flee, Joe grabbed him by his neck and dragged him into the apartment. He was short and skinny and so easily managed by Joe. The kid was wearing a white jacket and white pants, like that worn by a busboy or delivery guy.

Joe threw the kid to the floor, covered by the hooked rug that Mrs. Wang had given Gary when he started his drive from LA to NYC for the beginning of his first year at Columbia.

"So, you got your own turf now, huh Duc? Selling product to all these college kids. Product you got through my suppliers. You don't think I would find out, mutherfucker? You know I know everything!"

Duc stood on his knees in front of Joe. "Just trying to get new territory for us *Dai Low.*" Dai low was Cantonese slang for "big brother," used in Chinatown gangs to denote the chief, the Big Bro.

"Oh yeah? And when were you going to tell me about this new territory that you discovered?"

"I was gonna get around to it. Just wanted to get it going first. I was gonna tell you, Smokey Joe, I swear on my ma's urn."

"What are you packing?" Joe asked. "Hand it over."

Duc reached into his jacket pocket and pulled out a large zip-lock baggie. He handed it to the tall, angry figure hovering over him like a black storm cloud.

Joe took the package to the kitchen cabinet to examine the contents. "Ecstasy," Joe mumbled to himself as he took a taste of the white powder.

Meanwhile Gary, peering past the slightly ajar closet door, noticed that while Joe had his back turned to Duc, the latter had taken a .35 caliber handgun from his jacket. Gary burst out of the closet and pounced on Duc. "He's got a gun, Joe!" Gary and Duc wrestled on the floor, but Duc quickly managed to squirm away from Gary. Just as he pointed his gun at Gary, a BANG sounded from behind Duc. His arms fell to his sides and the gun dropped to the floor. He looked up to the ceiling with a facial expression that almost resembled what he was peddling…ecstasy. He toppled over on top of Gary.

Joe rushed over to Gary, a Glock in his hand. "Shhh, don't say anything. Listen." For several seconds, Joe stood there, intently listening for any sounds of movement or voices in the dormitory that may have been caused by the gun shot.

Joe reached down and pulled Duc off Gary. Duc's face was locked in an expression of wide-eyed horror mixed with abject amazement. Joe bent down and looked more closely at him,

"Is he dead," Gary asked, fret wracking his face.

"Yeah."

Gary got up from the floor and hurried to his phone sitting on the kitchen table and picked it up.

"What do you think you're doing?" Joe asked.

"We have to call the police, Joe. We have to report this. We can say it was self-defense, which is the truth."

Joe raised his Glock and aimed it at Gary.

"Put that fucking phone down right now. You're my brother but I will shoot you if I have to. I will try to only wound you, but I will shoot."

Gary put the phone down. Joe put his gun down.

"The cops know my business, my reputation," Joe said. "How we going to explain this?" He pointed at Duc. "They'll see it in the worst way. A drug deal gone wrong. And they'll just look at you as an accessory to the murder. Aiding and abetting. What we tell them happened won't mean shit to them. We'll both be put away for the rest of our lives."

"So, what are we gonna do then?" Gary asked, shaken, bewildered.

"We're going to dispose of the body. And then we're going to pretend that this never happened."

Joe searched Duc's pockets and found his wallet. "He's illegal so hardly anyone will notice or care that he's missing."

Joe looked around the apartment. "Help me put him in the center of this rug," he said to Gary. The two of them lifted the body, a small pool of blood on the linoleum floor the only sign that a few minutes ago this person had a life.

"Let's roll him up in this rug and we'll carry him to my car."

Gary was too dazed to argue with his older brother and did as told. As they rolled the body up in the rug, he wondered what his mother would think about how her rug was being used. *Never in her worst nightmare...*

"Okay, now we're going to haul him to my car in the parking lot right outside. So, wipe that shocked look off your face and smile at anyone you know passing by."

The brothers lugged the rolled-up rug out of the dorm room, down the hallway and the flight of steps (avoiding the elevator), out the dormitory and to Joe's red Mercedes SUV GLC 63. Gary remembered how their mother's favorite color was red; she said it symbolized luck and joy. Joe popped open the trunk with his key fob. They placed their unlucky cargo there, cargo turning redder every minute.

Joe drove. Gary had no idea where they were going. Neither he nor Joe spoke during the drive. The only sound was the hip-hop playlist that Joe plugged into the car's sound system from his phone. The music only made Gary's jangled nerves even more jingly.

They left Riverside Drive and entered a large park called Fort Tyrone.

"Shouldn't we find some place further out from the city?" Gary asked.

"I don't want to be driving around too long with a dead body in the trunk. Who knows what might happen. This is as good a place as any."

The park had a lot of woods, stone outcropping, deep gullies, and ravines. Joe came to an isolated area and pulled the car to the side of the road. "This looks like a good spot."

The two got out of the car. They both looked in all directions for any signs of others in the area. "Let's go." They quickly lifted the rug and carried it fifty yards into the woods. Late September and the tree leaves' colors burned bright with the promise of decay.

"Let's put it here, under this rock ledge," Joe said. They lowered their burden and concealed it as best they could with leaves and dead branches.

Joe drove back to the campus and stopped to let Gary out. Staring straight ahead behind his sunglasses he said, "Thanks."

Gary opened the car door, turned to Joe, and said, "I don't want to see your face ever again."

A little over three weeks later, Gary was watching the local news. The discovery of a body in Tyrone Park was the top story. Gary jumped up straight and stared slack-jawed at the TV screen. A gentleman wearing a trench coat and holding a microphone stood in front of the ledge under which the body had been found.

"Police have not yet been able to identify the deceased but believe the death was the result of foul play. Channel 7 will keep you abreast of any developments as the investigation proceeds. Back to you, Lori."

Gary stood there, his mind jumping from one possibility to another. Wouldn't Joe's DNA and fingerprints be all over the body? Could a strand or two of his hair be clinging to the rug? Or microscopic skin flakes? Wouldn't the authorities have Joe's DNA and fingerprints on file, assuming that he had been arrested before? Gary wouldn't admit it, but he worried about his brother. Then a realization slapped him across the face: his DNA, fingerprints, hair, skin flakes would also be all over the body and rug too. If he ever got arrested for anything, the police would run his DNA and fingerprints through the national crime database to find any matches obtained from prior investigations.

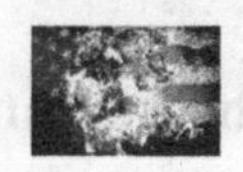

If he were ever lucky enough to see Manny again, he would tell her that was why he had no choice but to run.

Chapter Fourteen

DIM SUM

Gale Sturmstrom appeared on the TV screen with the Chryon caption underneath her that read: BREAK IN 5-YEAR-OLD MURDER CASE.

"CNN has breaking news to report about a case long gone cold. NYPD says that it has a DNA match—two in fact—with that found on an unidentified body discovered in Tyrone Park in 2015. The match has led police to seek the arrest of two suspects, who have been identified as—"

Gary sat up from the floor in the department store entrance, gasping. He was awakened by what he thought was a shout, and then he realized that it was *his* shout that had penetrated his deep sleep. He shook his head to cast off the nightmare. He then remembered where he was and what had happened the day before, the present coagulating into grim reality; still, Gary would take this reality over that dream. Similar nightmares had afflicted him over the past five years, dreams in which the authorities seem to be closing in on him and Joe for the murder of Duc. Thinking about it yesterday, Gary roused it from the dark grave that it refused to stay in. In any case, here he was, back to nowhere.

A church bell tolled nearby. He looked at his watch, seven o'clock in the morning. He could hardly believe he had been sleeping in his marble sanctuary for over eight hours. That he was able to sleep so soundly on the hard floor in the department store entryway indicated how traumatic and exhausting yesterday's events had been. He rose and stretched his arms above his head and bent up and down to get the soreness out of his back. He was starving and decided he had no choice but to venture out for food.

He stepped out of the entryway and looked around. He spotted a food cart about thirty yards down the street and walked toward it. He stopped when he came to a newspaper kiosk. On the cover of the *New York Post* was the loud headline: GARY THE RED HAS FLED THE FEDS. Taking up about half the cover page was a picture of him, the same Columbia student ID photo, and the People's Republic of China's flag behind him. *Damn, I can't walk around like this.*

A little way past the food cart was a table displaying sundry clothing items, obviously hot. He hurried to the table and picked up a cotton bucket hat with a kangaroo insignia on the front, and a cheap pair of sunglasses.

"Sixty dollars," the man with a Nigerian accent said to Gary. That price was highway robbery, but he wasn't in a mood or position to haggle.

He then went to the food cart and bought a gigantic marble cruller donut. He wolfed it down along with some coffee in a paper cup.

After nourishing himself and feeling a bit sturdier, he thought: *Now what? Manny, that's what.*

He walked several blocks until he came to the News Corp Building where Fox News was headquartered. The time was 7:43 a.m., about when Manny would be showing up for work. A few minutes later, he spotted her.

He called out her name. She stopped and squinted, not recognizing him because of his hat, shades, and mask.

"Manny, it's Gary."

Her eyes opened wide, and she immediately began to run toward him.

"Stop!" He raised his hand. "We can't make a scene here. Someone might be watching. Follow me to Bryant Park."

Manny followed ten yards or so behind Gary to the park where they stopped at a stone bench surrounded by maple trees. They both ripped off their masks and embraced each other with a long kiss.

They sat on the bench in the shade of the enclosing trees that hid them from prying, spying eyes. Manny reached out and caressed Gary's face, like she wanted to make sure it was really he.

"I thought you said I wouldn't see you again?"

"I couldn't stop thinking about you," he said. "I had to see you. Fuck the FBI. I had to see you."

"Gary, why did you run?"

Gary raised his eyes from hers and gazed over her head like the answer was written there in thin air. He wasn't sure where to start, so he started at the beginning. "About five years ago, my brother Joe showed up at my dorm room…"

As he told the story, he couldn't help but notice the shock and alarm transforming Manny's face. After he finished, neither said anything for several moments.

"You look…" Gary paused, not sure how to describe the look on Manny's face, "like you just saw a terrible car crash."

"Gary, I'm just trying to wrap my head around this…this murder." She shook her head a couple of times.

"Manny, the guy was pointing a gun at me. Thank God Joe saw it and reacted in time. Otherwise, I wouldn't be sitting here with you now."

"A murder in your dorm room," she said. "And then you…you helped dispose of the body? I just can't picture you, or the person I thought was you, doing that…I just don't know what to think." She averted her eyes from his. Her fingers skirmished with themselves.

"Joe forced me to do that. I had no choice. Don't you see?"

She nodded but her stunned expression remained. She glanced at her watch. "Damn, I was supposed to be at my desk twenty-five minutes ago. I'm one of the few working in the office, so it'll be noticed." She rose from the bench. "Gary, you have to give me time to absorb all this."

Gary half-laughed. "Time is one thing I have plenty of. But I don't know when we can see each other again. I can't even call you. I'm sure the Feds got their eyes on you. Tracking your phone calls, trying to figure out where I am. Hoping you'll lead them to me."

Manny grimaced, as if to say, "Wonderful..."

"I know I have to fight this. I can't just hope it all goes away. But I don't know how to fight back. I mean, I know that Copper File is at the bottom of it, but I don't know who or where his source is. It's like trying to fight a ghost."

Gary stood up and Manny took hold of his hands.

"You'll get to the other side of this. I know you will. I'm sorry, but I have to go."

She leaned over and gave him a quick kiss on the lips. She let go of his hands and walked back to the avenue. She turned one last time and looked back at him before disappearing.

Still standing in the lover's bower where they had hugged and kissed, Gary watched her go until she was out of sight. He could tell by her face, her voice, and that last perfunctory kiss that she saw him as a different person, suddenly a stranger. And how else could he have expected her to react? A sad, sinking feeling overwhelmed him because he knew that things had just forever changed between them. She was gone for good.

He got up and walked aimlessly, unmoored. His spirit, his self-identity was slowly escaping him, like air from a leaky balloon. He passed a kiosk and stopped to glance at the headlines, hoping not to see another photo of himself. Fortunately, no such stories appeared, at least not on the front page. He did notice *The New York Times* headline: BIDEN'S DOUBLE-DIGIT LEAD OVER TRUMP ERASED BY CHINA REPORTS.

Gary had almost forgotten over the past couple of days that an election was going on. He experienced a spasm of guilt that he might cost Biden the election through no fault of his own, even though he was completely innocent of these absurd charges. But he had bigger worries than that now. Where could he go, he wondered. No place. But he couldn't just stay on the streets.

As he shuffled along the sidewalk, drained and dejected, he thought again how he had to find some way to show the Copper File to be complete fiction. He had to get to Copper but how could he do that? There was probably an all-points bulletin out all over the country with his name and photo. He couldn't rent a car, get a plane or train ticket. Unless he had failproof fake ID, like a driver's license or passport. But where and how could he obtain one of those? And who would get it for him? He didn't know anyone underground or on the periphery of civil society who could pull that off.

Gary stopped dead in his tracks. His mouth slightly opened as the neurons in his brain crackled with an idea so crazy and improbable and dreadful that he had no doubt that it would work. There was a place he could go, a person to see. For the life of him, he didn't want to go there. Everything in him resisted the idea. But he knew he had to.

He walked to Penn Station and caught a subway to Canal Street. Sitting in the three-quarters empty subway car, his thoughts alternated between his losing Manny and the person he was going to try and find…alternating between a desolate and barren rock that was his lost love and the hardest place he could imagine crashing into, the person the subway was carrying him to. His plan energized him but at the same time his nerves jangled with the subway's rollicky rhythm.

He exited the subway stop at Canal Street and walked east. The further he walked the more the signs outside the stores and restaurants were filled with

Chinese characters. A short while later, he took a right onto Mott Street and entered the heart of Chinatown. On an sunny October Indian summer day like this, the street would usually have been filled with bustle and hustle, the small shops busy with locals and tourists, the sidewalks crowded with open displays of knocked-off perfumes, watches, handbags, electronics. Pungent aromas wafting from dim sum restaurants would have teased the nostrils.

Instead, the street was eerily quiet and sparse with people. The pull-down storefront gates signified, like silver coins placed on a dead person's eyes, the death of whatever business had once lived there. They also provided the perfect surface for spray paint. When Gary saw the large black ZZ graffiti letters on one such gate, he knew that he was in the right neighborhood to find the person he hoped and dreaded meeting.

Several kids were out in the street, playing games and idly passing the time even though they were supposed to be in cramped tenement apartments pretending to do online school work since all the schools had been locked down. Gary approached one of the older looking boys. Being Asian, he stood out with his close-cropped hair that was dyed baby chick blond.

"Hey, can you help me with something?" he asked the kid.

He looked at Gary suspiciously. "I guess so."

He had a tall, lanky frame his body was trying to grow into. He wore baggy jail-jeans and a T-shirt adorned with K-POP SUCKS and a large red X over a group photo of the Korean boy band BTS.

"I'm looking for somebody who hangs with the Zombie Zoo, or Double Z's, whatever people call them around here."

The kid shifted his feet and looked away. "I know shit about zombies except what I see on TV."

Gary pointed to the spray painted ZZ. "What's that mean?"

"Hey dude, if you're Po, I wanna see a badge."

Gary reached into his pants pocket and pulled out his wallet. "I don't have a badge, but I have one of these." He took a twenty-dollar bill from his wallet. "I just want to know where the ZZs hang out, that's all. If you tell me, I'll slip this to you and be on my way."

The kid studied the twenty dollars. "Go to 35 Mott. To the basement entrance. There's usually some Zombie Zoo there, playing cards, numbers, whatever. If that's what you're really looking for. A guy named Penny runs it." The kid snatched the twenty-dollar bill from Gary's hand.

"Thanks," Gary said as he walked away.

"Nice doing business with you and thanks for the Andy Jack," the kid said. "Maybe see you in the next life."

A few minutes later, Gary walked down the four steps to the below street level entrance to 35 Mott Street. Mei Lai Wah Hair Salon occupied the above ground establishment. He knocked on the door. The bass thud of a Chinese version of gangsta rap with Mandarin lyrics sounded behind the door. No one answered, and he knocked again, harder this time.

Finally, the door cracked open and a bloodshot eye peered through the small opening at Gary. The eye was set in a face that had the color of, well, an old penny but with dark freckles sprinkled across it.

"What?" the face asked in a high-pitched voice.

"You Penny?"

"You mean Dollar Bill? Penny no go by Penny. Dollar Bill who he is now."

"Whatever, are you him?"

The eye stared at Gary for a few seconds. "What biz you got with Dollar Bill?"

"I don't have any business with Dollar Bill. I'm looking for someone he knows…somebody who goes by the name Smokey Joe. You know Smokey Joe?"

"Every dick around here knows Smokey Joe."

"Get the word to him that Gary is looking for him. You expect to see him anytime soon?"

"He be by here sometimes."

"Tell him I'll be hanging out at Columbus Park over on Mulberry Street. Around the playground there."

"So, you like to swing, huh? Okay, if I see him, I tell him."

"You do that."

As Gary walked away from the salon, he turned and saw the person who had been behind the door leaning over the iron railing that ran along the steps leading to the basement. His torso was bare, and the most noticeable thing about him, at least in this neighborhood, were the dreadlocks he sported.

Gary crossed over from Mott Street to Mulberry Street via Bayard Street. Just as he got to the park, a black 2010 Lincoln Town Car came huffing and puffing around the corner of Mulberry and Bayard. The tires screeched as the car cut the corner at a fast speed. Gary became alarmed when the car jumped the curb and ran over a trash can. The driver slammed the brakes and the car skidded to a halt two feet from Gary.

The driver charged from the vehicle, not even bothering to turn the engine off. He was wearing nothing but drawstring pants. Gary noticed the freckles and dreadlocks and realized this person coming toward him was Dollar Bill formerly known as Penny.

"Okay, Gary, you wanna meet Smokey Joe?" Penny shouted in mid-stride.

Penny was smiling wide, showing his two eye teeth that were turned outward like fangs and shining with gold caps. Gary nervously smiled back. Before he could utter a word, Penny got within a foot of him and threw a right uppercut into Gary's stomach. Every wisp of breath left him. He bent over and fell to his knees. The world went dark as one of Penny's cohorts came up behind him and threw a pillowcase over his head. Gasping for breath, Gary felt himself being lifted from the ground and hauled to the Lincoln Town Car, into which he was unceremoniously dumped. Penny's two companions held Gary down, and the car rumbled back onto the street and sped away.

A few minutes later, Gary felt himself being hauled out of the car. His two escorts held his arms and rushed him down some steps.

"Take this stupid pillowcase off," Gary's muffled voice demanded. "I know exactly where we are—35 Mott Street.

"Shut the fuck up, or I'll Kung Fu your ass," Penny said in his wound-up voice.

The three ZZs ushered Gary into the windowless basement. Occupying the large room with a twelve-foot ceiling and bare floor were a pool table, a makeshift bar backed by a welcoming array of top shelf liquor bottles, and a giant leather sofa placed in front of a cabinet containing a Samsung UHD Smart TV with eighty-five-inch QLED screen that would normally retail for $9,999.99 but cost the Zombie Zoo nothing since it had been stolen.

A card table with a rack of poker chips and a Las Vegas style card shuffler took center stage. Surrounding the table were a dozen country club upholstered chairs that were designed to make its occupants comfortable and in no rush to leave until the House had won its take, which it always did if given enough time. A hanging shaded ceiling light shined down brightly on the green baize felt surface. The cognoscenti knew this illegal gambling parlor as the Zombie Zoo Lucky Lounge.

"So, Smokey Joe put you up to this kidnapping or you guys bounty hunters for the FBI?" Gary asked, getting right to the point after the pillowcase came off.

Penny burst out laughing. "You are crazy whacked out, Poindexter. Hey, Raze, you hear that? We bounty hunters. Why don't you turn me in, and I'll turn you in, and we get crazy Asian rich quick?"

Raze was leaning against the pool table and holding the pillowcase. He didn't laugh or respond but just stared at Gary. His hair naturally spiked in a dozen different directions. His teeth were small and seemed crammed in the front of his mouth, like a piranha's. His face was unadorned except for the scraggly goatee that matched his slight physique and a scar as thick as a caterpillar running from behind his right ear to the middle of his throat. Something about Raze's cold, coal-black pupils made Gary slightly uncomfortable, but he wasn't about to show it.

"Look, Dollar Bill or whatever you call yourself, I'll cut right to it. My name is Gary Wang, and my older brother is Joe Wang. I guess you know him by some silly street name, Smokey Joe. I think the last thing you wanna do is fuck with Smokey Joe's brother. I need to talk to him. So where is he?"

Penny grinned. "He's standing right behind you, Poindexter."

Gary turned. Standing in the entryway that led into the basement room was none other than his brother, Joe.

Chapter Fifteen

BROTHERLY LOVE

Joe was dressed all in black: black loafers, black slacks, black t-shirt, black Honghol Etoile sunglasses. Joe's predilection for dark clothing engendered his sobriquet "Smokey," that and his uncanny ability to elude the NYPD and escape their clutches like smoke dissolving into thin air. In his right hand, he held a leather leash attached to a chain collar around the thick neck of a Shar-Pei.

"Hello, Joe," Gary said in a calm tone.

Joe didn't say anything but walked past Gary, slightly brushing against him as he passed. He grabbed one of the card table chairs, turned it backwards and sat down. His Shar-Pei sat at his feet, on guard. Behind him, highlighted by ceiling track lights, was the life size photo of a shirtless Bruce Lee on the verge of a rage rampage.

Penny looked at Joe. "You never told me you had a baby bro, Smokey Joe."

"I thought I did…once. But not anymore, Penny," he said matter-of-factly.

Penny scowled. "C'mon *Dai Low*, you know what I go by now. It's Dollar Bill."

"Man, I can't keep up with all your name changes," Joe said. "Last month it was Mr. Dime."

"Why don't you go back to what they called you in high school, the Gnat?" suggested one of the other ZZs.

"Hey Bullet Head, you dis' me again and I'm gonna slap down your roody pooh candy ass in broad daylight right in front of your *maa mi*!"

Bullet Head, who was six feet two inches tall and weighed two hundred and ten pounds, laughed heartily at that impossibility. His close cropped, bowling ball shaped head appeared to be jammed onto his broad shoulders, obviating the need for a neck.

Penny's nickname derived from the color of his complexion, the result of his African American GI Joe grandfather hooking up with his Vietnamese grandmother in Saigon's Hotel Majestic bar in 1972. No one, including Penny, knew what the name given to him at his birth was.

"You go by Penny," Joe said with finality. "When you put ten times more than the pathetic amount you put in the ZZ till last month, maybe we call you Dollar Bill."

Penny frowned, and Bullet Head smirked.

Gary stood next to the card table, listening to the banter and completely ignored by Joe, Penny, and Bullet Head. Raze, though, continued to stare a hole through him.

"I seen him before," Raze muttered.

"What's that?" Penny asked.

"I say I seen this joker before. On the news."

Penny stared at Gary. "Ah shit yeah, now I recognize you. You're Biden's China money man. Hey, Smokey Joe, your little bro maybe can lend us a few million. Sounds like he's jacked big time."

"Yep, he's in the news and in some deep, deep shit too," said Joe. "Why else you think he'd dare to show up here?"

"Ah, so your bro's a commie," said Penny. "We don't like commies, Poindexter. That's what our parents and grandparents were running from. But you know, you look a little too bougie to be a commie. Look more like you belong in like Forrest Hills with like a tennis racket."

Everybody including Joe laughed at that.

"Funny enough, he actually was a pretty good tennis player. Yeah, Penny, my little brother used to be the All-American chink success story. Straightlaced, straight As, goody-two-shoes. Got to the Ivy League."

"Ha, every Chinese parent's wet dream," Penny said.

Joe continued. "Always work and no play, making the grade, making his parents proud. He was the shining example."

"And I guess you was the family black sheep embarrassment," Penny said with a laugh.

"What would Mama and Baba think about you now, Gary, my *sai lou?*"

"They would think their son is in trouble and needs his brother's help," Gary said.

"And what was it you told me five years ago, last

time I saw you, little brother? Remember? Something like 'I don't wanna see your face ever again,' if I recollect right. And now you got the nerve to slink in here and ask for my help without so much as giving me my props, after not talking to me for five years? Table sure has turned, hasn't it?"

"It always does, don't it?" Penny said.

"Why didn't that senile old white dude and all those round eye *gweilo* you were busting your ass for help you?" Joe asked. "They don't wanna have anything to do with you, right? They're avoiding you like you some kinda Chinese virus. And now you're just like us, just another thug hiding from the law. Get the fuck outta here, Gary."

Gary stood in the middle of the room, the center of Joe and his crew's collective disdain. Even the dog seemed to eye him with contempt.

Gary nodded, turned, and walked toward the door.

"Hold it," Joe said loudly.

Gary stopped and looked at him.

"Just one question's been on my mind: why did you run? Not like you."

Gary looked Joe straight in the eye. "Duc, that's why."

Joe didn't say anything.

"You know what I did for you that day. What do think they would find after they arrested me and ran my fingerprints and DNA through the system?"

Gary didn't say anything more because he knew Joe knew the answer to that.

"And so, I couldn't let them arrest me. I ran to save my ass. And just so happens I saved yours too. Saving your ass…again."

Joe looked at Gary and nodded a couple of times.

"Stay right there... Penny, Bullet Head, Raze, split for a while."

All three rose and did as told. As he left, Penny said to Gary, "Hey, little bubba, don't take that punch in the stomach personal. I just had to smudge your shine a little bit, Poindexter, so you know you're not in Forrest Hills anymore."

After the crew left, Joe turned to Gary. "Okay, I know I owe you...owe you a fucking lot. What goes around comes around. Those Buddhist classes Mama made us go to turned me on to karma."

Gary chuckled. "Yeah, I remember those classes. That time the lama busted you for playing Resident Evil 4 on your Gameboy and kicked you out for good."

"Yeah, well something must have sunk in because I'm sitting here dicking around with you. So let me ask you, how's a gangbanger like me gonna help a fugitive like you."

"I don't need anything from you but a place to stay for a day or two, until I can figure out what to do. I know how you feel about me, so believe me, I don't plan on hanging around long." Gary intended to ask Joe for much more, but he thought it best to ease into that request after he and his brother had gotten more comfortable with each other, gotten to know each other again.

Joe rubbed the dog's head and stared at the floor while Gary stood before him like a beseeching pauper before a prince. "C'mon, let's go," he finally said to Gary. "Genghis, car." That was all Joe needed to say for Genghis to hop up, tail wagging, and lead them to the door and out to the parking lot.

They stopped at Joe's car, a Mercedes Benz S560, stealth black, of course, all kitted-out and with tinted windows. They got into the car, Genghis in the back seat but with his blockhead between the front seats, his tongue lolling from his mouth. When Joe started the car, misty Miles Davis flowed from the four speakers. Gary was surprised that Joe the gangsta was still the jazz aficionado that he had been in high school. Joe left the parking lot and headed south toward downtown.

"How'd you know about me, where to find me?" Joe asked Gary, breaking the silence.

"Mama told me. Some friend of hers in Flushing heard about you."

"I'm sure that made her proud."

She wouldn't have been surprised, Gary almost said. Joe had left home just after he had finished high school, just after their father discovered an ounce of powder in Joe's desk drawer. Their father stood in the doorway to the bedroom that Joe and Gary shared, screaming in the middle of the night, "Get out of this house! You're no son of mine. No son of mine is a dope dealer. Get out!" Old man Wang in a t-shirt and underwear, saliva spraying from his mouth, bellowing, "Get out!"

Gary reflected with astonishment on his brother's rise to the heights, or rather his sinking to the depths of the underworld. It had all started with the girlfriend Joe shacked up with, after that night he got kicked out of the house. She told him that with his looks he should try modeling. After a stint in LA, the agency sent him to New York, where the cokehead who headed the New York office used him to pick up the dummy dust from his dealer. After seeing the amount of cash changing hands, Joe decided dealing sure beat couriering, and modeling too. He was off to the races after that.

As Joe drove, Gary noticed that he constantly

looked into the rearview mirror. *Probably worried that he's being followed by the cops or a rival gang...who knows.*

A few minutes later, after no conversation interrupted Miles, Joe pulled up in front of a newly rehabbed limestone and granite, pre-war condo tower on John Street.

"We're home," Joe said.

Gary wasn't sure whether he was talking to Genghis or him. A valet appeared out of nowhere and took the keys from Joe before they exited the car.

"Good afternoon, Mr. Wang," the masked, liveried doorman said as they entered the building.

"Hey Oliver," Joe said. Meanwhile, Genghis sniffed Oliver's pants legs and wagged his thick tail as Oliver reached down and rubbed his small ears.

"Lookie here, we got Mr. Wrinkles," Oliver said in the silly voice that humans often adopt when talking to dogs.

The three walked through the polished limestone walled lobby with a large abstract painting front and center. The elevator took them up to the twenty-fourth floor and Joe's apartment.

"Whoa!" Gary exclaimed when he entered the apartment. He was stunned that his thirty-two-year-old brother was living in a place like this. Light poured in from the floor-to-ceiling windows that afforded a view of New York harbor and the Statue of Liberty, and shellacked the bare parquet wooden floor. Assorted tan leather furniture filled the den in front of them. To the left was the kitchen with granite countertops, stainless steel cabinets, a block island with inlaid electric range, and subzero refrigerator.

"Nice kitchen," Gary said.

"The real estate agent called it an Open Chef's kitchen, whatever that means." Joe shrugged. "That tag alone probably cost me an extra ten grand."

Gary sensed Joe was more relaxed and less aloof now that he was home.

"So, you cook?" Gary asked.

"Shit yeah, don't you remember the meals I'd throw down for you and Baba while Mama was in the hospital with her lymphoma? That mean Chicken Kiev I put together?"

"Sure. I'm glad you never noticed me shoveling it to Midge under the table." Midge, the family Pekinese at the time.

Gary was glad to see a smile brighten Joe's face, as brief as a lightning flash against a storm cloud.

"C'mon, I'll show you the room you can use," Joe said.

Gary followed him into a bedroom that contained only a king size bed and chest of drawers.

"You can use the bathroom we just walked past," Joe said.

Gary nodded and then looked at Joe. "Thanks man. I, uh…" he paused, searching for the right way to say that he owed Joe one.

"You can chill here a couple of days. After that you're on your own. Last thing I need is the heat busting my ass trying to bust yours."

Joe shut off whatever brotherly sentiment might have been welling up within Gary from a deep reservoir that he thought had gone dry years before.

After Joe left the room, Gary sat on the bed and wondered what to do next. He first thought about changing the clothes he had been wearing for a day and a half. Although Joe was bigger than he, Gary figured that he might have some clothes that he could fit in, even if they were loose and baggy on him.

He walked to Joe's bedroom and found no one there. Unlike the rest of the apartment, this room had a personal touch. A large-platted map of Hong Kong covered most of one wall. The chess set from Joe's days of competing in Los Angeles County public school tournaments sat in a credenza. Propped on his desk was a framed photo of his mom, dad, and five-year-old Joe standing on Victoria Peak with the Hong Kong skyline behind them. Next to that photo was one of Joe, Penny, Raze, Bullet Head, and a couple of other ZZs kicking it at Jones Beach, the stem of a Colt 45 bottle stuck between Penny's golden fangs.

Another photo was a Rolex ad in which Joe stood on a busy trading floor with a ticker tape in the background. He was wearing a fancy striped shirt, sleeves rolled up, talking into his headset mic, and holding a piece of paper so the Rolex watch was prominently displayed. The tag line was, "When time is the most expensive thing you own."

The items in the room brought back to Gary the Joe he had grown up with. Not Smokey Joe, Zombie Zoo *dai low,* but his older brother who had taken the training wheels off his first bike and had given him a push. The brother who had knelt over Gary as he had lain in the street after having been hit by a car that fortunately had only been going fifteen miles per hour. He had been only six years old at the time, but Gary could still remember how briny Joe's tears had tasted as they had fallen onto his face. The brother who had beat up the neighborhood bully, a white kid who had for six straight mornings extorted Gary's lunch money on the school bus because Gary was a nerdy Asian kid who he knew wouldn't fight back. The brother who had taught Gary how to play tennis.

In that room, at that moment, his brother had come back to Gary, pinched from a time warp, the memory of him immediate and fleshed out. And then he saw it.

"Wow, look at that," Gary murmured to himself. On the dresser top was a photo of Joe and him, Joe's arm around his shoulder, after they had won Westwood's summer league doubles tennis tournament. They had won eight straight matches to get the trophy, which Gary had prominently displayed in his apartment den. That moment, captured by the camera that had been aimed by their father, was one of the proudest, happiest moments in Gary's life.

Gary reached to pick up the photo. As he did, he saw the Glock 9 that had been stashed behind it. Gary started as if he had seen a poisonous snake. The handgun snuffed out his trip down Memory Lane. He immediately set the picture down.

"What the fuck you doing in here?"

Gary turned and saw Joe in the doorway. He stood with his arms crossed over his chest.

"Nothing. I was wondering if, uh, you might have, uh, an extra set of clothes I could change into."

Joe rummaged in his closet. "Here, try these," he brusquely said as he tossed Gary a blue sweat suit. "And don't be wandering in here again."

Gary said thanks, took the clothes, and went to the other bedroom. Weariness weighed him down and he fell onto the bed. He tried to forget the Glock. And then for no reason at all, he remembered the first time he had ever flown a kite. He remembered Joe's face, his snaggle-tooth smile because he had lost his two front teeth, as Joe had watched the kite flutter and flap when it took to the April wind like some exotic, princely bird that really didn't want to leave the two boys. The kite hovered over Manhattan Beach, orange and red against the blue of the sky.

"Run, Gary, run!" Joe had shouted. "Let the string unwind. Don't look back. Help the wind."

The string had gone taut, the cross sticks had bent, and Gary jumped high in the air as if the kite were pulling him up with it, spreading itself to the wind.

When Gary had suddenly stopped, Joe had hurried to him. Gary vividly remembered Joe's puckish grin, his eyes dancing, and the small indenture between his eyes. Joe had hugged his little brother and Gary had kissed that place between his brother's eyes.

The kite had suddenly dipped once, shuddered, and then zoomed into the sun. The string had zipped through Gary's fingers, stinging them—he specifically remembered that lying in the bed. Remembering, he was with the kite, as high as the kite, the cross sticks against his chest, the string the only thing connecting him to this earth.

And then he fell sound asleep.

Chapter Sixteen

ONE OF THE GANG

"We got a lead on Wang," Fisherwood said to Cummings.

"It's about time, Peckerwood," Cummings said.

"Wang's got an older brother in the New York area. Joe Wang, goes by Smokey Joe. Runs a criminal enterprise out of Chinatown. Controls a gang called Zombie Zoo, otherwise known as the ZZs. He's what they call *dai low*, you know the boss, like the Don with the Italians."

"Hmmm, that's interesting. What's he running?"

"Deals drugs mostly…coke, MDMA, lately fentanyl. A couple of illegal gambling joints. He's all over the place. Sunset Park Brooklyn, Bensonhurst, Flushing, Atlantic City, East Brunswick. NYPD thinks he's got a couple of dozen soldiers scattered in safe houses across his territory."

"Where does he usually hang out?"

"If he's got a headquarters, it's probably Chinatown. ZZs have a sort of clubhouse on Mott Street. Locals know it as Zombie Zoo Lucky Lounge. We don't know where he resides. Wherever it is, he's probably got it under a false name or some corporate or LLC name. But get this Boss, one of the street urchins in the neighborhood tells us he saw a face he hadn't seen before coming out of the joint with none other than Smokey Joe. Just a couple of days ago."

"Really? So, you think it could be our man?

"Maybe. The kid said the guy was wearing a hat, sunglasses, and mask, so he couldn't really give a description."

"Hmm, sounds promising."

"And this Smokey Joe must be pretty damn smart 'cause the NYPD has never been able to nail him with anything."

"I guess you could call him a drug kingpin, huh?"

"I dunno, Boss. Do they still use that term anymore since Nancy Reagan?"

"You making fun of me, Peckerwood?" Cummings was in a more jocose mood now that they had this lead to work with. "You set up surveillance on—what did you call it—Zombie Zoo Lucky Lounge?"

"We're staking it out this evening. We'll have eyes on it 24/7. Ears too. Got a microphone transmitter stuck to the side of the building that's sensitive enough to pick up farts. Set up a Stingray so we can intercept calls and texts going out of or into that location. Just got the warrant for it yesterday."

"Okay, Karl, sounds like we're finally cooking

with some gas."

"Funny, isn't it?" Fisherwood asked.

"What's funny?"

"How criminals seem to run in families. Like it's genetic."

"Well, Peckerwood, funny or not, I'm not gonna be laughing 'til we got Wang under lock and key. And his brother too while we're at it."

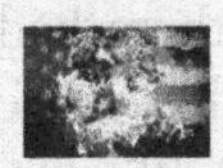

Manny lay in her bed, a book propped on the pillow in front of her. She tried to read the latest tome about Trump and how awful he was, written by a former member of his administration who had been so mesmerizingly disgusted by what he witnessed that he could not tear himself away from the lofty administrative position from which he was able to observe it all, as well as profit from it. But she couldn't keep her mind on the book and off the vacant space next to her, the space Gary would have occupied a couple of days ago.

She gazed at the small, open closet where his clothes hung next to hers. She once again thought that she ought to do something with his clothes and possessions since it was over between them. Pack them up and store them someplace out of sight, where they wouldn't be a constant reminder. Hide them so she could forget. She wouldn't admit it, but she didn't want to forget. His toothbrush still accompanied hers in the coffee mug that sat next to the bathroom sink.

Where could he be? *Alone, out on the streets, nowhere to go.* Could he survive in the present dystopian version of New York City that sci-fi writers thought wouldn't happen at least for another couple of decades, when the energy ran out, a climate change tsunami drowned Lady Liberty's torch, or zombies took over. She had no doubt about Gary's intelligence, but he wasn't the most practical person she'd ever met. And he wasn't exactly a take-charge kind of guy either.

Worry caused her to leave her bed and wander in her pajamas and slippers into the den. She sat on the sofa where the two of them had so often sat, talking, laughing, having morning coffee, watching TV. His bright blue Go Joe 2020! sweatshirt hung over the couch. She took it, clutched it to her chest, and deeply inhaled his scent.

She asked herself, for the hundredth time, if she had overreacted to what he had told her in Bryant Park. His recounting of the killing stunned her numb, like her central nervous system had shut down. Later that day, after the initial shock wore off, she re-evaluated her initial reaction. She conceded Gary's brother had put him in a bad situation. Gary wasn't the one who shot the guy who was about to shoot him. And he said Joe pulled a gun on him when he tried to call the police. He was an innocent bystander forced to do something he never wanted to do. Wrong place, wrong time…wrong brother.

And now he was out there alone, probably thinking she abandoned him. The worst thing was she had no idea how she could reach him. She called his cell phone several times, hoping against hope that he might answer even though he said that he was going to dispose of the phone after their last conversation.

At that moment her phone rang. She saw it was Gale calling. She hesitated to answer, but then thought Gale might have some new information about Gary.

"Hello, honey, you doing okay?"

"Why do you ask?"

"Well, I mean, your boyfriend, Gary. You know, the news about him on the lam from the FBI. I was worried about you."

"You don't need to worry about me, Gale."

"Listen, Manny, I know you must know where he is. I offered it before, and I offer it again: I'd like to interview him. Get his side of the story out there."

"I don't know where he is."

"C'mon dear. Can you at least propose it to him? I think it would help his case."

"I told you I don't know where he is or how to reach him. And besides, why would he trust you to tell his side of the story, as you put it?"

"What do you mean, Manny? That's what I do. I tell stories, true stories that are relevant, have import, that people want to hear."

Manny picked up Gale's condescending tone loud and clear. "Why would a Trumpster like you give someone like Gary a fair shake or benefit of the doubt? I know you relish all this. It's killing Biden's poll numbers, and you love it." Manny was done treading gingerly with Gale regarding her motivations.

"Look honey, I know you're under stress, but the way you're speaking to me, you know, is borderline rude and insulting. I'm a professional journalist. I was doing this when you were still in diapers. I knew what "objective" was before you knew how to spell it."

"I don't know what you once were, Gale, but I know what you are now. I've been in this business long enough to see the tricks. Like, you interview someone, but you edit it so that his statements are all chopped up and taken out of context. You always got some expert, some in-the-know somebody countering everything he says. But you never challenge the so-called expert. You only do that to the lucky person you're interviewing. And the camera's always close on your subject, or let's say victim, because you hope everyone can see when he's nervous or uncertain, like he's lying. You don't think I've watched *Sixty Minutes* before?"

"Scott Pelley is a dear friend of mine, and I don't appreciate your impugning his journalistic integrity." Gale huffed and puffed with indignation.

Manny laughed. "Journalistic integrity! That's an oxymoron if there ever was one."

"Well, aren't we high and mighty? Self-righteousness doesn't become you, young lady."

"If Gary were ever stupid enough to let you interview him, Gale, you'd slant it so that no one had any doubt that he was an agent of China doing Xi's bidding."

"Let me ask you, are you one hundred percent sure he's not?"

"I think it's time we end this call, Gale, before it gets nasty."

"Hmm, I thought it already had. Just remember, girl, when you told me this Wang guy was your boyfriend, I advised you to get another one."

Manny ended the call without a goodbye. She held Gary's sweatshirt to her face and cried.

Gary opened an eye just in time to see the digital clock on the bedside table click to 3:39 p.m. He bolted straight up in a panic, wondering where he was. After a few seconds, he remembered he was in Joe's apartment. He had been asleep for almost two hours.

He lay back in the bed. As he watched the phantom play of afternoon light and shadow dancing across the ceiling, he reassembled the events that led him from Goldsmith's Department store to here. He wished it were all a bad dream. His situation might have changed, but he was still a fugitive, on the run.

He got up, sat on the edge of the bed, and rubbed his neck, still stiff from sleeping on marble the night before. He thought of Manny. He considered leaving there and going straight to her apartment. But of course, that was a stupid idea since the FBI had her place staked out for sure. Besides, why would she have anything more to do with him since she saw him as aiding and abetting the cover up of a murder?

He rose and walked to the window. The inhospitable sunlight bouncing off the Hudson River caused him to shut his eyes and turn away.

He then heard knocking on the apartment door. He left the bedroom and was surprised to find Joe and Genghis had left. He walked to the door and peered through the peephole and saw Penny's face in all its wide-angled splendor. Penny looked right at the peephole, as if he thought he might see inside from the outside looking in. His dreadlocks draped down from under his New York Giants cap.

"Where's Smokey Joe?" Penny asked after Gary let him in.

"How did you get into the building?" Gary asked.

"Me and Oliver are tight, that's how," Penny said. He walked past Gary and hollered, "Hey, Smokey Joe."

"He's not here. I haven't seen him since like two hours ago."

"Shit!" Penny shouted as he swung his arm through the air in frustration. "Where'd everybody go?

Raze gone. Bullet Head gone. Lizard Skin dis'pear. Damn, is some kinda thug holiday going on?"

Penny let out another loud and long, "Sheeeit!" He shook his head as he scratched the back of it. Then his eyeballs slowly rotated up until they locked onto Gary.

"I guess that leaves you, Poindexter. C'mon with me, little brother. I need your help."

"What the fuck you talking about?"

"Don't get bugged out. I need you for something. Ride shotgun while I make a drop-off."

"You're out of your mind if you think I'm going anywhere with you."

"C'mon, do it for *Dai Low*. Least you can do to repay him for getting your ass off the street and out of the FBI's clutches."

Gary admitted to himself that Penny had a point. He was planning on asking Joe to help him execute a plan he had in mind to clear his name. Helping Penny do something for Joe would grease the wheels. "What is it you want me to do?"

"Just ride with me, that's all. I got to go to Brooklyn."

Brooklyn sounded safe enough to Gary. Woke hipsters voting Biden.

"Okay, whatever. I'll make the ride with you."

"Stay cool, my man," Penny said to Oliver as he and Gary exited the building. They got into the decrepit Lincoln Continental, its black paint peeling. Penny put his wraparound shades on and laid some rubber as they drove off.

He set the tone by cranking up Cardi B's "WAP." By the time she got to the part about a bucket and mop, Gary had enough.

"Hey, man, you got something else to play. That

shit's making me queasy."

"Oh, you want something a little more tame and retro? You look like a Kool and the Gang sort. Sorry, Poindexter, no gots."

They crossed the Brooklyn Bridge, the grand old spinster dame ushering travelers across the East River, now glazed with sunlight. As they sped down Shore Parkway, Penny, in a mood to chatter as usual, turned the radio down. "Hey, I tell you I'm gonna be a daddy?"

"Oh, that's terrific," Gary barely managed to say. "Lucky kid."

"Gotta marry the bitch though. Her daddy not letting his precious little girl be a baby momma. So, get this: I'm over at their apartment in Queens, and Daddy pulls out a twelve-gauge shotgun and tells me I'm gonna marry his daughter or he's going to shoot me dead. I kid you not!" Penny turned to Gary with a big golden fang smile. "So, dig it, it's really a shotgun marriage for real! I thought that was just a saying."

Gary didn't say anything but stared straight ahead.

"Hey, let me ask you this, Poindexter, since you're an educated man. So, my girl is showing a bump, and I see all her friends touching it and saying, 'Oh girl, congratulations.' How come they don't come up to me and pats my dick and say, 'Good job?'"

Gary couldn't help but shake his head and smile sort of. But he quickly turned back to serious. "Okay, Daddy-O, so you going to tell me anything about what you've gotten me into? Like where exactly are we going?"

"We're going to a place in Brighton Beach. And we're not going there to swim and get a suntan. Doing a transaction."

"And what exactly are we transacting?"

"Fifty thousand Fentanyl pills, that's what. Worth 225 K. Got 500 bottles of it in the trunk."

Gary looked at Penny with alarm. "Are you kidding? You're carrying that?'

"Fuck yeah. What you think I am, the Avon lady?"

"What if we get pulled over?"

"Why I'm driving fifty miles an hour the whole way. No Po going to pull me over for DWA, and that's Driving While Asian in case your Columbia U ass didn't know."

"So, whoever we're meeting is going to hand over $225,000 in cash?"

"Something like that. Smokey Joe got his costs down real low, like five bucks a pill. See, he's got the connection for the raw stuff in China, and he hooks them up with the hombres in Mexico who turn it into pills. Controls the supply chain. We sell it to this guy we're meeting for fifteen dollars a pop and he street-tails it for like forty-five a pill. We both triple our money. Easy as pie."

Even though Gary knew that Joe was dealing drugs, it finally hit him square in the solar plexus what exactly that entailed.

"How long you been working with Joe?" Gary asked.

"Ah, a couple of years now. I started out a look-out, worked my up to mulin' the stuff. Now, *Dai Low* lets me score the deal. Your brother's a smart cat. Makes us all plenty of jack. Got enough turf for us to have plenty to do and plenty to take and make."

"Didn't he have to take that turf from somebody else?"

"Sure. A goon called Jack Fong controlled a lot of it. Ran a gang called Ghost Monkeys. But he no playa, just a sissy-slut. Didn't take Smokey Joe too long to bump him off his roost."

"Bump him off? Did Joe kill the guy?"

"Nah, Smokey Joe didn't kill him. He never killed anybody. He just sicced Raze on him. All I know is Jack Fong ain't around no more. Departed to parts unknown."

Gary didn't bother to correct Penny about he never killed anybody. There was Duc, and Gary hoped that he was the only one.

Penny sensed uneasiness in Gary's silence. "Look, let me tell you, Smokey Joe plays the game as clean as anybody can play it. He don't even touch the stuff. He stays pure when it comes to that. He won't deliver it, don't like to even see it. And yeah, sometimes he's gotta make a point, but he always let's Raze or Bullet Head or one of the other ZZ's handle that part of it."

"You ever kill anyone, Penny?"

"Nope, 'cause he who kills usually gets killed. If somebody dis me, I'll take them on hard, mess them up good. I ain't leavin' 'til I get even-stevens. I might get thrown in jail for it, but when it comes to capin' a dude, well, that's not my play. I'd rather be judged by twelve than buried by six, if you get my drift."

Fifteen minutes later, they were driving down Coney Island Avenue with Brighton Beach and the Atlantic Ocean before them. Many commercial establishments along the Avenue announced themselves with both Cyrillic and English letters. Penny parked in front of a building facing the ocean. The Art Deco building's terra cotta façade displayed a mosaic panel over its entrance that depicted an angry Neptune aiming his foreshortened trident at onlookers.

Penny turned to Gary after he parked the car, all

business now. "Okay, here's the low down, Poindexter, so listen good. There's a private club here…I guess like what dagos call a social club. Called Matushka Rosa, which means Mother Russia I think, whatever. Has a restaurant that all the Ruskies love, but you have to know somebody in the know to get in, you know like Rao's. The dude we're meeting is Evgeny Balagula. Some call him Wooly Bully 'cause—well, you'll see. And some call him Little Stalin 'cause he's paranoid as shit about everything and everybody. He hasn't killed millions of people like the real Stalin, but I tell you, you don't wanna be on the other side of his craziness. Otherwise, he's a decent guy we done a lot of biz with and I think—"

"Hold it, what did you say? Something about we're meeting?" Gary asked. "We as in you and me? I said I'd come along for the ride. Nothing more than that. I don't want to be any part of some drug deal."

"Man, you think I brought you along just for your personality? So, I could have someone to chit chat with? Your bro always wants two ZZs cutting a deal. For backup in case something doesn't go right. And just to make sure everything's on the up and up and nobody skimming or pulling some kinda other shit like that."

"So, Joe doesn't trust you?" Gary asked with a rhetorical chuckle.

"Listen, we might be comrades-in-arms, but no one trusts no one a hundred percent in this game. If he does, he'll be taken out real quick on a long ride to the cemetery. Now put your mask on and let's go and close this deal so we can get back to doing nothing."

When they got out of the car, Penny unlocked the trunk and retrieved a silver metal suitcase, which reminded Gary of the metal suitcase that the FBI agent put his stuff into when they raided his apartment.

"We're going up to the restaurant," Penny told the guy at the reception desk in the small lobby.

They got off the elevator and walked down the hallway to a nondescript office door with no number on it. Penny pulled out his cellphone. "Hey, Penny here to see Evgeny. Outside the door. Okay."

A few moments later, a big guy with slicked back blond hair that hung to his shoulders opened the door. He was wearing a tight-fitting pinstripe suit and vest but no tie.

"Hey Vitaly," Penny said.

"Wazhappnin' little man," Vitaly said, his combo of street slang with a heavy Russian accent having an almost comic effect to Gary's ear.

The Russian escorted Penny and Gary through a restaurant that one would never have guessed was behind the office door with the scrapes and black smudge marks. Ten tables with white embroidered covers filled the room. Chairs dressed in lace linen cloth and with satin gold-colored bows tied around the backs. A large zinc bar with gleaming liquor bottles ran along the far wall. Several vases filled with gladiolas, gilt framed mirrors, and a large painting of St. Petersburg circa 1898 set the ambience. It was empty this time of day.

Vitaly led them to a small office off to the side of the restaurant, next to the kitchen. The windowless office had unadorned concrete walls, a bare floor, one overhead fluorescent light. The room contained a metal desk, some metal chairs, and a beat-up fabric-covered sofa. It looked like maybe a supply clerk's office or an office that wouldn't leave any trace or trail should its occupants have to make a quick getaway. The air smelled of cigar smoke. A baseball bat leaning in the corner was the only decoration.

"Hey, my fav half-breed," Balagula said as Penny and Gary entered the room.

Balagula had a thick, raven black mane of hair that fell down to his broad shoulders and belied his forty-six years of age. He was wearing shorts, a white Cuban guayabera shirt, unbuttoned enough to show a thick mat of chest hair and a diamond-encrusted necklace bearing a twenty-four-carat gold Star of David pendant. The dark hair on his legs cascaded all the way down to the Crocs on his feet. Yes, Crocs and orange juice orange to boot.

"Wazup, Wooly Bully," Penny said as he gave Balagula a soul-handshake followed by a shoulder bump. Balagula was four inches taller than Penny and had to lean down into Penny's shoulder.

"So, you brought some candy for me?" Balagula asked in his Yiddish accent as he looked at the suitcase in Penny's hand.

"Sure, 50,000 gum drops."

"And for you my friend I got some cabbage," Balagula said with a laugh. "Two hundred and twenty-five thousand dollars' worth of cabbage. Cabbage for candy."

"That's what we do," Penny said.

"Who's this guy?' Balagula asked as he pointed at Gary.

"Uh, this fine young man is Poindexter."

Balagula laughed. "Poindexter?"

"Don't he look like a Poindexter?" Penny asked.

"Funny name." Balagula looked Gary over, appraising his worth on the fly, making Gary feel like a thoroughbred racehorse at one of the auctions that he imagined Balagula regularly attended. Gary figured that not knowing his real name made Wooly Bully suspicious of him.

"He's a funny guy," Penny said to break Balagula's attention on Gary.

"Hey Poindexter, take that mask off," Balagula said. "Masks make me nervous. I like to see the lower half of a man's face. Women on the other hand, I kinda find it sexy. Is that weird?"

"Hey Wooly Bully, whatever floats your boat," Penny said.

Gary did as requested, or rather ordered, and took his mask off. As friendly as Penny and Balagula appeared to be, tension filled the room like low background static noise.

"Come relax, my friends." Balagula said in his baritone voice as sat down behind the metal desk. Gary and Penny sat on the sofa.

He then said something in Russian to Vitaly. Vitaly took the case from Penny, sat down on a chair, opened it, and began counting the bottles. Gary assumed that whatever Balagula said to Vitaly it included: "Make sure these fuckers aren't fucking me."

Balagula propped his Crocs up on the metal desk. "You know, Penny, I hardly do deals like this anymore. Getting too old, I guess. It's gotten to be more identity theft, ransom hacking, that kind of action. All of it is kind of impersonal, you know. You like to touch and smell what you're selling, right? My father was a rag merchant, so I guess that's where I get it."

"I hear you Wooly," Penny said. "Any eighteen-year-old punk can pull off stealing someone's credit card number. That's Pee Wee league shit."

As Vitaly counted the merchandise, Balagula eyed

Gary more closely. He then pulled out his phone and began fiddling with it. “Excuse me guys, I have to check something.”

Balagula rose from the desk. He walked toward the door. Just as he passed the sofa, he quickly pivoted, pulled a Beretta 9mm handgun from the back of his shorts and pressed it against Penny’s forehead.

“What the fuck did you bring this guy here for?” Balagula yelled.

Penny still had his wraparounds on but behind them his eyes were as wide open as if someone rammed a cattle prod up his ass.

“Whadaya mean? He’s with Smokey Joe’s crew.” Penny was as frantic as a shocked cow on its way to the slaughterhouse.

Balagula said something to Vitaly, who immediately whipped out a handgun and aimed it right between Gary’s eyes.

“I thought I recognized Poindexter. Face has been all over the news. Gary Wang. I just looked him up on my phone and it’s him all right. And I happen to know Wang is Smokey Joe’s last name. This asshole is Joe Wang’s brother. You’re fucking meshuga bringing this guy to meet me.”

“I’m telling you Wooly, he’s cool.”

“The FBI has probably followed you here and waiting outside the door right now.”

“No way, man. C’mon, take it easy with the gun.”

Balagula’s eyes narrowed. “Or maybe you two are informants. You think if you hand my head on a platter to the FBI, they’ll go easy on Joe’s brother. Is that what this is all about? Is that the play?” He pressed the handgun harder against Penny’s temple and twisted it.

“No fucking way! You’re overreacting, man!”

"I got no choice now. You left me no choice, Penny. You see that, right? I can't let you two leave here alive and talking. Sorry, my friend, but like they say, 'It's not personal, just business.'"

Balagula turned and said to Vitaly in Russian something that Gary feared probably translated to: "Good thing these concrete walls are soundproof. You do him and I do Penny."

"Hey, you're making a big mistake," Gary suddenly blurted.

"Oh yeah, college boy?" Wooly said sarcastically.

"What you're saying is crazy," Gary continued. "But say it is true, say the FBI has been trailing me. Then they would know that I'm here. If what you say is true, then they know it's you I'm meeting. And if I don't leave here alive, then they would know that it was you who murdered me."

Balagula stared at Gary for several seconds.

Vitaly's gun aimed a foot from his forehead didn't keep Gary from calmly saying, "Let's just do this deal. You take the pills, we take the money, and we all go on our separate merry ways."

Balagula still kept his gun pressed against Penny's temple.

"Going through with this deal should tell you we aren't informants or any bullshit like that. If the FBI had trailed me, they wouldn't be waiting outside the door. They would have busted it down by now." Gary managed to speak even though his mouth was as dry as cotton. His armpits, though, were plenty wet.

"And what do you think Smokey Joe will do? Yeah, he is my brother. He knows where we are. You think he would take you killing me and Penny lying down? You want a World War III nuclear gang war on your hands?"

Still staring at Gary, Balagula pulled his gun away from Penny. He said something in Russian to Vitaly, who put his gun back into his jacket's inside pocket.

Balagula sat down and again propped his feet on his desk, "You two are lucky I got a degree from the Moscow Institute of Physics and Technology so I can quickly estimate probabilities." He emitted an exaggerated laugh that weirded Gary out.

Balagula asked Vitaly if he had finished his count of the pills and did it pan out.

"Da," Vitaly said.

Balagula pulled a satchel out from one of the desk drawers and handed it to Penny.

"There's your money. I still don't like you bringing this fugitive along with you. Now beat it."

Gary grabbed the satchel from Penny, who looked at Gary like he was crazy.

"We need to count it first," Gary said.

Balagula snickered at the notion that he might have short changed them.

Gary emptied the satchel filled with hundred-dollar bill blocks onto the floor and knelt to count them. Each block contained fifty hundred-dollar bills, which meant there should have been forty-five blocks to add up to $225,000.

Gary looked up at Balagula, who stood over him. "You're short a block. Five grand."

"Oh, am I?" Balagula nonchalantly replied.

When Balagula reached into one of his pants back pockets, the same place where he placed his gun, Gary for a moment wondered if not only was Balagula going to tell him to kiss his ass but change his mind and blow both him and Penny away. He stopped breathing. But instead of a gun, Balagula pulled out the forty-fifth stack and tossed it at Gary.

"Ah, I must have forgot about that one," Balagula said with a sinister grin.

Gary took a C-note from the stack, wadded it up and then put it into mouth. He chewed it up like it was a piece of flank steak, all the while staring at Balagula until his grin melted away. Even Penny, who had been replacing the blocks of money back into the satchel, stopped to gawk at Gary.

Gary spit the slobbery, balled-up bill into his hand and, after examining it, flung it toward Vitaly. Vitaly folded his beefy arms up and hopped away from the moist dough as if it were ostrich shit.

Balagula pouted and then smiled at Gary. "Yeah, like Penny said, you're really funny, man."

Chapter Seventeen

HE AIN'T HEAVY

"Goddammutherfuckinshit!" Penny shouted after he and Gary had gotten in his car and sped away from angry Neptune and his trident. "Wooly Bully! We stared the mutherfucker down! Little Stalin can suck my little dick!" Smiling with amazement, he triumphantly pounded on the steering wheel with each word he spoke. But his hands had been trembling when he put the key into the ignition.

"That Russian goon was just waiting for Balagula to give the signal," Gary said. He twisted his neck around to dispel the residual tension in it. He could still see the deathly dark hole of the pistol barrel pointed between his eyes.

"Man, I never thought I'd come that close to dying," Penny said. "I could see Wooly Bully's trigger finger itching to pull. My heartbeat's still going a mile a minute!"

"Okay, dude, but slow down," Gary said. Penny's heart rate and the Lincoln's rpm were in synch. "You're going too fast. I don't want some cop asking why we're carrying $225,000 in a metal suitcase."

"That was some quick thinking on your part, little brother," Penny said after slowing the car. Gary ironically had to thank that gun pointed at him for focusing his mind like never before on one single, crystal-clear thought: Convince Wooly Bully not to splatter his and Penny's brains all over the concrete walls.

"Thanks. One thing I've learned from being in politics is that the only way you get out of a Mexican standoff is figure out what leverage you got and use it to the max."

"Damn, it worked. And Wooly isn't any pushover sucker either. And eating money like that, what was that about? That was some cool shit."

"They call it bread, don't they," Gary said, suddenly Mr. Cool Shit. "I saw it in a John Woo movie once. The guy ate the Triad dude's money to make sure it wasn't counterfeit. And then he spat it back at him."

Wow, that really was an inspired badass move, he thought. It came from somewhere inside him that he had never known before. Certainly not something the Gary Wang of a year ago would have risked. Wherever it came from, he wanted to go there more. He rolled down the window to let in some air. The sun was setting, and the purple-bottomed clouds blushed a dusky pink. He stuck his elbow out the window and set the seat back as far as it could go. He had just one-upped a notorious gangster and lived to tell about it...as close to Upekkha as he had been in many days.

"And I can tell you Smokey Joe is going to be proud at how you pulled that off. I guess you and him have more in common than I thought."

"Glad I could help." Gary's voice lacked the irony it would have had four hours ago if he had been congratulated for helping his brother unload some product. He happily accepted the congratulations because he knew his older brother would be amazed, pleasantly amazed at how he had handled Balagula, even with a gun pointed at his forehead. He knew that Joe had always viewed him as book smart but street dumb. But what he had just done with Balagula, saving not only his own life but Penny's too, couldn't be found in any book.

Twenty-minutes later, they were back in Joe's apartment, using the key that Oliver had given Gary. They made their way to the den. Gary plopped onto the large couch, psychologically exhausted, while Penny went to the wet bar. A few minutes later, he ambled over to Gary with two drinks in his hand.

"Got something for you, Poindexter. Help you relax. Try this." Penny sat on the couch and handed Gary one of the drinks.

"Damn, what is this?" Gary asked with a sour face after taking a sip.

"Wild Irish Rose mixed with Ginseng. I call it a Chirish, my signature cocktail. You heard of a Black and Tan. This is a Red and Yellow. Not your cup of tea, I take it?"

"No thanks."

After gulping down half his drink, Penny played with his phone and suddenly a loud eruption of sound followed. A Chinese rapper named Jony J did his thing over the four state-of-the-art wireless speakers in the corners of the room. The base beat oscillated though Gary's body. Jony J's rap was a mishmash of English and Fuzhounese dialect.

The music took Gary back to his days in Hong Kong at the Academy. Days spent at seminars and lectures, writing papers, reading ancient Han dynasty texts. At night he and his buddies would hit the clubs and dance until sweating to Tizzy T, the Higher Brothers, and vintage TriPoets. Trying to drink away his bookworm inhibited self. Trying to make it with the girls and usually with no luck. He smiled remembering eating deep-fried pig intestines on a skewer at some street stand at 3 a.m. And now here he was, just three years later, lucky to be alive. It seemed like another lifetime ago; it could have been if Vitaly had jumped the gun.

Would he go back there and then if he could? he asked himself. He surprised himself and answered no. As terrible as his current circumstances were, he had growing confidence that he would fight his way through it and come out a stronger person on the other side. He had truth on his side. Perhaps he was being naïve, but he believed that was all he needed in the end.

"Time to get down!" Penny shouted. He reached into his back pocket and pulled out a small glass pipe and vial. He took a small rock of coke from the vial, put it in the pipe and lit it. The column of smoke hurried from his mouth as fast as it had gone in. "Ahhh…

"Now I'm gonna load one up for you, Poindexter. Celebrate your score on Wooly Bully. In fact, I'm not going to call you Poindexter anymore but Kid Cool. How you like that?"

Gary had tried cocaine before, but never in the

form of crack, which is what he assumed Penny was smoking. He had never had much use for illegal substances, after trying coke a couple of times. The effect on him had been far from bliss, and he had always felt ridiculous leaning over a mirror with rolled legal tender jammed up his nose. He had too much self-control to enjoy the self-abandonment that drugs induced.

"C'mon man, it won't bite you," Penny exhorted as he held the pipe in Gary's face. "You're tighter than teenage twat. It don't bite, only kisses." His dark wraparound shades and giddy goofy smile endowed Penny's face with a quasi-demonic aspect.

Gary considered for a moment and then once again surprised himself by saying, "Gimme that damn pipe."

Penny leaned over and positioned the pipe in Gary's hand. "Okay, Kid Cool. Now here, put your finger over that hole there."

Penny lit the bowl. "Now pull it in slow and easy," he said.

Gary did as told and felt something like a scratching, hairy rodent burrowing down his esophagus before his mouth exploded open with a hoarse pop. Penny laughed hysterically. Gary attempted it again, this time taking it in slower.

If someone had asked Gary at that moment why he had done something so stupid as to take a hit off a crack pipe, he probably couldn't have answered. Stress was an obvious reason. And anger. Anger at being falsely accused. Anger at having his name splattered all over the media for something he hadn't done. Anger at losing Manny. Yes, he thought he was going to get through this, but that didn't mean that he didn't have the right to rage.

Mix some anger and stress with a dash of self-pity and there you have it: a man who doesn't care anymore. *Fuck you!* was all he had to say. *Fuck you Fisherwood. Fuck you FBI, fuck you Danny Copper, fuck you Gale Sturmstrom and all the others lying about me, fuck you Columbia University and Confucius Academy of Global Understanding, fuck you Joe Biden, and finally one big fuck you to Gary Wang.* The only thing in his life that he left off his "fuck you" list was Manny. But she was gone, gone, gone, and that was all the more reason to fire one up.

He drew in the narcotic smoke as deeply as he could. And it felt great. All the stress, all the anger was blown away by a tornado of gray smoke funneling from his mouth. Everything seemed the same, but nothing felt the same. The space between his ears expanded, became lighter, like a balloon filling with chilled helium. The cranium balloon expanded until it lifted from the chair the tired body attached to it like a string.

The music suddenly was not just good but fucking unbelievable. Gary stood, twitching his shoulders and snapping his fingers, causing Penny to laugh and clap his hands. Unlike a drowsy margarita high, this high awakened him, releasing energy locked up somewhere. The energy converted to a purifying, clarifying light that left Gary and shellacked everything. Such a happy, gleaming light, but cool and sparse like the moon's.

Gary skated his feet and swung his arms. He was back in one of the Hong Kong nightclubs dancing to Tizzy T or Jay-Z. He lifted his hands and twirled them over each other, dancing a modified boogaloo that gradually became shadow boxing. "Fuck that Fisherwood guy," he murmured to himself as he threw a right cross, his hips turning all the way into it. He danced to the music, punched to the beat, smiling like a man who had nothing left to lose.

"Hey, Penny, load me up one more. One more is all I need."

"Yeah sure...just one more, that's what they all say," Penny said with a laugh.

Before long, the two had reached the zenith of giddy garrulousness. Now any topic was open for conversation.

"Hey, Kid Cool, let me ask you something. How come you turn out as starched as a politician's white shirt and Smokey Joe turned out, you know, smokey? You gone good and Joe gone bad. You suck from the same tit, grow up in the same house. You peddling political dope, and Joe peddling dope dope. How'd that happen?"

Gary thought for a few moments. "The simple reason is that Joe was a mama's boy."

Penny turned his head quizzically and stared at Gary while his brain digested that nugget of information. He then burst out laughing. "Oh yeah, that's a good one. Smokey Joe a mama's boy."

Although Gary laughed along with Penny, he recognized that he and Joe exemplified that age-old brother trope, from the Smother brothers to the Cuomo brothers: which one did Mom love best? Gary and his mom had a close and loving relationship, but he suspected from early on that her connection with Joe was different and deeper. Her emotional radar seemed a little more sensitive to whatever was affecting Joe, like when he lost a tennis match or failed a class.

Joe was the spitting image of her, lucky to get her good looks, and maybe something that simple had drawn her a little closer to him. Maybe she gave Joe more attention because he needed it more. "Don't worry, son, you'll get over it and one day be a great man. Come give Mama a hug."

But who could really know why, and Gary had come to accept it. On the other hand, his father openly doted on him, the successful one, over Joe, the problem son. Gary got over the hurt from his mom maybe favoring his brother more, but Joe would always resent his father's championing of Gary and constant denigrating of himself.

"Speak of the devil and up he pops," Gary said to himself when into the room marched Joe with Raze and Genghis trotting behind him.

"What the fuck's going on in here?" Joe asked.

Penny jumped from the sofa to his feet.

"Partying down, Smokey." Penny had the loaded pipe in his hand. "We just transacted with Balagula."

Joe went to the receiver and shut off the blaring music. He strode over to Penny and slapped the pipe out of his hand. The pipe flew through the air and shattered against a wall.

"Hey, what's up with that?" Gary protested.

Joe then turned back to Penny, who cowered as if he were trying to hide within himself. Joe grabbed Penny by the throat and squeezed until Penny's freckles seemed to expand and his eyes bugged out. He gargled words that couldn't quite make it out of his constricted throat as his hands took hold of Joe's wrist, trying to wrench free from his grip.

"What do you think you're doing, turning my brother onto that shit," Joe said through gritted teeth. He worried Penny's head back and forth with one hand and then finally flung him to the floor. "You little punk, trying to hook my brother onto that shit."

Penny began crawling on all fours, and Gary attempted to intercede. "Joe, he didn't mean anything, we were just—"

"You shut up," Joe shouted, cutting Gary short.

Joe gave Penny a swift kick in the rump as he crawled away. "Don't you ever give that shit to my brother ever again." Raze put his hand over his mouth to stifle giggles. Penny got up and ran to the door and exited the apartment.

"Get your butt to your room," Joe ordered Gary, as if they were back in high school and his parents weren't around and so he had dominion over the household.

Gary, flummoxed by the dope and Joe's surprise attack, spluttered an incoherent remark. He shambled back to the bedroom and fell onto the bed.

Joe still thinking he can order me around like that. Who does he think he is?

He lay there, waiting to come down, wanting to come down as he was dead tired but oh so terribly wide-awake. The cocaine would not let him sleep, so he lay supine on the bed and clenched his hands like a patient receiving shock treatment. His heart palpitating, his nerve endings quivering, and his head throbbing.

He thought about Manny and an avalanche of ugly thoughts cascaded down upon him. He tossed and turned onto his side and hoped that his thoughts, like the colors inside a kaleidoscope, would rearrange themselves if he shifted his body. The hope that he had clung to seemed to have drifted away with the crack smoke. The happy radiating light had turned inward into a garish spotlight searching him out. Now there was no pretending. But there was no joy in the knowing and his grip tightened further. No way out. No place to hide. The cocaine made him grind his teeth. How he wished he could fall asleep.

Suddenly his chest heaved, and his ribcage protruded like a set of horns as he held in his breath. A plaintive wail sounded, like a note in a whale tune, dying among the quiet of the early evening. Along with the wail came a single tear, breaking, clear, and warm. It swirled around his eye socket, traced the slope of his cheek, careened past the corner of his mouth, and hurried over his chin and down his shuddering throat. Then the darkness came.

Gary roused from a deep sleep and glanced at the clock. 2:13 a.m. What had awakened him? A sound…it was a sound of some kind. There, he heard it again. A grinding noise seemed to be coming from down the hall. Someone was sick. He looked and sure enough, the door to Joe's bathroom stood half open, the light on, and Joe on his knees, his head hanging over the toilet.

Gary walked to the bathroom door. "What's the matter, Joe?"

The look on Joe's face only said, *Oh, it's you again.* He turned and sat on the floor, his arm resting on the toilet rim. Gary noticed blood trickling from Joe's mouth.

Joe closed his eyes and rubbed them before saying anything. "Ulcer. Bleeding ulcers. They get rowdy on occasion."

Gary leaned against the doorjamb. "Must be from stress, huh? You got some blood on your chin, by the way."

Joe wiped the blood away with a piece of toilet

paper. "Stress? Now why would I be under any stress?" he asked, with a faint snicker.

"I don't know much about your life, Joe, but I know enough to know that it's not a walk through the park."

Joe smiled in a sickly way. "Yeah..." Without his sunglasses on, or his entourage backing him, but simply sprawled on the bathroom floor, he looked much older than his thirty-two years. Gary felt a sharp pang of sorrow for his brother. A rumpled and crumpled specter in black pajamas, marring the bathroom's gleaming chrome and white tile.

One of Joe's entourage did in fact enter at that moment. Genghis waddled in and up to Joe so he could give him a consoling lick in the face. "Hey there, buddy," Joe murmured as he rubbed Genghis's neck.

"Why you doing this, Joe? How did you end up like this?"

Joe looked at Gary and laughed. He laughed until he clutched his sides and began choking. He leaned over the toilet and spat out more blood. After recovering, he sat back against the tile wall and took a couple of deep breaths.

"And why are you doing what you're doing, Gary? And what exactly is it you're doing?"

"Working for the Biden campaign. Or at least that was what I was doing before all this happened." Working for the Biden campaign suddenly sounded so foreign, unreal, irrelevant to and detached from the real world, Chinatown, Brighton Beach.

"So, you're selling a product like I am. The product you're peddling is some promises some old white dude who's been around for fifty years is making. That right? You're hustling people to fork over dough, saying this loudmouth is going to help them. Has he ever really helped anybody before? I deliver what I promise. All your boss has ever done is make speeches."

"That's bullshit, Joe. How can you compare what I do to selling poison? Ruining people's lives?"

"Listen, Gary, the people I sell to don't have any lives to ruin. And that's not my fault, brother. Hell, if it's anybody's fault it's politicians like your man Biden. Most of my customers don't have jobs and those that do, well, those jobs really aren't worth having. Their mothers are skanks and their daddies unknown. Dusk comes around and they go inside 'cause when the stars appear so do the bullets too. So why take away their only chance to get away from it all for a little while? That's all I'm doing, see, giving them a first-class ticket to some, you know, resort island for a couple of hours or so."

"You're better than that, Joe. You were raised better. You were meant for something better."

"What were you meant for, Gary? To be sucking on a crack pipe like you were doing a little while ago?"

"Hey, didn't you just tell me that junk is just a first-class ticket to Club Feel Good? So, why'd you go ape shit like you did?"

"Because you're my brother."

"A brother who hasn't spoken to you in five years. Why do you give a damn?"

"Because I used to look up to you, that's why." Joe paused, as if his answer surprised himself.

Gary shifted uncomfortably in the doorway. "You used to look up to me?"

Joe coughed and put his fist to his mouth to keep the blood from coming.

"Look, Gary, I'm gonna be straight up with you about this." He paused before continuing. "I mean you were everything. So damn smart in school. A fine tennis player. Weren't you voted most likely to succeed in high school or something like that? It almost made me sick sometimes. But still, I was proud of you." He shook his head and exhaled.

"And so, when I see you toking off that pipe with Penny, it was sorta like, you know, seeing someone take a prized trophy that you'd had since you were a kid and smashing it to pieces. That's why I went off. Am I making any sense? It's late, and I'm sick and maybe I'm blabbing too much. I'll be sorry in the morning for what I'm saying."

"You really hated my guts back then, didn't you?" Gary asked.

"Look man, my head was really twisted then, okay. I was flunking in school and thinking I was stupid 'cause no one said it was ADD. Baba was breathing down my neck non-stop, sticking his face in mine, asking me why I couldn't be like you. You remember all that, don't you?"

"Yeah. I wanted to say something to Baba about it. But I never did. I guess it wouldn't matter if I told you I felt bad about that."

"Nah, I didn't hate you, Gary. It just made me more determined to succeed in something, in fucking anything. I knew it wasn't gonna be academics or something straight 'cause, like, there was no way I was going to play second fiddle to you. So, I found my own gig. Found something I was really good at. And here I am. Just look at me...successful beyond my wildest dreams. Leaning over a toilet, puking up blood.

"But enough about me, man. You told me you

came to me for some help. We haven't talked since. How do you think somebody as grimy and crimey as me can save you from the Feds?"

Gary sat on the edge of the bathtub and looked intently at Joe. "I need to make a cross country trip to see somebody, the asshole at the bottom of all this. But I can't rent a car, buy a plane or train ticket. I'm sure my name is on every no-go checklist. I need some fake ID, really good fake ID, like a driver license or passport."

"You're going after that Copper guy, right?" Joe asked, fully in the know about his brother's problems. "Don't kill the guy, Gary. That'll only make it worse for you."

"Believe me, I have no intentions to do that, at least if I don't have to. Can you help me?"

"When did you get so ballsy, *dai dai?*"

"Taking after you, I guess, *ge ge.*"

Joe leaned his head against the wall and looked up at Gary. "Give me a day or so. I'll get what you need. Now go back to bed."

"You always got to be the bossy big brother, don't you?" Gary said with a grin. Weary Joe grinned too.

Chapter Eighteen

MEANWHILE ON THE STUMP

Gale Sturmstom stood with a couple of dozen other people in a demarcated area at the back of the arena that was reserved for the press. Her CNN production crew was with her, ready to record the event and get her thoughts afterwards. She had been in the CNN trailer in the parking lot since she arrived early that morning. The last thing she wanted was to mingle with her peers, to use that term loosely, including local yokel reporters. She couldn't tell you how many times she'd been hit up at rallies like this by budding journalists looking to get their feet in the door at CNN. She emerged from the trailer only after she got word that the main event was about to start.

Suddenly, the crowd stirred, and a wave of anticipation moved over the 24,635 people, some of whom had lined up over fours before, so that they could stand at the front of the dais. Her pulse picked up. After catching a pre-dawn, first class flight from La Guardia to Madison, Wisconsin and then being ferried via limo to the rally site and sitting in the trailer for the past three hours, she was more than ready for the show. And then, there he was. Finally.

He strode onto the stage at the outdoor arena in a long black overcoat, long blue tie. Thousands in a sea of red, white, and blue erupted into cheers and applause. Len Greenwood's "God Bless the USA" blared from the giant speakers. He roamed the stage like a hungry blond bear in search of honey sweet luv from the mostly maskless audience packed together like bees in a comb. He threw in a couple of hip shakes to the music just for fun and to the delight of the crowd. He turned to face the people behind the stage as he clapped his hands and gave thumbs up. He stopped to point here and there with a wink and wide smile at some individual or another or, more likely, to no one in particular. Sturmstom would not admit it, but she was mesmerized.

Red, white, blue… The sea of red MAGA hats and Trump signs, the nearly uniform white complexion of the crowd, the perfect unearthly blue sky. He turned to face the throng and raised his fist ensconced in a black leather glove. The chant USA! USA! USA! spontaneously exploded like verbal fireworks.

Sturmstrom couldn't help but wonder if a white guy in a long black coat and holding up a fist in a black leather glove appeared a bit too, oh, what was the right word? Fascist, perhaps? She found the audacity almost breathtaking.

He gripped the edges of the podium with both

hands, slightly bent over and craned his neck, thrusting his large jaw forward with a self-satisfied smile. He looked first left and then right, reminding Sturmstrom of an unblinking heron looking for fish. Like any good performer, he let the chants go on for another thirty or so seconds before speaking.

"Wow, I can't tell you how great it is to be in Wisconsin! I love Wisconsin, and Wisconsin loves me. Am I right?" He paused and cuffed his hand to his ear as the crowd joyously cried, "Yes!" Sturmstom smirked at the showmanship.

"Beautiful fall afternoon. You know, I kinda like these outdoorsy things instead of being cooped up inside. Look at you all, so many beautiful faces. I thought you'd all be home watching Wisconsin play Ohio State. I guess not. Who can miss a Trump rally? Wisconsin versus Ohio State. I wish I could tell you that I want Wisconsin to win, but I'm gonna be in Cleveland tomorrow." Light chuckling shimmered over the crowd like wind over one of the nearby corn fields.

He then focused on the teleprompter and read in monotone the scrolling words. "After being hit hard with the Wuhan virus, our country has entered into a V shape recovery with the strongest expected economic growth this quarter going back decades. Jobs are coming back much faster than economists had ever expected. We have turned the corner and Operation Warp Speed will have us back to normal quicker than the so-called experts predicted. Joe Biden meanwhile touts a radically progressive agenda of higher taxes, more regulations, open borders, new transgender dictates…"

He paused from reading the teleprompter to

address the crowd directly. "Let me tell you, when Ivanka was a young girl, you think I'm gonna let some pervert say he's a woman so he could take showers with her in the locker room?" His eyes did their crazy eye dance of incredulity as he lifted his hands. "You all know my beautiful daughter, so you wouldn't be surprised if some crazy pervert wanted to take a shower with her. I mean, this is insane!" He then left the podium and prowled around the stage like an angry bear, exceedingly disturbed by the thought of that crazy pervert being naked with nubile Ivanka.

Sturmstom nodded. How did all these goofy, bizarre notions disable the brains of so many people, she wondered. Hell would have to freeze over before someone convinced her that a person with a penis could be a woman and a person with a vagina could be a man. It would be like her waking up one morning and declaring herself Japanese. Anyone who didn't accept her new racial identity was of course nothing but a racist.

Back to the podium, teleprompter, and monotone. "Before the Wuhan virus, we built the greatest economy the world has ever seen. If Joe Biden is elected—" another break from the teleprompter— "Ain't gonna ever happen—" back to the teleprompter— "he will do whatever he can to take your guns, let criminals loose, and drastically cut military spending. And no beautiful wall!" The last Biden desiderata elicited a long stream of boos from the throng.

Back to improvisation. "Sleepy Joe wants to bring back catch and release. You know what that is, you catch them if they touch one foot in the country and then release them—can you believe this? Ask them to come back four years later for a court date. Yeah, right." Crazy dancing eyes and comic grimace grin.

"Tell me what percentage come back? Would you say one hundred percent? No, you're a little off. Like, how about two percent." Crowd laughed. "And those people you don't want because how smart can they be to show up four years later. Two percent. Two percent. Two percent come back. Those two percent are not going to make America great again, that I can tell you. Crazy." More laughter and applause. Sturmstom couldn't suppress a smile.

Back to reading the teleprompter. "Americans everywhere are heeding the battle call to stand up for our values and founding principles and push back against the woke critical race theory that has infected our country in a way worse than Covid-19." Sturmston would have applauded if she had been in her Parc Flamboyante apartment by herself.

Away from the teleprompter and back to addressing the crowd like they were some pals he was chatting with in the men's grill room at Mar-a-Lago. "Have you seen the polls lately? Got me ahead for the first time." The crowd roared with approval. "I think I've been ahead the whole time, but you know these polls. We haven't peaked and only five weeks before the election. But who can vote for a guy who's taking tens of millions from the Chinese? Joe and Xi are butt buddies, what we called some in high school. No offense to any gays out there—who I love by the way, and they love me—but that's what we called them." He paused until the laughter subsided.

"Taking money from Xi. The guy who caused the Kung Fu flu. Have to thank that kid Wang though. What's his name—Gary? How many Chinese guys you know named Gary? Did you read that Copper File? Some crazy stuff in there. About Hunter and Creepy Joe in that hotel. I'm not going to tell it with all the kids in the audience. But man, some crazy stuff. I gotta give Sleepy Joe some credit. I mean he's seventy-eight years old. Thank God for Viagra I guess." It takes over a full minute for the uproarious laughter to die down.

"So, I have to thank this Wang kid for all this Chinese money going to Joe. Failing Fox News did everything it could to suppress it, but CNN was beautiful. Connected all the dots. Anyway, I told FBI Director Barney that when he finds this Wang kid, I want him to bring him to the White House so I can give him a medal."

He then put his hand to his brow to block the sun and pointed with the other hand toward the press area. "Speaking of CNN, one of my little spies tells me that Gale Sturmstom happens to be here today. Gale, you out there?"

Sturmstom felt like her body turned to stone. She couldn't move or speak. All the other press members looked at her; some smiled, some scowled. One put his hand over her head and signaled to Trump where she was.

"There she is. Hi Gale. Thanks for all the good work you do. Actually, most of you guys back there have been fantastic. Except failing Fox News, of course. They're just terrible." The crowd booed lustfully.

"But back to the best reporter in the White House press corp, Gale Sturmstrom. You know, she's like fifty or something like that. No offense, Melania, but if I were single, I might just slip her my phone number. Just saying." Low level prurient giggling burbled up throughout the arena. He again put his hand over his eyes and looked back to the press area, "Love you, Gale. Thanks for your support."

Forty-five-year-old Sturmstome lowered her head, mortified. Her face throbbed with embarrassment and her chest cavity seemed to have shrunk to the size of a coffee cup. She detected snickering from others in the press area. He had just given her career the kiss of death.

Once again, he turned back to the teleprompter and the canned monotonous campaign screed. An hour later, the show ended with Bruce Springsteen's "Born in the USA" playing loud. Sturmstrom used to joke that if anyone had paid attention to the lyrics, they would have stuck with Len Greenwood. But no jokes now. She hurried back to her trailer, not bothering to do a post-rally report.

He stood beside the outdoor stage set up the night before in a Macon, Georgia Walmart parking lot. For some inexplicable reason, a campaign staffer had selected a number from the electronic group LMFAO to play for the assembly. Arrayed in a semi-circle in front of the stage were forty-two socially distanced automobiles. Even inside the autos, the extra virtuous had donned masks. Red, white, and blue Biden/Harris signs decaled many of the autos and campaign banners fluttered in the breeze. When he stepped up on the stage, the cars honked their horns in unison.

Being a warm October day in Georgia, he had discarded his tie and suit jacket. His trademark aviator sunglasses, which he thought made him look sixty-eight years old instead of seventy-eight, shielded his eyes. He waved at his supporters, most of whom he couldn't see because they remained in their autos. He waited a few awkward seconds for someone to silence LMFAO's "Party Rock Anthem" before he began to read off the teleprompter. He did a passable job of plodding through the speech, in the beginning stumbling over only a couple of the names of Georgian politicians who were in attendance. He gave this same speech at other stump stops, except here in Georgia he tossed in some y'alls and occasionally dropped the "g" off gerunds. He made a couple of jokes, which had no chance because whatever laughter the punch line may have provoked was trapped inside the cars.

He improvised only once, and that's when he said, "And boy, how lucky am I to have a running mate like Kamala Harris."

The car horns honked loud and long. He smiled and raised two thumbs up. "I love this honking." He leaned into the microphone so that he could be heard above the cacophony. "Honkies for Kamala. Catchy isn't it. Honkies for Kamala."

With that, the horns abruptly went silent.

"Oh, I guess that didn't come across right," he mumbled aloud. "Okay where was I?" he asked himself as he focused again on the teleprompter.

Chapter Nineteen

CLOTHES MAKE THE MAN

Gary sat in his Toyota Corolla rental, parked at the curb in front of a townhouse in the Lower Queen Ann section of Seattle. The townhouse belonged to Danny Copper. Copper had purchased the property five years before, when the money had been a bit more liquid and flowing, and since then it had appreciated considerably. He was doing everything he could to come up with the monthly mortgage payment, and recent fees from both the FBI and Global Fission had certainly helped in that regard.

Gary had driven from his motel room to the townhouse at around eight o'clock that morning so that he could observe the comings and goings of Copper. At 8:48 a.m., Copper left his townhouse for a jog. As usual, Copper attired himself with flair: psychedelic colored spandex, neon green running shoes, a Union Jack tank top, lightweight triathlon sunglasses. A tie-dyed bandana encircled his head, the hair on which was tied up in a man-bun. He could have been the Master of Ceremonies for the lighting of the Burning Man.

Since the day before, Gary Wang had become Clifton Chong, which was the name on the driver's license Joe handed to him along with a passport and a thousand dollars cash. "You're going to need some walk around money."

"Joe, I don't know how to thank you, but—"

"Just don't get yourself caught or killed," Joe said, interrupting Gary before he got too mushy.

"Ha, well, I don't plan to."

Joe put his hand on Gary's shoulder. "You sure you don't want me to go with you?"

"Nope. I can handle it. And I don't want to put you at any more risk. You've done enough for me already."

"Hey, you did something for me too, little brother. You got me thinking, believe it or not. Our toilet conversation."

"Really? What do you mean?"

"You're right, Gary. I'm better than this. Time to make a change. Besides, my stomach is going to crawl out of my mouth if I don't."

"You mean you're quitting this business? Not going to deal anymore?"

"I got more money in the bank than I know what to do with. You got to me. Going to piss a lot of people off me quitting, people who depend on me. But fuck it, now is the time."

"Damn Joe, the only thing that might make me as happy as hearing that is getting the FBI off my case and clearing my name." He and Joe hugged for the first time in decades before Gary departed on his mission.

Finally, Copper returned from his jog. As soon as he entered his apartment, Gary exited the car. "It's go time," he said to himself as he walked up to the front door. He wasn't worried about Copper recognizing him since he was wearing his bucket hat, sunglasses and mask. Still, he was nervous and wondered if he could really do what he was about to do.

After Gary knocked twice, Copper opened the door. He held a large plastic container of post-workout liquids.

"Yes, what can I do for you?" Copper asked Gary.

"Hey good morning, Mr. Copper. I work for the federal government in collecting 2020 Census questionnaires. Our records show that you haven't completed the survey. Do you have a couple of minutes to fill it out, and I'll take it from you and turn it in?"

"Oh, well, I'm actually a British citizen, so I didn't think I had to do the survey. I threw the thing away when I got it."

"If you're a legal resident, you're supposed to do the survey."

"Oh, okay, well come on in and let's do it right now. Just keep that mask on." Copper slurped his drink through a straw and turned to go back into his apartment. When he turned back around, Gary had a gun pointed at him.

"Do what I say, or I'll blow your head off right here and right now." Gary said this in the same tough guy tone he had practiced while waiting in the rental car. "Get your hands up."

Copper calmly raised his hands, the drink in one of them. "Could you be so kind as to tell me why you're so angry?"

Gary had seen Copper in action before, that night when he had taken on three Proud Boys, so he knew to keep a safe distance.

"Just move back into the apartment NOW!"

Once in the apartment, he ordered Copper to drop to his knees; he didn't want a Jujitsu kick arcing through the air into his face. Copper did as told. Gary quickly scanned the apartment and his eyes alighted on the oven in the kitchen.

"Crawl on all fours to the kitchen. I don't plan to kill you, but I will if I have to."

Once Copper had gotten to the kitchen, Gary told him to lie flat on his stomach with his hands at his side.

"If you're planning on robbing me, I should inform you that you had better luck getting blood from a stone than money from me," Copper said, with his face to the floor.

Gary quickly stood over Copper and slid the gun into his belt. In one fluid movement he pulled a pair of handcuffs out of his back pocket, slapped one cuff onto Copper's hands and the other cuff onto the steel handle soldered to the oven door. He didn't waste a millisecond since he knew that at that moment, he was most vulnerable to a counterattack. Relieved once he executed this maneuver, he sat in a chair at the small kitchen table across from the oven.

"You can sit up now," Gary said.

Copper sat up and looked at the handcuffs. "I can't say that this is the first time that I've found myself shackled."

Gary removed his hat, sunglasses, and mask. "Yeah, I know. I was with you the last time that happened when we had dinner in New York."

Copper stared at Gary for a few moments, disbelief

in his eyes.

"Ah, Gary Wang, as I live and breathe. So, you're packing heat now? You've come a long way from that budding scholar I knew at the Academy, my friend."

"I'm not your fucking friend. And by the way, this is not a real gun. I was worried an MI5 guy like you would have noticed that right off. But I guess you've lost a step or two." Gary contemptuously tossed the imitation semi-automatic pistol at Copper.

"Okay, now that you have me exactly where you want me, what exactly is it that you do want from me?" Copper asked.

"I want you to tell the truth, that's what."

"I think I've done that sufficiently, at least in the FBI's eyes."

"Who and where is your source?"

Copper smiled. "Come now, Gary. You know I can't tell you that. Don't be silly."

"Oh okay. Let's see if you find this silly."

Gary left the kitchen and found Copper's bedroom. A couple of minutes later, he returned with an armful of clothes retrieved from Copper's closet. He dumped them on the kitchen table then searched the kitchen drawers until he found a large knife.

"You ready to get silly, Danny?" Gary said as he held up the knife.

The sangfroid melted off Copper's face. "Now, now, Gary, I don't want you to hurt yourself with that. Akaishi Kido sushi knives are not toys."

"It's not me I'm planning to hurt."

"So, you planning to lop off one of my ears or fingers with that?" Copper couldn't hide the nervousness in his voice.

Gary picked one of the items in the pile of clothes,

an olive-colored blazer. He held it up for inspection. "Hmm, double-breasted? Is that still in style, Danny boy?"

"In certain circles, yes. Careful mate, that piece of linen there cost me a pretty quid, thirty-five hundred pounds as a matter of fact."

"I think it might need a bit more tailoring." Gary slashed the knife through the back of the jacket.

Copper gasped.

Gary next picked up a Thomas Pink custom-made jacquard Tattersall shirt.

"Very dandified, Danny. Bold colors. Dashing."

Copper reached his free hand out toward Gary, grasping the air. "Please, that shirt was given to me by my girlfriend when I made Officer Agent II. Lot of sentimental value. I once wore it—"

Before Copper could finish—slash, slash, slash—the shirt was good for nothing more than house cleaning rags.

Copper's face collapsed with horror. "You bastard!"

Next up was a pair of super 130s wool Mocha trousers.

"No, please no." Copper pleaded. Beads of sweat popped out on his forehead.

Gary held up the pants and knife. "Who's your source, Danny?"

Copper moved his eyes back and forth from his favorite pair of trousers to Gary. "I can't… you know I can't."

A rapid succession of slices reduced the pair of pants to kite tails.

Copper cried in anguish and his head fell against his un-cuffed hand.

"Hmm, let's see what else we got here." Gary sorted through the pile. He held up and examined a printed deco diamond tie. "I can make some quick work of this."

"Okay, just stop! Please stop!" Copper's chest heaved for breath. "I'll tell you. My contact lives in Hong Kong. Her name is Meng Quilong. She went to the Academy. She may even have been there when you were there."

Gary asked for her email and phone number, which Copper summarily provided.

"Very good, Danny. We're making progress. This your laptop?" Gary opened the laptop on the kitchen counter. All he had to do was hold the knife up for Copper to give him the username/password.

"Eureka," he muttered when he saw the file "Meng." He inserted a thumb drive into the USB port and sucked away the file's contents.

"Now who was her source? Where was the sludge flowing from?"

"I don't know."

"Of course, you know. You didn't just take what she was telling you at face value. I know you're not stupid, Danny. So don't take me as stupid."

"I tell you I don't know."

"Okay, whatever. But I'm having so much fun with this, why stop?" He next selected a dark blue wool tuxedo jacket with satin lapels. "Nice," he said as he raised his knife. "I can see you in this. Sort of James Bondish."

Copper began yanking his cuffed hand from the oven door handle, over and over, panicking like a trammeled slave-rower on a sinking galleon. "Don't! For God's sake, don't!"

"Then tell me. Tell me, and I'll go and leave you to your precious wardrobe."

"Uh, Meng mentioned some guy who was plying her with intelligence. A Russian. GRU guy. Something like that."

Gary stood with the knife in his hand, his mouth open, completely dumbstruck by what Copper just told him. "A Russian agent was the original source of all this. Are you fucking kidding me?"

Copper blushed and remained silent.

Gary stood there for a few seconds, shaking his head in disbelief. He turned and started walking to the door.

"Hold it, where are you going?" Copper shouted.

"I got what I need." Gary walked to the door and opened it.

"But what about these?" Copper said, pointing at the handcuffs with his free hand.

"I'm sure you'll figure it out."

Gary intended to make an emergency call to the Seattle Police about a man in a serious fix at Copper's address once he landed at JFK five hours later.

He closed the door and walked to his car. Before he drove away, he pulled the small tape recorder from his windbreaker and hit play. The voice of Copper saying, "Yes, what can I do for you?" sounded from the recorder. Gary listened to the whole tape as he drove. He couldn't keep from smiling all the way to the airport.

Ramon Aruba sat in Director Cummings office and had just finished playing the recording of Gary's encounter with Copper, for the benefit of Cummings and Fisherwood.

"So, there you have it, sirs. All just basically a big hoax, to use the President's favorite word. I'm sure your forensic voice technicians will confirm that those voices are in fact that of Gary Wang and Danny Copper."

Cummings mused to himself how handy these gadgets were. First Danny and now Wang turning the tables, or recorder in this case. Pocket recorder—don't leave home without it.

"How did this tape get to you?" Fisherwood asked as he leaned over to Aruba sitting next to him. "I'm sure you know that meeting with a fugitive from the law can be considered aiding and abetting."

"It was couriered to my office," Aruba said. *Nice try, Fisherwood.*

"You know Copper will claim that he said all those things under duress," Cumming said.

"Duress…you mean the wardrobe massacre?" Aruba said, smiling.

Fisherwood guffawed. "I admit I almost felt sorry for the guy. Such agony!"

"That thumb drive I gave you off Copper's laptop more than backs up everything that Gary Wang has asserted. And that includes that the ultimate source of this China tale was an officer in the Russian GRU. This whole thing was just another cheap Russian disinformation effort to influence the election. They probably have about a hundred of these going at any one time. Putin has to be laughing at all this disruption he's caused…again."

Cummings pressed his fingers together, shook his head, and frowned at Putin's election hijinks.

"And these signed affidavits that you have presented to us are from the three Chinese nationals that phone intercepts show Wang called?" Cummings asked.

"Yes, they confirm what Wang said. He was calling some friends from the Academy of Global Understanding to try and set up a meeting between Biden and Xi."

"Because they signed these affidavits doesn't mean diddly squat, as my grandmother in Alabama used to say," Fisherwood said. "I mean, they're in China, outside US prosecution. Say we found out they were outright lying? Nothing we could do about it."

"If you don't accept the affidavits, you should talk to them yourselves. I'm surprised that you haven't already approached them."

"We've been trying," Cummings said. "But all kinds of hoops and ladders we have to get around before they let us talk to any of their citizens. And our two countries aren't exactly on friendly terms right now, and we are the FBI. They're probably more than happy to let you do that, however. I'm sure they'd like to clear up the charge that they're trying to corrupt the US election."

"And we all know they want Biden to win," Fisherwood added sourly.

Aruba took a deep breath. "So, gentlemen, given what I've presented and what we all know now, I request that you call off the investigation of my client, so he can start to put back the pieces of his life that have been shattered to smithereens by these lies."

"Just one thing, Ramon," Fisherwood said. "Why did Wang flee if he's so innocent?"

"I can't answer that because I haven't asked him."

"Well, I think that's a pretty damn important question."

Aruba shrugged. "Maybe he was scared how a Chinese guy might be treated when the pandemic is called the Chinese virus, at least by some, not to mention the President of the United States.

"Look guys, you know, and I know that this info that I've handed over is going to get leaked to the media sooner or later, and it's more likely to be sooner. So just ask yourself what that will do to the FBI's reputation. Pursuing some twenty-eight-year-old campaign worker because some guy gets paid by the opposition to put together the quote—the Copper File—unquote. We know Copper is a money-grubbing fraud, but you're going to tell the world that the FBI didn't know any better? Really?"

Neither Cummings nor Fisherwood answered that question.

Cummings found even more foreboding the prospect that as this investigation dragged on, Slade McClintock would drag his butt in front of his committee to explain what in tarnation was going on with this Wang matter.

"We will present what you have given us today to the election task force, Mr. Aruba," Cummings said. "We will fully consider its implications regarding our current investigation. We will be in contact with you thereafter. Have a good day, sir."

"Hello, Manny, it's Ramon."

"Ramon! Long time no talk. How you doing? Anything strange or wonderful?"

"Ha, well, actually both. I have someone here on

the speaker phone with me."

"Yeah, who's that?"

"Gary."

Long pause on the other end of the line. "Gary?"

"Hey Manny. Yep, it's me."

"We're calling because we got a scoop for you. Telling you first because you're our favorite journalist."

Manny, still a bit shaken by Gary's voice, managed to say, "Yeah, I bet that's a short list."

"The news is that the FBI has dropped its investigation of Gary," Aruba said.

"What?" Manny shouted. She veritably leapt from her desk on the Fox News floor into the air, drawing attention even amidst the usual commotion. "Oh my God, really?"

"I'm sending you an email with the particulars, like a press release," Aruba said.

"We want you to get the credit, Manny," Gary said. "You'll not only get some kudos from the higher ups there, but you'll really piss off your mentor, Gale."

"Mentor, right." Manny laughed, knowing that Gary was in on that joke. "I think after that Trump rally debacle, she might be asking me for a job."

"So be looking for my email, Manny, and let me know if you have any questions. Tell the people there to get it out before the FBI spills it to their favorite lackey reporters."

"Will do for sure, Ramon. And Gary, do you have a cell phone now so I can call you?"

"Not yet, but that's the first order of business."

"I guess I'll have to say this in front of Ramon, then: Get your ass ASAP over to my apartment. I'll check out early and meet you there right now."

"Yes ma'am…see you then."

After the call ended, Aruba smiled at Gary with one eyebrow salaciously arched.

Chapter Twenty

TAKE THE KING'S CASTLE

November 2020

She ran down Amsterdam Avenue screaming. The middle-aged woman was wearing lingerie even though an evening autumn chill was in the air. She stopped where Gary and Manny stood at Amsterdam and 95th street. She placed her hands to her face, reminding Gary of the figure in Munch's "The Scream," and bellowed: "Trump is going to win!"

"What, I can't believe that," Manny said.

Gary noticed that others gathered because they too had heard the news that had driven the woman to madness. They appeared as unnerved by that news as a small herd of cattle at the sight of a wolf. In solidarity with the locals, of whom Gary figured ninety-five percent had voted for Biden, what few restaurants were open had cut their wine and liquor prices in half as a way evidently to exemplify their social justice bona fides. The heated outdoor seating areas were filled with customers guzzling away their shock and sorrow.

"We better get back to your apartment quick," Gary said. "People are going nuts. There could be trouble."

They passed others wandering dazed into the streets, some in pajamas or robes. Many stood on their terraces or hung out windows and banged on pots and pans in agitation and anguish. As they walked further north, they heard the bells of the Cathedral of St. John the Divine tolling out of schedule to sound the alarm. Gary had read that ages ago, parishioners would have understood that the impromptu tolling of church bells signified that demon spirits had been loosened unto the land and all should seek immediate sanctuary in the church. Even though no one on the Upper Westside of Manhattan was ignorant enough to believe in demons and angels, he was surprised to see that dozens had spontaneously gathered within the great walls of the cathedral to seek succor. He and Manny stopped for a few moments outside the cathedral to listen to the organist play on the giant pipes a rendition of Mozart's Lacrimosa ("weeping") from his Requiem.

Once at Manny's apartment, the two sat on the sofa and watched the election returns with grave countenances.

"The people have spoken, Matt, loud and clear. The average working stiffs—the elite's derogatory term they use when describing Americans in flyover country—are not going to let things go back to pre-2016."

"So speaks the ten-million-dollar a year cable TV pundit with fake eyelashes," Gary said.

"You're right, Stephanie," the co-anchor said. "The working-class carnage that President Trump so eloquently described at his first inauguration will perhaps be a thing of the past now."

Trump had made a clean sweep up the southeast coast battleground states, taking Florida, North Carolina, Georgia, at least according to the official Associated Press tally. Pennsylvania seemed to be a safe Democrat pickup. Two other toss-up states, namely Iowa and Ohio had also been projected for Trump.

At eleven o'clock on the night of November 3, the various news services had Trump with 256 electoral votes and Biden 244. All eyes were on Arizona with eleven electoral votes and Nevada with six. If Trump won those two, his total would be 273 electoral votes, three more than the 270 needed to win the presidency. At the stroke of midnight, Nevada was called for Trump, and he had surged comfortably ahead in Arizona.

"I can't believe this, I just can't," Manny said, on the verge of tears.

Gary shook his head. "That China bullshit story cost Biden the election." His voice was filled with remorse and guilt.

"Gary, there was nothing you did. It all was done to you. Besides, the press release from the FBI ending the investigation should have made that moot."

"I guess there's still an outside possibility that the mail-in and absentee ballots that haven't been counted yet will go to Biden. Big margin of Democrats over Republicans in that category." Gary knew that he was clutching at straws in the middle of a tornado.

"Most of that has been counted and the late ones will have to go like sixty-five percent or higher to Biden," Manny said. "Fat Chance of that happening… Sometimes you have to hope for voter fraud," she said. Gary knew that she was joking, at least mostly.

"If the Trumpsters ever got wind that something like that happened, there'd be civil war," Gary said.

"I think there might be anyway," Manny said somberly. "C'mon, let's go to bed. Maybe we'll wake up in the morning and Trump winning was just a nightmare we somehow had together."

Gary imagined the wail of woe that would rise up tomorrow in New York City, excepting Staten Island of course.

The next day, although Trump had not officially been declared the victor and the vote counting in Arizona had not been finalized, all assumed it was a foregone conclusion that he had won. Protest marches sprung up spontaneously throughout Manhattan. Manny and Gary joined a march down Avenue of the Americas, where fortunately the traffic was Covid light. The day was sunny and unseasonably warm, so the street scene couldn't help but get a little festive, protests or not.

Manny and Gary ambled along hand in hand, both feeling a bit guilty that they were too much in love to keep up the seething anger at the election outcome.

The protesters represented a mix of Blacks, Latinos, Asians, but Whites were the largest constituent and most of them were in their twenties. They had the good grooming and healthy, well-fed looks that indicated to Gary that they were college kids or recently so.

"You think we're walking cliches?" he asked Manny.

"What? Come again?"

Gary chuckled. "I mean, I'm just looking at all these people. I guess what you would call our demographic cohort, right? Everybody has the basic same style. We all look like we buy clothes from like Old Navy, H&M, UNIQLO."

"Ah, you mean stores that sell overpriced stuff that's made to look like it came from a thrift shop? Like these jeans with the knees ripped out that I paid sixty bucks for at Forever 21?"

"Exactly. They allow you the privilege to overpay for their clothes that signify that privileged is the last thing you want to be."

"Hey, let me tell you, boyfriend, after growing up in a row house in the bad part of Queens with a mother who worked her tail off cleaning houses and a dad who moped around doing a lot of nothing, I got no problem getting me some privilege."

Gary laughed. "I hear you babe."

But he didn't laugh at a different element that moved as a unit within the flow of people. They were white kids mostly, and dressed all in black. Many wore helmets and goggles, some carried umbrellas, while the more militant wielded black plastic body shields and metal batons that were good for breaking windows and perhaps bones.

He knew a few of their ilk from college. They seemed to have paradoxically found something nihilistically meaningful in committing violence and destruction, a meaningfulness that had been missing in their middle to upper middle-class lives, which had mostly centered since sixth grade on getting into an elite university, like Columbia. Raising a fist in the air, smashing a Target store window—a place where he would bet that their families often shopped—released the inner rebel, made them feel like they mattered.

They would condemn his working for the Biden campaign as a manifestation of his capitalist bourgeois degeneracy, just as the Chinese Red Guard had condemned his father. The ones he knew had played the game throughout high school and college as well as they could have. But dressing in black, cursing and spitting into the face of a cop a foot away from them, made them feel fierce, a feeling they had never before experienced in their sheltered, well managed, well provided lives. They were now something that they had never been, a force to be reckoned with. He saw first-hand how that intoxicated them.

But overall, the atmosphere was more benign than malign. So much so that Manny suddenly began singing a song, Johnny Nash's "I Can See Clearly Now."

"Hmm, that's an interesting song to just start singing out of the blue," Gary said. "Why'd you pick that one?"

"My mama used to sing it to me as a lullaby when I was a little girl. I like the Jimmy Cliff reggae version better though. I don't know, I guess I could use a comforting lullaby after last night."

Even with her mask on, Gary loved how her singing voice was both poignant, sometimes on the verge of breaking, but still strong. The soulfulness that she poured into the words roused him to do something he didn't do often, and that was sing. He lowly sang along with her but wondered if she even noticed because she stared straight ahead as she sang. Others strolling along with them began to pick up the chorus and sing too.

The two eventually made their way to Union Square. On the dais there, speakers spoke, musicians performed.

Somebody named Benny Calabrese, who touted himself as "The Woke Comic" even attempted a stand-up routine: "So a Wall Street guy, a Catholic priest, and a lobbyist for Exxon walk into a bar. They're all three white, of course. Perfect epitomes of the patriarchal, white supremacy, imperialistic, racist, anti-gay—except maybe the priest, if you get me—anti-everything socio-economic power matrix…" Benny stopped here, out of breath. "So the Wall Street guy wants to be Mr. Big Shot naturally and tells the bartender that he wants to buy a round for him and his pals. But then he goes 'Shit, I left my wallet in my squash bag at the University Club. Would you accept a check, bartender?' The bartender, who happens to be a Black chick with Cherokee ancestry, says 'The only checks we take here is when dudes like you *check* their white privilege at the door.'"

The total lack of response didn't keep Benny from grinning ear to ear. "Can't you just see the look on Wall Street dude's face."

The lame joke caused Manny and Gary to turn and grimace at each other, which made them both laugh.

Suddenly their attention was diverted to the bizarre sight of a Chinook helicopter moving over the midtown skyline. The roar of its two massive rotary blades could be heard more than a mile away.

"Wow, look at that," Gary said as he stood. "It looks like it's hovering over Trump Tower. We have to check that out." He and Manny caught a taxi and within a few minutes were in front of Trump Tower on Fifth Avenue. They got there just as a crowd of spectators started to build. They gazed in awe and amazement at the helicopter as it gingerly positioned itself over the tower roof.

A rope dropped from the Chinook and a crew of eight men rappelled on it down to the roof. Something long and black dropped from the tail opening of the copter to the men on the roof. A football field long roll of black canvas then descended and covered half the front of Trump Tower's fifty-eight stories. The black sheath displayed a gigantic white skull and cross bones. The Chinook then rose and sped toward the horizon.

"Oh my God!" Manny said.

"Who in the hell could get a permit from De Blasio to pull that stunt off?" Gary asked.

"A woke tech billionaire probably," Manny said.

"You think that's supposed to be a symbol for poison?" Gary asked.

"Or a pirate logo," Manny said.

"Trump would probably like that since he thinks he's some kind of modern-day swashbuckler."

By now hundreds had amassed on Fifth Avenue between 56th and 57th street. Three large dump trucks filled with sand had been parked on the street in front of the entrance to Trump Tower. A row of large concrete blocks with NYPD stenciled on them had also been arrayed on both sides of the trucks, along with metal police barricades. All this had been set up after Trump received the Republican nomination as protection against a terrorist act like a car bomb; but Gary didn't think it would do much to contain a crowd like this, which seemed to have erupted out of nowhere and was on the verge of transmogrifying into a mob.

A squad of policemen, numbering eight, stood at the entrance. They wore helmets and protective body vests underneath their shirts. They held to their chests Colt AR-15 A3 heavy barrel rifles. The crowd pushed right up to the metal barricades, which were usually used for parades. Having arrived before most, Manny and Gary were near the front.

Gary could hear the squad's captain frantically speaking into the radio transmitter attached to his shoulder "We need backup! Gotta be at least a thousand protesters in front of Trump Tower. Get the Strategic Response Group here immediately. Repeat immediately. " Precinct Headquarters response could be heard over the crowd noise: "Roger that. SRG a little spread out. Outbreaks all over the city. But help is on its way. Hang in there."

Three guys wearing black suits and ties, sunglasses and radio earpieces appeared. Obviously Secret Service agents who guarded Trump's three-story penthouse. They pulled their suit jackets back enough so all the world could see the handguns holstered to their belts.

Hoping to record some brutish police abuse, the protestors held up their camera phones at an angle, creating a sea of what could have been mistaken for progressive Sieg Heil-like salutes. Those in the front line of the crowd contorted their faces in hate and screamed curses and insults at the policemen, saliva spraying from their unmasked mouths.

"How many Blacks have you killed today, you racist pig?"

"Is your mother proud that you're a murderer?"

"I'd love to catch you out of that uniform. I'd bust your head wide open."

One of the policemen was Black, and special abuse was reserved for him.

"Traitor!"

"Fucking Uncle Tom!"

"Look at your skin! Look at your skin! What color is it? White?" So shrieked a young white woman, who happened to be standing next to Manny. She and Manny exchanged glances.

"Let me guess, Barnard College?" Manny asked.

"Nope, N.Y.U, American Imperialist Lit," she calmly replied before she turned back to spraying insults and spit at the Black officer.

Meanwhile others behind the first line of protestors began chanting, "Pigs in a blanket, fry 'em like bacon!"

"This is getting tense," Manny said to Gary. "Maybe we ought to split."

"It'll take us forever to get through this crowd," Gary said. "Let's start moving. We can catch a subway at Lex and 53rd."

An NYPD helicopter appeared and hovered over the crowd. Then a voice over a loudspeaker from a NYPD van sounded a few blocks down Fifth Avenue. "You are ordered to disperse immediately by orders of the Mayor and the NYPD." A line of officers two deep stretched across Fifth Avenue. They wore helmets with face visors and Kevlar vests. They carried bulletproof Plexiglass shields, two-foot-long polycarbonate batons, flash and tear gas grenades, pepper spray canisters, rubber bullet guns. As they marched, they tapped their batons against their shields and shouted in unison, "Move back! Move back!" as if it were a war chant.

Manny and Gary had unwittingly joined the flow of people moving straight into the advancing police line. “Oh shit,” Manny said.

Some protesters stood several feet away from the marching officers. The ones dressed in black took the point, seizing the opportunity to become real social justice warriors, ready to fight. A hard rain of rocks, bottles, and whatever else the protestors could find greeted the oncoming police. Tear gas grenades popped off and the air quickly became burning and asphyxiating. Many protesters, the veteran ones, donned gas masks.

Manny leaned her head into Gary’s chest. “I can’t breathe. Like I’m suffocating.”

Occasionally, a stream of yellow pepper spray would piss out from behind the wall of shields at any protester who had gotten too close. As rubber bullets flew, the disembodied, eerily calm recorded voice sounded every sixty seconds: “You are ordered to disperse immediately by orders of the Mayor and the NYPD,” while underneath that continued the steady command, “Move back! Move back!” But the street had become so packed with people that they had trouble moving back.

Gary, with Manny coughing uncontrollably against his chest, almost stumbled amidst the commotion, barely avoiding being trampled by the herd.

The mad medley of curses, shrieks, screams, and shouts was broken by the sound of a gunshot. A police officer went down.

Chapter Twenty-One

WAR, IT'S JUST A SHOT AWAY

The gunshot caused screams of panic to supplant screams of righteous indignation. The crowd surged back unto itself. Bodies bumped into bodies.

Gary almost tripped over two people sprawled on the ground. He wrapped his arms tightly around Manny, knowing that if he fell then he and Manny could end up dead under the stampeding feet.

The NYPD column stopped to give attention to the fallen officer. Fortunately, his vest had stopped the bullet and he appeared not seriously injured. But the police commander in charge ordered a retreat.

"Damn, don't leave!" Gary said out loud as he turned and saw the thin blue line that separated chaos from order dissolve. But he knew the last thing the NYPD wanted was to engage in a live ammo skirmish with civilians. The nation could not afford the sight of kids dead in the street.

Many protestors, not sharing Gary's alarm, cheered triumphantly and shot their fists into the air as the police beat a hasty but orderly retreat to their armored vehicles parked on 54th street. They celebrated their victory by smashing storefront windows and looting shops up and down Fifth and Madison Avenues.

Trapped in the human flow, Gary searched desperately for a way to get Manny and him out of this riot before they were injured or killed. She clung to him, her nails digging into his arm.

As the crowd thinned some, they passed the owner of a men's clothing store standing in front of his shop, pleading with the marauders. "I came from Pakistan. Look at my skin," he said as he pointed at his face. "I'm a person of color. Black lives matter. Please, everything I have is in this store. I came to this country with nothing and now this is everything." He reached his hands out in supplication to the looters as they nonchalantly walked through the shattered store windows with armfuls of clothes. "I voted for Joe Biden. I hate Trump. Please, this is everything. This is my American dream."

On his way out, one of the black-clad kids with a bandana around his lower face stopped to yell at the store owner: "This is just stuff, man. Just clothes. From some sweatshop in Indonesia. All you think about is profit, profit, profit. You got insurance." Before he exited, he shouted to one of his comrades, "Hey Chad, lift one of those cashmere sweaters for me while you're at it."

Manny by now had gotten over the effects of the

tear gas, thanks to the wet rag a sympathetic protestor had given her. Given the surrounding mayhem, she and Gary decided the safest thing to do was go back to the others in front of Trump Tower. At least police would be trying to maintain order there.

By the time they found their way back, the mood of the crowd had gone from restive to surly. Word must have reached the officers in front of Trump Tower that the cavalry wasn't coming. "Abandon your post. I repeat, abandon your post," the captain shouted over the din to the other officers.

"C'mon!" Gary said, agitated as he watched the officers rush into the tower and exit out a back entrance to Madison Avenue.

The police departure incited the crowd to swarm over the barricades and to the building entrance. Gary and Manny stepped aside as they rushed past them. Some were gleeful, giddy, even giggly in their ability to chase off the cops with their big rifles; others had in their faces the narrowing eyes of the wolf.

Finding the doors locked, several picked up one of the police barricades and began ramming it into the glass door.

"Heave ho!"

Bash.

"Heave ho!"

Bash.

A Black guy, attempting to resemble a 1960's Black Panther with a large Afro, black turtleneck, black-framed sunglasses, and introducing himself as an adjunct professor of sociology at local Hunter College, mounted one of the concrete blocks with NYPD stenciled on it. He held up a megaphone and began a call and response with the congregation.

"What do we want?" he asked.

"Justice!" the collective answered.

"And if we don't get it?"

"Burn it all down."

Evincing some degree of megalomania, he then issued forth a proclamation. "To commemorate this revolt, I declare the area from 50th to 59th Streets to be an autonomous homeland for the Pursuit of Justice and Equity for all peoples subjugated under the jackboot of the FUSA, the Fascist United States of America. Y'all can substitute your own F-word if you like. We dedicate our new autonomous homeland to the Lenape, the native tribe from whom those pointy-nosed Dutch crackers stole it four hundred years ago!"

The crowd burst into cheers.

"That guy has a fine future as Commissar," Gary said, to inject some humor into the dire situation. Manny had regained her nerves enough to smile. The two luckily found a bench to rest on before recovering enough to try to get their way back home. Notwithstanding their uneasiness, they were also spectators transfixed by the melee around them.

"To support the birth of this new nation," the Commissar continued, "we will need provisions of food, water, clothing, blankets. Look around you, this is the land of plenty. Go now and confiscate what is rightfully yours and bring it back here so that we can distribute it to each according to zirs, hirs, eirs, vers needs. And I beg your pardon if I left out your preferred possessive gender pronoun."

Behind him, some of the more creative types had rearranged the large gilt block letters TRUMP TOWER over the entrance into TRU POWER.

After multiple efforts at battering down the entry

doors with the metal police barricade, the glass finally broke and the rammers waved to the jubilant throng. The crowd then rose like a wave toward the opening and poured into the building.

As was his wont, President Trump sensed the perfect opportunity to throw some gasoline on the roaring fire with a well-timed tweet, and he seized it: "Watching NYC chaos. Horrible! My beautiful building being overtaken by mob. Mayor De Blasé nowhere to be found. Tough guy Cuomo hiding. We cannot rely on them or anyone else. Rise up citizens. Take back your city!"

Eddie Cavalini, resident of the Sunnyside neighborhood on Staten Island, was on his couch watching with apoplectic disgust the live news streaming of the assault on Trump Tower, when the President's call-to-action tweet pinged on his phone. The master had just blown his dog whistle. Eddie knew exactly what to do next; in fact, he had been waiting for this moment for months. He sent the message throughout the social media grapevine to members of the Staten Island Defenders of Liberty. The subject line of the message was "A call to arms Patriots!"

Like conquistadors entering a Mayan temple (which had the similar zigzag outline as Trump Tower setbacks), many of the rioters upon storming into the building were awe struck by all the gold, or rather highly polished brass, emanating from the seven-story atrium interior that, like a cathedral, allowed the spirit to soar in flights of luxurious fantasies. Golden elevator doors, sunset golden pinkish marble walls, golden escalator handrail. The mirrored skin of the atrium reflected the gilt sheen back and forth. And as with the conquistadors, all this golden glow corrupted the protestors and sent them into a frenzy of covetousness.

After hauling off pretty much anything that wasn't nailed down in the lobby, including the bronze reception desk emblazoned with the double golden letter T and the fifty-foot-tall Christmas tree with all its glittering ornaments, the invaders went from floor to floor banging on apartment doors. Whoever was foolish enough to open the door was then led down to the lobby and deposited into a makeshift holding pen made from the police barricades.

The adjunct professor/ersatz Black Panther/Commissar pronounced another edict: "Anybody homeless out there? Well, y'all c'mon on up 'cause we got a nice Trump Tower apartment waiting for you!"

Manny looked at Gary with disbelief.

A procession of the disheveled approached the entrance to claim their condos as the well-groomed erstwhile owners of those condos were being paraded in a line out of the building. The Commissar took the key from each person exiting and handed it to the person entering. To add insult to injury, he asked the donors to tell the recipients the number of the apartment that they were tendering.

The first homeless person in line was Gabriel Arguello. When he received his key, he clasped his hands together and raised them above his head before the adoring crowd as his soiled pants slid down past his butt.

"Gabriel, tell us all your story," the Commissar asked, "so we can all appreciate our generosity."

The Commissar held the megaphone up to Gabriel, who attempted in a halting, barely comprehensible manner to tell his benefactors that he had been diagnosed as schizophrenic five years before. He had voluntarily left the Kingsbridge Heights Apartments in the Bronx where he had been housed/treated. He had recently decided to switch his medication from Risperdal to Oxytocin, which made living a life of freedom on the streets really not all that bad. His audience welcomed his progress with gracious applause.

The Venezuelan organic hibiscus-based energy drink magnate who had handed his keys over to Gabriel was none too happy. Standing there in his silk pajamas, bathrobe and Hermes scarf, he couldn't believe that the same thing that had happened to him in Chavez's Caracas was now happening to him in New York City.

The twenty-six other newly homeless who had opened their doors when the knock came, walked in a single file through the crowd. They bowed their heads in humiliation as they were pelted with verbal contempt.

"Eat the rich!" chanted those who lined the gauntlet that the condo owners walked through. Gary mused that the original romantic rebel, Jean-Jacques Rousseau, would have been amazed that his 18th century slogan had somehow become *au courant*. Plastic bottles and sundry refuse found from garbage cans were hurled at them. A former public relations associate and now trophy wife, who thought she had sufficiently disguised her age with all kinds of cosmetic treatments, including injections of a substance that made her lips look like two conjoined bright red Saveloy sausages, defiantly spat one "Fuck You" after another like machine gun fire at her tormentors. One of the Jacobins threatened to whack her collagen and Botox-filled head with his skateboard.

Another of the pariahs sent in exile from his cherished abode, a music executive with Sony, glanced up at those castigating him with sneers, jeers and some rotten eggs found in a nearby dumpster, and was shocked to recognize a face.

"Oh my God, Gisele is that you? I haven't seen you since you went off to Brown. Gisele, what's happened to you?"

Gisele, who had recently declared *their* androgyny and changed *their* name to Billie, used to babysit this persona non grata's twin daughters in this very tower. She lowered her face now pink with embarrassment, hoping none of her cohorts had noticed this rich asshole's acting as if he knew her or that she had once baby-sat for wealthy people. "Eat the rich!" she screamed directly at her interlocutor, so as not to leave any doubt in anyone's minds regarding her commitment to income equity.

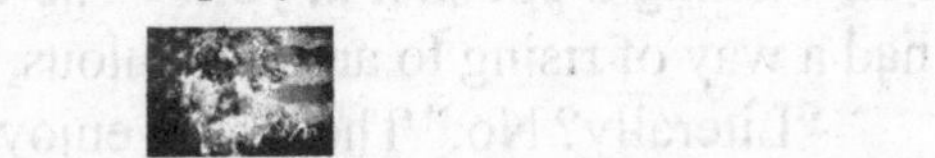

A caravan of sixty-three SUV's and pick-up trucks displaying Trump banners, the Stars and Stripes, and a couple of Confederate battle flags crossed over Verrazano Bridge, on its way to Trump Towers to launch the counterattack. Two hundred and fifty-six angry white men stared ahead with uniform grim faces in contemplation of the mission before them: take back not only the king's castle but also their country.

An emergency phone call came through to Gracie Mansion. "Mayor, Governor Cuomo is on the line," Mayor De Blasio's deputy office aid informed him.

The mayor rolled his eyes at the staff around him. "Over twenty minutes late as usual," said the chronically late mayor. "Pipe him in, Phil."

"Mayor?"

"Hello Governor."

"What the hell is going on down there, Mayor?"

"I should tell you first, Governor, that I have you on the speaker with a few members of my staff and—"

"I don't care who's there with you. I'm talking to you. Just you and me. Now again I ask you, what the hell is going on down there?"

"People are upset, Governor. This country has re-elected a dictator who is racist, xenophobic, anti-transgender and—"

The governor cut him off. "Upset? I get upset too a lot of times. I'm upset right now with you. But I don't loot, burn shit down, and take pot shots at NYPD cops. Am I taking a pot shot at you?" The Governor's voice had a way of rising to an incredulous, whiny pitch.

"Literally? No." The mayor enjoyed displaying his superior wit to the governor, especially in front of his aides.

"What do you mean 'literally'? Is that supposed to be cute, funny? Look, I'm sitting here watching television and I think I'm seeing a video to that Billy Joel song, you know, what is it? "Seen The Lights Go Out on Broadway." I'm expecting Trump to send up an aircraft carrier into New York harbor and bomb everything to kingdom come. He might say he's from

New York, but he hates every single thing about it."

"Except his buildings," DeBlasio jibed.

"Speaking of which, I don't like what's going on at Trump Tower. Now tell me, Mayor, what are you going to do to bring this insurrection under control?"

"I think insurrection is too strong a word, Governor. NYPD's on it. It's going to take some time to do it correctly. I think the best thing to do is let the rage burn out, let the people blow off some steam and simmer down some. It's not like citizens are being gunned down or anything. Yes, some property is being damaged or whatever, but insurance covers that."

"Blow off some steam? What are you saying?" The Governor whined in staccato as he pounded each word "And by the way, people are getting gunned down every day in the Bronx, but that's another topic for another time. Listen, I'm going to talk to you straight. One Sicilian to another."

The mayor hit the mute button and said to his staff, "He's doing that Godfather shit again.

"My Italian ancestry actually comes from Benevento on my mother's side, as I've mentioned to you several times before." The half-German Mayor was a bit defensive about being called Sicilian.

"Whatever, that's south enough for me," the Governor replied. "But what I'm telling you is you're going to have *crescere un paio di palline...capisce?"*

"Sorry, Governor, but I don't understand anything you just said."

"You're going to have to grow a pair of balls, Mayor." The Governor's voice rose to a crescendo of annoyance.

The mayor winced and shook his head in disbelief. He twirled his finger around his temple to indicate what he thought of the Governor's mental state.

"Look, Governor, playing it tough and hurting some people who are simply protesting this despicable human being who is destroying our democracy—"

"Cut the crap, Mayor. I asked for this call really for one reason only: I'm calling out the National Guard. This city is out of control. I was hoping to gain some confidence that you knew what you were doing and had a plan to stabilize the situation. You have failed to convince me of that. I am immediately issuing an order for the Second Battalion, 108th infantry regiment to deploy out of Farmingdale ASAP. They were mobilized yesterday for exactly this kind of election unrest, so they will be on their way shortly. Am I clear?"

"It's your call, Governor." The mayor sighed at his staff. He raised his hands palms up and shook his head.

"I suggest you hold a press conference to inform everyone. I will be issuing a press release shortly. Adjutant General Major Helms will be following up with you after this call with the details of the deployment and operational logistics. Have the right people at NYPD participate in that call. Have a good evening, Mayor, and prepare for a very long night."

After he hung up, the Governor said to the strawberry blond aide sitting on his lap. "So whadaya think about how I handled Block Head?"

"So rough and tough, you sexy luv Gov."

"Okay, now go type up a press release, Ms. Collins." He gave her a playful light slap on the rump as she rose from his desk.

Chapter Twenty-Two

ARMAGEDDON DEFERRED

Before Ms. Collins had time to finish her typing task, the convoy of troop-carrying National Guard trucks and armored personnel carriers had already departed from the military base at Farmingdale, Long Island and was rumbling its way down I-495 toward Manhattan. Two thousand fully armed soldiers were prepared to take back the streets. Their first objective was Trump Tower.

Simultaneously, the Staten Island Defenders of Liberty landed on the lower east side of Manhattan after traversing the Verrazano Bridge into Brooklyn and then crossing the Manhattan Bridge. The caravan paused at City Hall Park, where members disembarked from their vehicles so they could do one final check of their weapons and gear before engaging the enemy…that is protestors. Some also took the time to guzzle another beer or Red Bull, smoke a cig or stogie or maybe a joint off to the side. AC-DC's "Highway to Hell" sounded from somewhere.

The general vibe among the group was that of a football team in the locker room before the state championship game, i.e., upbeat but tense. A lot of backslapping, jocular jousting, and jostling, but a quiet intensity underneath it all. They gathered in small groups to chat about how the Giants sucked or joking who wouldn't take a run at Nancy Pelosi since, you know, she didn't look all that bad for eighty, anything that would settle their nerves a bit. And even though most of them had been preparing for this scenario for months if not years, the basic background humming thought behind more than a few was, "What the fuck are we about to do?"

Captain Edward "Eddie" Alfonse Cavalini, Amazon warehouse worker and part-time security guard, strutted amongst the militia members under his command. Like most of his troops he had donned a camouflage uniform and military boots that maybe worked in Iraq or Afghanistan but in Manhattan were nothing more than a hip-hop fashion statement. But unlike most of his guys who wore baseball caps or camo boonie hats, his head bore a brown Army Ranger ballistic proof helmet bearing night vision goggles, even though there wasn't much night in Manhattan even at nine o'clock p.m. His plate carrier vest held magazines for the AK-47 that he held; barrel pointed downward.

The captain delivered a pep talk to his boys, basically declaring that democracy was at stake and, just like the Minuteman of yore, it was up to them to protect it. "As our founding father, Thomas Jefferson put it, 'The tree of liberty must be refreshed from time to time with the blood of patriots and tyrants.'" He left out the part "It is its natural manure" since that sounded kind of weird. After that, all the men joined in chanting "USA!... USA!... USA!"

All revved up, the captain shouted with gusto, "Okay boys, this ain't no party, this ain't no disco. Saddle up and onward we go! Booyah!"

At Trump Tower and newly founded Lenape Independent Autonomous Republic, which no one realized until too late had the inauspicious acronym LIAR, the scene had turned sort of Woodstockian. The crowd spread all the way from 55th to 58th streets, many taking a seat on asphalt. Bottles of wine, beer, and liquor had been confiscated (looted) from various stores in the vicinity as well as edibles and distributed to the partisans, so that most everybody was enjoying a nice buzz on a lovely evening. A cloud of marijuana smoke slowly rotated over the scene. Groups here and there gathered around trash can fires where maybe someone strummed an acoustic guitar and people sang songs once sung by protest troubadours like Pete Seeger, Bob Dylan or Joan Baez (certainly not, however, "The Night They Drove Old Dixie Down ").

The Commissar added to the felicitous mood by informing all that a cavalcade of stars from Hollywood, the music industry, Silicon Valley, professional sports, in other words the whole schmear of American so-called ruling elite, had stirred up a tweet hurricane with congratulations to the congregation of courageous patriots.

"Listen, I got one here from Lebron James. Dig this: 'Hey, I'm over in Beijing doing promo for the NBA, but I just wanted y'all to know that I've been watching what's going down in NYC. I stand with you sisters and brothers and whatever you might call yourself, shoulder to shoulder. Fight the good fight to save democracy!'

"And here's another one from talk show host and funny man Steve Colbert: 'Amazing watching you warriors storm the Devil's lair. I almost wept. Cynics always say no. But saying yes brings things. Saying yes is how things grow. And here's my promise: Anyone who sends me a selfie of themselves taking a dump on Trump's 18-carat gold toilet will get a guest appearance on my show!'

"Okay, now that's sure a motivator," the Commissar said with a chortle as he paced. "But now listen up people; I got some heavy shit to lay on you. A little while ago, Governor Cuomo issued a press release saying he's called out the National Guard and they're on their way to Manhattan. Tanks in the street and all that fucked-up shit."

A low murmur shivered over the crowd.

"Now stay calm. We are engaged in civil disobedience, just remember that. We're not looking to pick a fight with the National Guard. We're not looking to turn this into Kent State or another Tiananmen Square or nothing like that. But if you do go down fighting, you'll go down in history as heroes and heroines and brave non-binaries. If there's one true thing that slave fucker Tom Jefferson said, it was that the tree of liberty is watered with the blood of tyrants and patriots, or something like that."

No rousing affirmation arose from his audience that death there in front of Trump Tower was a worthy and noble ending. "Like, you know, whoever said that was part of the deal?" one social justice warrior in the crowd whined to another. Instead, nervous chatter sounding like highly amplified termites chewing on wood emanated from the assembled patriots who were not excited about the prospect of being manure for the Tree of Liberty.

"Manny, we gotta get out of here," Gary said. "You're okay now, right?"

"I'm fine. Got some tear gas breath, but otherwise okay. Let's go."

A perimeter of police barricade had been set up by some of the protestors around the protestors for no stated purpose, other than evidently to keep unwelcome intruders out. *Evidently*. Manny and Gary approached an opening in the fence and were met there by three black-clad men holding rifles.

"Yeah, what's up?" one of the guys wearing a black ski mask asked in a less than friendly tone as he blocked the exit.

"We're on our way home," Gary said.

"We've been here for like five hours," Manny said.

"Sorry, no one leaves."

"What do you mean no one leaves?" Gary asked with irritable disbelief.

"It's not safe out there," the guy said.

"It's sure not going to be safe here soon when the National Guard shows up," Manny said.

Gary pulled down his mask so his voice wouldn't be muffled. "Hey, last time I checked this was still a free country. Why do you want people to stay here for? For cannon fodder? Get out of our way or else we're going to have a real serious problem right here and right now."

"That's right, Gary," Manny said. He sensed that she was impressed with his show of forcefulness.

The gatekeeper studied Gary's unmasked face. "Hey, you're Gary Wang, right? Wow. I didn't know you were here. Yeah, you can leave, but you have to do us all a favor first."

The guard left the other two at their posts and led Gary and Manny to the building entrance. He whispered something to the Commissar who looked Gary over. The Commissar then approached Gary and put his hand on Gary's shoulder.

"Thanks for all you did, brother. I really don't care for either of those two old white clowns, but you helped the lesser of two evils. Like they say, the enemy of my enemy is my friend."

Gary didn't say anything, only nodded, thinking that he had to get Manny and himself out of there.

The Commissar lifted his megaphone and said to the crowd: "Hey people, I've got a surprise for y'all. We have a celebrity amongst us. Gary Wang! You know, the cat who got Biden all that extra dough from the Chinese."

The protesters responded with faint applause and a couple of "Yeah!"

Gary wondered if they knew that those charges about Biden and the Chinese were false, and if they believed they were true, why were they applauding him?

"Gary wants to say a few words to you." The Commissar then handed the megaphone to Gary. "Speak truth to power, my man."

Gary looked down, trying to come up with

something worth saying to the crowd, which was growing restless. The megaphone feedback static squeaked and squawked.

"Hey, uh, let me first say that all those reports about the Chinese giving Biden money were all just a bunch of lies. And, I'm not up here because there's anything special about me. I'm just a guy who got caught up in some terrible shit that really had nothing to do with me. The whole thing is too weird to even try to explain to you. I'm up here because the guy with the gun standing over there said that if I spoke to you then I could leave. And I don't get what the gentleman was just saying about peaceful civil disobedience when there are people like that guy carrying weapons. So, all I'm trying to do is get out of here with my girlfriend and go home. And that's what I think all you should do."

The Commissar looked at the armed guard and said, "What is this guy, some fucking agitator?"

As Gary spoke, National Guard trucks pulled up at the Grand Army Plaza, which covered two blocks at the intersection of Central Park South and Fifth Avenue. Troops poured out of the trucks and grouped into formations. They all put on gas masks.

Those on the fringe of the crowd nervously eyed the National Guard activity. Someone shouted, "The National Guard just showed up!"

"So, they're here, the National Guard," Gary said, continuing his address. "This is not the time or place to make a meaningless and stupid last stand that could get a lot of people killed. That could set back our cause years, even decades. So, let's go home everybody and continue the struggle tomorrow when our heads are clear."

He paused at the sudden sound of windows shattering four stories above him. He, Manny, and others near the entrance fled the falling shards of glass. About a dozen or so silhouette figures crouched in the space where the windows once were; the barrels of semi-automatic rifles pointed out of the jagged opening toward the Grand Army Plaza. The exploding windows were loud enough for the National Guard troops to hear two blocks away. The soldiers crouched, took cover, and released the safeties on their M16s.

The centrifugal force of panic propelled the protestors outwards in all directions.

"Company C, take position on the east side of Fifth Avenue and advance toward Trump Tower," the National Guard Sergeant Major shouted. "Fire if fired upon."

Manny ran from the entrance. She turned and expected to see Gary behind her, but he was nowhere in sight. "Gary!" she called over and over. She spun in a circle, calling his name in all directions while people fled past her. "Gary!"

The Defenders of Liberty convoy at that moment was barreling down Fifth Avenue, unaware that it was entering a potential live fire zone five blocks away.

And then darkness fell. Yes, it was already nighttime, but this darkness was all encompassing, instantaneously and simultaneously snuffing out every speck of light within a mile radius. Like someone had hit the light switch after saying goodnight. And when the lights went out, the formidable tower lost its meretricious shine and blended in with the foreboding banner draped over its top half, the skull and crossbones turning a ghostly shade of pale. The crowd, which a millisecond before had been dispersing in all directions, trampling over the gates, shouting and falling, suddenly stopped. An exhilarated but alarmed gasp rose from them, like that heard at a firework show finale when the crackling weeping willow sparkles drift slowly down over the amazed onlookers' heads. But no illumination shimmered across their awe-struck faces. Their eyes strained to soak in whatever photons of light might be lurking around.

What terrified them more than anything was that their phones no longer worked. Nothing happened when they tried to turn on their phones' flashlights. Nothing happened when they tried to make a call for help. Nothing happened when they tried to video this preternatural event for the sake of posterity. Nothing happened when they turned their cameras up to the skies to take a photo of stars that had not twinkled over Manhattan since the Northeast power outage of August 2003. Nothing happened because the Central Processing Unit inside each phone had been burned to a crisp.

The looters and rioters who were having fun several blocks over, stopped in the middle of their looting and rioting when the night turned utterly black. They quickly realized that their revolting revolutionary acts would not be captured by their buddies' phone cameras or by the pack of journalists who were always on the edge of destruction like hyenas waiting to pick over the carcass. "Hey Carly, don't tell me you didn't get me bashing that cash register open?" They then sulked off into the darkness, since after all what was the point of a revolution if it wasn't televised or at least put on YouTube?

The Defenders of Liberty militia halted dead in its tracks. Any vehicle made since 1980 and thus dependent on the electrical circuitry of semiconductor chips came to an abrupt and automatic stop. Although the frying of the vehicles' electrical innards was almost simultaneous, it wasn't exactly so, which resulted in a massive pile up of SUVs, pick-up trucks and a Hummer or two. Hoods smashed into trunks.

Captain Eddie Cavalini, who naturally was at the front of the column in his stalled Ford F-150, turned and saw wreckage as far as his eye could see, which in the dark wasn't very far. Many militia members lay injured on the avenue, moaning and groaning. Others fled helter skelter, filled with the primal fear of what they couldn't see. Captain Eddie threw his helmet onto the pavement in agonized frustration upon witnessing the dissolution of the regiment that he had spent three years training in the art of urban warfare. But the spooky inkling that maybe divine intervention was at work did cause him to pause and wonder.

The National Guard troops huddled befuddled near their personnel carriers, not having any idea what to do since all communication both within and outside the unit had ceased.

Meanwhile, 4,664 miles east, Vladimir Putin sat in the Kremlin's Presidential Executive Office. He and Sergei Valitnikoff, Director of Cyber Warfare for the FSB, were focusing on a video monitor live streaming the action around Trump Tower as relayed by one of Russia's satellites.

"I swear on Lenin's tomb, our little experiment is exceeding all expectations," Putin said to the Director. His soulless eyes glowed with demonic intensity.

"Yes, yes," replied Valitnikoff. An overweight guy

with bushy salt and pepper hair and mustache, he could barely stay in his seat that was too small for him anyway. "An electromagnetic pulse attack without the need for a high-altitude nuclear explosion to do its trick. Just a couple of short laser bursts from a low-orbiting satellite. What a technological breakthrough!"

Putin's thin, devious smile stretched across his oval-shaped face. "And it's so precise. The outage limited to less than a kilometer radius. No needless mass collateral damage. Just think how we can use this on the battlefield."

Valitnikoff could barely contain his giddiness. "And we'll put out the usual phony fingerprints making the Americans suspect the Chinese are behind it, my President."

Putin smirked. "Or maybe that chubby little North Korean punk. Anyway, so what if they know it's us? The damage is limited. No one got killed. Not enough to start a war over."

"And it might make them think twice about fucking around with us," the Director added. "Poking their noses under our tent, like in Ukraine or Venezuela."

"Besides, my friend Donald would be happy if he knew that I saved his precious building, so why would he retaliate if he knew for certain it was us?" Putin said.

The Cyber Warfare director laughed boisterously. "You may have saved his presidency too. The last thing he needs is the US's largest city going up in flames. Trump will call this a 'Putin ex Machina!'"

Putin had never studied Latin, so he didn't get the pun, but he liked the way it sounded anyway.

"When we planned this last year, I didn't think Donald had a chance after he talked about injecting bleach to stop Covid," Putin said. "And Biden? What was that old goat going to do about it?"

Again, the jolly Director laughed more than necessary to flatter his boss. "This is just the Russian Republic's way of congratulating our American friends on their really chaotic election that no one really believes in."

Putin leaned back from the monitor and smiled at Valitnikoff. "You know, I think the Hero of the Russian Federation Gold Star medal is going to look nice on your barrel chest, Sergei."

Manny continued searching in the darkness for Gary amidst the fleeing protestors. "Gary!" She began to despair that the silhouetted armed gang standing behind the broken windows may have for some reason taken him hostage.

"Gary!"

She then finally got a response to her call.

"Over here, Manny."

Enough space had cleared that she was barely able to see him not far from the entrance. He appeared to be tussling with two guys in suits who looked like they were trying to restrain him. She raced over to them.

"Get your hands off of him," she yelled. They didn't need to see the snarl behind her mask to know that she meant business.

"They're Secret Service guys, Manny," Gary shouted, seemingly out of breath from grappling with the two accosters. One of the agents was trying to pin Gary's arm behind his back while the other hugged his torso.

"What do you want with him? He hasn't done

anything. Get your hands off him you!"

"He was trying to incite a riot," said the one embracing Gary. "We heard him and saw him. You don't do that at President Trump's home." The agent breathed heavily between sentences, tiring from wrestling with Gary.

"This Chinese spy has caused enough trouble already," the other agent said.

They finally managed to throw Gary to the ground. Manny rushed toward them. She pulled out of her pocket something that she aimed at the faces of the two Secret Service agents.

One of the agents jumped to his feet with his fingers digging into his eyes. "Goddamn, what is that shit? I can't see." The other agent rolled on the ground, cursing and shrieking.

Manny had squirted directly into both their faces a canister of pepper spray that she had found on the street earlier. Gary got to his feet and the two of them sprinted away.

They ran through the chaos. They tightly clutched each other's hands to make sure they didn't lose each other again. A skeleton with Day-Glo bones ran along beside them, laughing maniacally. Manny guessed the guy was still wearing his Halloween costume from three nights before. They almost tripped over a young woman, barefoot and wearing a white dress and blue denim jacket, on all fours, blood and tears dropping from her face onto the pavement. Those who had lighters flicked them on, creating a sea of fireflies. The movement of bodies had no direction or flow.

At one point Manny and Gary came upon some of the Staten Islanders. But the would-be Minutemen seemed too dazed and distraught to care that two of the "enemy" were in their midst. The men wandered aimlessly, and Manny got the impression that they only wanted to get back to Staten Island where they might have a slice and a beer and call it an unholy night.

At Eighty-Six and Columbus Avenue, they finally entered the light. Manny did a leaping joyful arabesque. Seeing the light made her feel like she could breathe again after her head had been underwater for five minutes.

She thought she might have startled Gary by her exuberant leap into the light. But he then comically attempted his own version of the ballet move and fell on his ass. Manny laughed so hard it almost hurt, and she forgot about the hell that they had just passed through, at least for a moment.

She bent down and put her arms around him to help him to his feet.

"I guess I'm no Baryshnikov," he said sheepishly.

"Hey, I give you kudos for the spontaneity, sweetie."

National Guard troops were stationed at the corner they neared. One of the troopers approached the two.

"Hey, curfew in effect people. Sorry, but gotta be off the streets."

"We're just trying to get back to our apartment, that's all," Gary said.

The soldier asked for both their IDs, and once satisfied that they did live a few blocks north, sent them on their way.

Gary took hold of Manny's hand. Although the temperature had dropped to the low 40s, his hand felt warm in hers. As they walked on, he began humming and then softly sang the opening line to "I Can See Clearly Now."

Manny glanced at him with eyebrows raised. "Now where did that come from?"

"Just really glad to be fucking alive," he said. "And here with you."

"Well, don't stop singing now that you started!"

She joined him on the next verse, which was a good thing since he didn't seem to know the words.

The two lovers walked down the avenue singing, their clasped hands slightly swinging, as they passed a smoldering car that had been set on fire earlier, the shattered store windows, the boarded-up restaurants, the burning piles of garbage, a discarded placard that read, "We The People are pissed off!" A copter overhead trailed them. Sirens wailing in the distance provided the backup vocals. The Guardsmen, nervously clutching their guns around an armored carrier parked at the next corner, made for an audience. Manny didn't need an audience.

"Shut the fuck up!" a voice out of the surrounding urban wilderness shouted.

Manny looked up and saw a weary looking, besieged New Yorker sticking her head out her apartment window. She and Gary stopped in the middle of Columbus Avenue.

"You got a problem?" Gary shouted back to her.

"Yeah, I got a problem. What right do you two lovebirds have to sing when this city, this country, this world is one goddamned hot mess?"

"Ignore her, Gary," Manny said. "Let's go."

Manny felt sorry for the woman. She hoped that later, while she lay in her lonely bed, this resentful observer would reflect on the ridiculous sight of two people singing amidst desolation and ruin. And maybe she would see that there is no better time to sing, to defiantly sing against the breaking up, the breaking apart, the breaking down. Singing is the soul going to a better place. It is between accepting and not accepting, both surrender and victory. And maybe this poor woman would realize that love is not a right but a gift, given not only from the beloved to the other, but also a free gift to the city, the country, and even the world. Just as light begets light, love begets love. Maybe she would even admit the corny thought: *Isn't that what the world needs now*?

Manny had suffered enough pain in her life to know she was being naive, like all lovers are. But she, with Gary's help, was going to do her damndest, despite everything, to make tomorrow a bright sun shiny day.

Michael Goodwin grew up in Memphis, TN. He received a BA from the University of Virginia, an MBA from Wharton, and attended University of Columbia's MFA program in creative writing. He lives in Connecticut and works at an investment firm in Manhattan. He is married with three children. His previous novels were Big Time, Junk, and When Vultures Dance.

CPSIA information can be obtained
at www.ICGtesting.com
Printed in the USA
BVHW072247090122
625811BV00005B/14